Shot i

Declan's iron grip on me went a little more lax as he tucked the phone back into the pocket of his black jeans. It was enough to let me sink my teeth into his arm. He pushed me back so hard I whacked my head against the wall and fell to the ground. I'd managed to draw blood on his forearm, which was already riddled with other scars.

I scrambled up to my feet, adrenaline coursing through my body. I was ready to do whatever I had to in order to fight for my life, but another curtain of agony descended over me.

"What's happening to me?" I managed to say through clenched teeth. "What the hell was in that syringe?"

He grabbed me by the front of my sweater and brought me very close to his scarred face. "Poison."

"Oh my God. What kind of poison?"

"The kind that will kill you," he said simply. "Which is why you have to come with me."

I shook my head erratically. "I have to get to a hospital."

"No." He grabbed me tighter. "Death now or death later. That's your only choice."

It was a choice I didn't want to make. It was one I wouldn't have to make. More pain erupted inside of me and the world went totally and completely black.

Berkley Sensation titles by Michelle Rowen

THE DEMON IN ME
SOMETHING WICKED

NIGHTSHADE

Nightshade

MICHELLE ROWEN

BERKLEY SENSATION, NEW YORK

THE BERKLEY PUBLISHING GROUP
Published by the Penguin Group
Penguin Group (USA) Inc.
375 Hudson Street, New York, New York 10014, USA

Penguin Group (Canada), 90 Eglinton Avenue East, Suite 700, Toronto, Ontario M4P 2Y3, Canada
(a division of Pearson Penguin Canada Inc.)
Penguin Books Ltd., 80 Strand, London WC2R 0RL, England
Penguin Group Ireland, 25 St. Stephen's Green, Dublin 2, Ireland (a division of Penguin Books Ltd.)
Penguin Group (Australia), 250 Camberwell Road, Camberwell, Victoria 3124, Australia
(a division of Pearson Australia Group Pty. Ltd.)
Penguin Books India Pvt. Ltd., 11 Community Centre, Panchsheel Park, New Delhi—110 017, India
Penguin Group (NZ), 67 Apollo Drive, Rosedale, North Shore 0632, New Zealand
(a division of Pearson New Zealand Ltd.)
Penguin Books (South Africa) (Pty.) Ltd., 24 Sturdee Avenue, Rosebank, Johannesburg 2196,
South Africa

Penguin Books Ltd., Registered Offices: 80 Strand, London WC2R 0RL, England

This is a work of fiction. Names, characters, places, and incidents either are the product of the author's imagination or are used fictitiously, and any resemblance to actual persons, living or dead, business establishments, events, or locales is entirely coincidental. The publisher does not have any control over and does not assume any responsibility for author or third-party websites or their content.

NIGHTSHADE

A Berkley Sensation Book / published by arrangement with the author

PRINTING HISTORY
Berkley Sensation mass-market edition / February 2011

Copyright © 2011 by Michelle Rouillard.
Excerpt from *Bloodlust* by Michelle Rowen copyright © by Michelle Rouillard.
Cover art by Don Sipley.
Cover design by Lesley Worrell.
Interior text design by Laura K. Corless.

ISBN: 978-0-425-23982-7

BERKLEY® SENSATION
Berkley Sensation Books are published by The Berkley Publishing Group,
a division of Penguin Group (USA) Inc.,
375 Hudson Street, New York, New York 10014.
BERKLEY® SENSATION and the "B" design are trademarks of Penguin Group (USA) Inc.

PRINTED IN THE UNITED STATES OF AMERICA

10 9 8 7 6 5 4 3 2 1

ACKNOWLEDGMENTS

Thank you so much to my brilliant editor, Cindy Hwang, and my fabulous agent, Jim McCarthy, for giving me the chance to show my undying love for vampires in this book.

Thank you to my bodacious betareaders:

Eve Silver, my writing buddy through both the highs and lows, who entices me to have stress-relieving powdered mini donuts far too often.

Bonnie Staring, my amazing friend, cat lover, cheerleader, rock star. Well, not really a rock star, but she's done some reality TV. And she literally has pom-poms to cheer various events. Which totally helps.

And thank you to my awesome readers who enjoyed my funny vampires in the past . . . I hope you like the scary ones, too!

1

LIFE AS I KNEW IT ENDED AT HALF PAST ELEVEN ON A Tuesday morning.

There were currently thirty minutes left.

"What's your poison?" I asked my friend and coworker Stacy on my way out of the office on a coffee break.

She looked up at me from a spreadsheet on her computer screen, her eyes practically crossed from crunching numbers all morning. "You're a serious lifesaver, Jill, you know that?"

"Well aware." I grinned at her, then shifted my purse to my other shoulder and took the five-dollar-bill she thrust at me.

"I'll take a latte, extra foam. And one of those white chocolate chunk cookies. My stomach's growling happily just thinking about it."

Stacy didn't normally go for the cookie action. "No diet today?"

"Fuck diets."

"Can I quote you?"

She laughed. "I'll have it printed on a T-shirt. Hey, Steve! Jill's headed to the coffee shop. You want anything?"

I groaned inwardly. I hadn't wanted to make a big production out of it since I hated making change. Unlike Stacy, math was not my friend.

By the time I finally made it out of the office I had a yellow sticky note clenched in my fist scrawled with four different coffee orders.

Twenty minutes left.

The line at Starbucks was, as usual, ridiculous. I waited. I ordered. I waited some more. I juggled my wallet and my purse along with the bag of pastries and take-out tray of steaming caffeine and finally left the shop, passing an electronics store on my way back. It had a bunch of televisions in the window set to CNN. Some plane crash in Europe was blazing. No survivors. I shivered despite the heat of the day and continued walking.

Five minutes left.

I returned to my office building, which not only housed Lambert Capital, the investment and financial analysis company where I currently temped, but also a small pharmaceutical research company, a marketing firm, and a modeling agency.

"Hold the elevator," I called out as I crossed the lobby. My heels clicked against the shiny black marble floor. Despite my request, the elevator was *not* held. The doors closed when I was only a couple of steps away from it, a look of bemusement on the sole occupant's face who hadn't done me the honor of waiting.

One minute left.

I nudged the up button with my elbow and waited, watching as the number above the doors stopped at the tenth floor, ISB Pharmaceuticals, paused for what felt like an eternity, and then slowly descended back to the lobby. The other elevator seemed eternally stuck at the fifteenth. Another bank of elevators were located around the corner, but I chose to stay where I was and try my best to be patient.

Finally, the doors slid open to reveal a man who wore a white lab coat and a security badge that bore his name: Carl Anderson. His eyes were shifty and there was a noticeable sheen of sweat on his brow. My gaze dropped to his right hand in which he tightly held a syringe—the sharp needle uncapped.

That was a safety hazard I wasn't getting anywhere near. What the hell was he thinking, carrying something like that around?

Glaring at him, I waited for him to get out of the elevator so I could get on, but he didn't budge an inch.

Behind thick glasses, his eyes were steadily widening with what looked like fear, and totally focused on something behind me. Curious about what would earn this dramatic reaction, I turned to see another man enter the lobby. He was tall, had a black patch over his left eye, and wasn't smiling. Aside from that, I noticed the gun he held. The big gun. The one he now had trained on the man in the elevator.

"Leaving so soon, Anderson? Why am I not surprised?" the man with the gun growled. "No more fucking games. Give it to me right now."

I gasped as Carl Anderson clamped his arm around my neck. The tray of coffees went flying as I clawed at him, but my struggling did nothing. I couldn't even scream; he held me so tightly that it cut off my breath.

"Why are you here?" Anderson demanded. "*I* was supposed to be the one to make contact."

The gunman's icy gaze never wavered. "Let go of the woman."

My eyes watered. I couldn't breathe. My larynx was being crushed.

"But she's the only thing standing between me and your direct orders right now, isn't she?"

"And why would you think I care if you grab some random hostage?" the gunman growled.

Random hostage?

Panic swelled further inside of me. I scanned the lobby to see that this altercation hadn't gone unnoticed. Several people with shocked looks on their faces had cell phones pressed to their ears. Were they calling 911? Where was security? No guards approached with guns drawn.

Fear coursed through me, closing my throat. My hands, which gripped Anderson's arm, were shaking.

"We can talk about this," Anderson said.

"It's too late for negotiations. There's more at risk than the life of one civilian."

"I thought we were supposed to be working together."

"Sure. Until you decided to sell elsewhere. Hand over the formula."

"I destroyed the rest." Anderson's voice trembled. "One prototype is all that's left."

"That was a mistake." The gunman's tone was flat.

"It was a mistake creating it in the first place. It's dangerous."

"Isn't that the whole point?"

"You'd defend something that would just as easily kill *you*, Declan? Even though you can walk in the sunlight, you're not much better than the other bloodsuckers." The man who held me prone sounded disgusted. And scared shitless—almost as scared as I felt.

Bloodsuckers? What the hell was he talking about?

How did I get in the middle of this? I'd only gone out for coffee—coffee that was now splattered all over the clean lobby floor. It was just a normal workday—a normal Tuesday.

More people had gathered around us, moving backward toward the walls and door, away from this unexpected standoff, hands held to their mouths in shock at what they were witnessing. I spotted someone from the office to my left rounding the corner where the other elevators were located—it was Stacy with an armful of file folders, her eyes wide as saucers as she saw me. She took a step closer, mouthing my name.

No, please don't come any closer, I thought frantically. *Don't get hurt.*

Where the hell was security?

I shrieked when I felt a painful jab at my throat.

"Don't do that," the man with the gun, Declan, snapped.

"You know what will happen if I inject her with this, don't you?" Anderson's voice held an edge of something— panic, fear, desperation. I didn't have to be the helpless hostage in this situation to realize that was a really bad mix.

He had the syringe up against my throat, the sharp tip of the needle stabbing deep into my flesh. I stopped struggling and tried not to move, tried not to breathe. My vision blurred with tears as I waited for the man with the gun to do something to save me. He was my only hope.

"I don't give a shit about her," my only hope said evenly. "All I care about is that formula. Now hand it over and maybe you get to live."

The gunman's face was oddly emotionless considering this situation. He wore black jeans and a black T-shirt, which bared thick, sinewy biceps. His face didn't have an ounce of humanity to it. Around the black eye patch, scar tissue branched out like a spiderweb up over his forehead and down his left cheek, all the way to his neck. He was as scary-looking as he was ugly.

"I knew they'd send you to retrieve this, Declan." Anderson's mouth was so close to my ear that I could feel his hot breath. His shaky voice held a mocking edge. "Who better for this job?"

"I'll give you five seconds to release the woman and hand over that syringe with its contents intact," Declan said. "Or I'll kill both of you where you stand. Five . . . four . . ."

"Think about this, will you?" Anderson dug the needle further into my flesh, prompting another wheeze of a shriek from me. "You need to open your fucking eyes and see the truth before it's too late. I'm trying to stop this the only way I can. It's wrong. All of it's wrong. You're just as brainwashed as the rest of them, aren't you?"

With his chest pressed against my back, I could feel his erratic heartbeat. He feared for his life. A mental flash of memories of my family, my friends, sped past my eyes. I didn't want to die—no, please, not like this.

"Three . . . two . . ." Declan continued, undeterred. The laser sighter from his gun fixed on my chest.

Several onlookers ran for the glass doors, and screams sounded out.

"You want the abomination I created that goddamned much?" Anderson yelled. "Here! You can have it!"

A second later, I felt a burning pain, hot as fire, as he injected me with the syringe's contents. It was a worse pain than the stabbing itself. Then he raggedly ripped the needle out and pushed me away hard enough that I went sprawling to the floor. I clamped my hand against the side of my neck and started to scream.

The sound of a gunshot, even louder than my screams,

pierced my eardrums. I turned to look at the man who'd just injected me. He now lay sprawled out on the marble floor, his eyes open and glassy. There was a large hole in Anderson's forehead, red and wet and sickening. He had a gun in his left hand, which he must have pulled from his lab coat when he let go of me. The empty syringe lay next to him.

Declan went directly to him, gun still trained on the dead man for another moment before he tucked it away, squatted, and then silently and methodically began going through the pockets of the white coat.

My entire body shook, but otherwise I was frozen in place. There were more screams now from the others who'd witnessed the shooting as they scattered in all directions.

Declan swore under his breath and then turned to look directly at me for the very first time. The iris of his right eye was pale gray and soulless, and the look he gave me froze my insides.

My throat felt like it had been slit wide open, but I was still breathing. Still thinking. A quick, erratic scan of the lobby showed where I'd dropped my purse and the coffees and pastries six feet to my right. Most of the people in the lobby were now running for the doors to escape to the street outside. A security alarm finally began to wail, adding to the chaos.

"You—" Declan rose fluidly to his feet. He was easily a full foot taller than my five-four. "—come here."

Like hell I would.

The elevator to the left of me opened and a man pushing an empty mail cart got off. The murderer's attention went to it. I took it as the only chance I might ever get. I scrambled to my feet and ran.

"Jill!" I heard Stacy yell, but it didn't slow me down.

I had to get away, far away from the office. My mind had switched into survival mode. Stacy couldn't get anywhere near me right now; it would only put her in danger, too.

I left my purse behind—the contents of my life scattered on the smooth, cold floor next to the spilled coffee and spreading pool of blood. I pushed through the front doors, fully expecting Declan to shoot me in my back. But he didn't.

Yanking my hand from my wounded neck, I saw that it was covered in blood. My stomach lurched and I almost vomited. What was in that syringe? It burned like lava sliding through my veins.

I was badly hurt. Jesus, I'd been stabbed in the throat with a needle by a stranger. If I wasn't in such pain, I'd think I was having a nightmare.

This *was* a nightmare—a waking one.

A look behind me confirmed that Declan, whoever the hell he was, had exited the office building. He scanned one side of the street before honing in on me.

I clutched at a few people's arms as I stumbled past them. They recoiled from me, faceless strangers who weren't willing to help a woman with a bleeding neck wound.

My heart slammed against my rib cage as I tried to run, but I couldn't manage more than a stagger. I wanted to pass out. The world was blurry and shifting around me.

The burning pain slowly began to spread from my neck down to my chest and along my arms and legs. I could feel it like a living thing, burrowing deeper and deeper inside me.

Only a few seconds later, I felt Declan's hand clamp around my upper arm. He nearly pulled me off my feet as he dragged me around the corner and into an alley.

"Let go of me," I snarled, attempting to hit him. He

effortlessly grabbed my other arm. I blinked against my tears.

"Stay still."

"Go to hell." The next moment, the pain cut off any further words as I convulsed. Only his tight grip kept me from crumpling to the ground. He pushed me up against the wall and held my head firmly in place as he looked into my eyes. His scars were even uglier up close. A shudder of revulsion rippled through me at being this close to him.

He wrenched my head to the left and roughly pulled my long blond hair aside to inspect the neck wound. His expression never wavered. There was no pity or anger or disdain in his gaze—nothing but emptiness in his single gray eye as he looked me over.

Holding me with one hand tightly around my throat so I could barely breathe, he held a cell phone to his ear.

"It's me," he said. "There's been a complication."

A pause.

"Anderson administered the prototype to a civilian before he tried to shoot me and escape. I killed him." Another pause. "It's a woman. Should I kill her, too?"

I tried to fight against the choke hold he had me in, but it didn't help. He sounded so blasé, so emotionless, as if he was discussing bringing home a pizza after work rather than seeking permission for my murder.

His one-eyed gaze narrowed. While talking on the phone he hadn't looked anywhere but my face. "I know I was followed here. I don't have long." Then finally, "Understood."

He ended the call.

Finally he loosened his hold on me enough that I could try to speak in pained gasps. "What . . . are you going . . . to do with me?"

"That's not up to me." Declan's iron grip on me went a little more lax as he tucked the phone back into the pocket of his black jeans. It was enough to let me sink my teeth into his arm. He pushed me back so hard I whacked my head against the wall and fell to the ground. I'd managed to draw blood on his forearm, which was already riddled with other scars.

I scrambled up to my feet, adrenaline coursing through my body. I was ready to do whatever I had to in order to fight for my life, but another curtain of agony descended over me.

"What's happening to me?" I managed to say through clenched teeth. "What the hell was in that syringe?"

Declan grabbed me by the front of my sweater and brought me very close to his scarred face. "Poison."

My eyes widened. "Oh my God. What kind of poison?"

"The kind that will kill you," he said simply. "Which is why you have to come with me."

I shook my head erratically. "I have to get to a hospital."

"No." He grabbed me tighter. "Death now or death later. That's your only choice."

It was a choice I didn't want to make. It was one I wouldn't have to make. More pain erupted inside of me and the world went totally and completely black.

2

I WASN'T SURE HOW LONG I WAS UNCONSCIOUS. THE good news—if I was forced to find some—was, aside from a brain that felt as if it was made from three-day-old oatmeal, the worst of the pain had subsided. I could, however, actually feel my veins now—the length and width of them throbbing just underneath my skin.

The poison was working its way through me.

Poison. But if I'd really been injected with poison, why wasn't I dead yet?

And where the hell was I?

I heard a noise, a steady hum against my ear. I was laying somewhere slightly soft, but without a lot of give. And I was moving. Well, *I* wasn't moving, but I was in something that *was* moving.

A car.

I opened up my eyes just a fraction, careful not to betray the fact that I'd woken up.

Yes. I was in a car—the backseat of a car, to be precise. As I raised my gaze just a little, I saw that Declan was behind the steering wheel.

No radio. Only the sound of the road beneath the tires. The level of heat I felt told me that this was a car that didn't have any air-conditioning—or it wasn't turned on.

So he'd dragged me out of that alley unconscious, thrown me in a car, and started driving. Had no one even tried to stop him?

He'd taken me out of downtown San Diego, not the middle of nowhere.

I hadn't had much experience with life-and-death situations before, other than dealing with the deaths of my parents five years ago. Beyond that tragedy, everything in my life had mostly gone according to plan, or, more accurately, *lack* of plan.

Get up in the morning, go to work, try to get along with everyone. Go home or go out for dinner with a friend. Go to bed. Dream about a more interesting life filled with adventure, then wake up, shower, and do it all over again. Mundane and predictable, sure. But at least I never questioned whether I'd live to see another sunrise.

I was questioning it now.

I heard once that your life basically consists of about seven major moments—moments when you made a decision that changed the trajectory of your existence. Perhaps the loss of a loved one. Or a traumatic event that pushed you onto another unexpected path. And usually, these moments were never anything you recognized as life-changing at the time. Sure, when you looked back you could pinpoint it and realize that, yeah, that's where things changed forever. The choice of a certain college. Saying yes to a job in another city. Going out on a date with the right guy—or the wrong one. Deciding to jaywalk and not looking both ways.

Smash. For better or for worse, your life was different from that point forward.

For me, as I lay motionless on the backseat of Declan's car, I knew my life had changed. It didn't take a rocket scientist to figure that out.

"If you're smart," Declan said without turning around, "you won't give me any more trouble."

Any *more* trouble?

I didn't answer. I squeezed my eyes shut again and tried not to move.

"I know you're awake." His deep voice had a rough-edge quality to it, like he smoked a couple cases of cigarettes every day even though I couldn't smell any tobacco. "Your breathing pattern changed."

Even if we were going fast, maybe I could jump out of the car. I'd stand a better chance hitting the pavement at eighty miles an hour than being in here with him. At the moment, I didn't have much to lose. Except maybe *time*.

Before I could scramble to unlock the door, Declan reached back to grab the front of my shirt. He pulled me like a rag doll between the seats, twisting my legs into painful, unnatural angles, and slammed me down next to him.

All without taking his eye off the road.

"Behave," he said. "Or I promise you'll spend the rest of this trip unconscious."

"Don't touch me." I slapped at his hand, not that it did much good. He finally removed it and placed it back on the steering wheel.

He didn't say anything else. Didn't ask me if I was okay, what my name was, or what I was doing in that lobby. Wrong place and wrong time didn't even begin to cover it.

Stacy had seen what happened. Was she okay? I wished I knew for sure.

"You can't do this." My throat felt raw and damaged.

He didn't reply. It was as if I was suddenly invisible.

"Where are you taking me?"

"Be quiet."

"You can't just kidnap me. I'm hurt. I need help." I touched my neck again and winced. I expected to feel a gash, an open wound, but luckily there didn't seem to be anything that bad. The blood had mostly dried. It did feel tender and bruised, all up and down the right side of my throat, though. I didn't need a mirror to tell me that.

My purse was gone so I didn't have my cell phone. No ID. No money. Nothing.

Declan kept his eye on the road as though he was competing in a staring contest with it. I turned to look out the window and saw another car passing us. I pounded on the window and tried to get the other driver's attention, then attempted to roll down the window when the man didn't as much as glance in my direction.

I stopped when I felt Declan's hand clamp down on my arm.

"Do you have a death wish?" he snapped. "Just sit there and be quiet, or else."

"I need to go to a hospital. You said there was poison in that syringe."

"Regular doctors can't help you. As soon as you explain what happened, they'll call some people interested in getting their hands on that formula, and trust me, you're not going to want to meet them. Go to a hospital and you will die."

I grimaced at how certain he sounded about that. "What do you mean? What people?"

"Be quiet."

"But—but I have to do something. I can feel it inside of me . . . the *poison*."

That earned me a momentary glance. "You can feel it? How does it feel?"

"It hurts like hell."

"I don't doubt it."

"The pain made me pass out."

"No, you passed out because you were hyperventilating."

I tried to breathe normally, but it was a struggle. Despite everything, this freak of nature hadn't been excessively violent toward me yet. Not compared to what he'd done to that Anderson guy, anyway. Did I think he wouldn't hurt me? Kill me? Not for a moment. But maybe he could be reasoned with.

"My name's Jillian," I said. "Jillian Conrad. My friends call me Jill."

Taking it to a friendly introduction level might make all the difference. Make him see that I wasn't just a random hostage. I was a normal person with a normal life and I didn't deserve any of this.

His lips thinned. "Jillian?"

I nodded eagerly. "Yes."

"Shut the fuck up, Jillian."

I winced. Okay, that didn't work so well.

His jaw tightened. Again his attention was anywhere but on me. Which was fine. I didn't need a full-on look at that ugly, scarred face of his again. I was petrified enough to begin with. All I had to do was hold it together and wait for my first opportunity to get away from him.

Damn it. What did they say? Never get in a car with somebody like this. It wasn't just a warning to little kids about strangers and candy. It was for anyone. As soon as the bad guy got you in their car, they had you under their control. He could be taking me anywhere.

"Should I kill her?"

He was an admitted killer. A sociopath. I'd never met a murderer before, never wanted to, outside of seeing them in movies or on the nightly news.

Maybe he'd been lying. Maybe it wasn't poison. To me, poison was cyanide. Something that would kill you in seconds. I wasn't dead. I was still breathing.

"Your name's Declan." I had a feeling he wouldn't confirm or deny it, so I wasn't surprised when his mouth remained closed. "Okay, Declan, we can figure this out."

"We can, can we?"

"Sure. But you really need to tell me what's going on."

"I'm driving."

"I see that." I swallowed and realized that I had my arms crossed so tightly, my fingernails digging into my skin so deeply that it hurt. "Do you have a Kleenex?"

"For what?"

"My neck. I'm still bleeding a little, I think."

"No shit. Yeah, you should mop yourself up so it's not a distraction for me."

Funny, he didn't seem the least bit distracted.

He didn't say or do anything for a moment. Then his right hand darted out so quickly that I jumped and pressed myself up against the door. But he wasn't reaching for me, he was reaching for the glove compartment. He popped it open and dug inside, pulling out a travel-sized container of tissues. He tossed it in the general direction of my lap. I pulled one out and dabbed at my neck.

Okay, so despite his looks and previous actions he

wasn't a complete heathen. He provided tissues when I asked for them. That was . . . mildly encouraging.

Yes, I was reaching. I knew it.

"You knew that guy? That . . . Anderson guy?"

He sighed. "You're not going to shut up, are you?"

"Maybe talking is what I do instead of freaking out."

The line of his jaw tightened. "What do I have to do to get you to close your mouth, apart from my making you?"

A shiver went down my spine. "Let me the hell out of this car."

"Any other options?"

I bit my bottom lip. "Answer my questions."

"And you'll be quiet for the rest of the drive?"

That all depended on where this monster was thinking about taking me. However, I didn't say that out loud.

"Yes." I used a fresh tissue to wipe at my face, under my damp eyes. Half the mascara I'd applied that morning came off in a black smear.

"Anderson was a chemist who specialized in the development of serums and toxins."

"You killed him." Bile rose in my throat at the memory of glassy eyes, a bloody wound, and a growing pool of blood.

"You're observant." Sarcasm. "He pulled a gun on me. I reacted."

"You could have just wounded him."

"I don't shoot to wound. I shoot to kill. Makes it harder for anything to go wrong."

That meant this wasn't the first time. Declan did this sort of thing frequently. Racking up a body count wherever he went. By the looks of him—scars, eye patch, and all—I never would have pegged him for a nice family man. I suppose the title of assassin suited him just fine.

"Should have wounded him," Declan continued under

his breath. "I fucked up. He kept that formula in his head and I had to go and shoot it off."

Seemed as if he was talking more to himself than to me.

I touched my neck again and pressed lightly on the injection point. It made me feel weak all over when I thought about what had happened. "He said he destroyed the rest."

"Only one sample left—the prototype. And you got it. Which is the only reason you're here right now."

"That's why you kidnapped me? Because of what's inside me?"

"Yes."

"It's important, isn't it?"

"Vital," he said simply.

I was important because of what was currently coursing through my veins. Ironically, the deadly poison was my ticket to getting out of this nightmare alive.

"So you're not going to kill me?"

"Not at the moment."

"But you were ready to kill me in the alley. You would have done it if you were told to, right?"

He eyed me sideways. "You ask too many questions. Are you some sort of reporter?"

"No. I'm . . . I'm a temp. I do office work. Whatever's needed, for however long they need me."

"And you get in trouble for talking too much, I'm guessing."

"Among many other things. My last job review stated I was hard to manage." I was pressed firmly against the door, as far away from Declan as I could possibly sit without riding on the outside of the car. My ankle felt sprained from when this monster had lurched me into the front seat. I noticed a small tear in the knee of my black pants. "What were you told to do with me?"

"Exactly what I'm doing. I collected the formula and I'm returning it to where I was supposed to take it in the first place."

"And where's that?"

"To see someone."

"Who?" I pressed. I wasn't feeling much braver, but talking kept my mind from wandering off in silence and imagining of all sorts of horrific outcomes.

"My father. He helped to order the development of the formula in the first place. Back when it was in a glass vial, not a living, breathing human being."

Why would his father be developing a formula like this? Who the hell was he? Dr. Evil?

"How long will I be a living, breathing human being with this poison in me if I'm not supposed to go to any hospitals?" I asked quietly.

"I don't know." Flat. Matter of fact. No sugar-coating the details.

"No estimate? Weeks? Days?" I swallowed. *"Hours?"*

"I said, I don't know."

"Okay. But what do—"

There was a sound then. A beeping—three clear tones that made me jump. Declan reached to his left wrist and pushed a button on his watch.

"What's that?" I asked.

"A timer."

"For what?"

That pale gray eye moved to me to show his bland disinterest in my endless string of questions. "I need to do something. It'll only take a minute. If you budge an inch from that seat, you won't like the results. Consider that a firm warning."

He pulled off to the side of the road, shifted into park, and got something out of his pocket—a small, black rectangular case, which he unzipped. I tensed when I saw it held another syringe. It was more of a pen needle than the one Anderson had.

"Relax," he said. "This isn't for you."

As he fiddled with a small glass vial, one of a half dozen that sat in the padded case about the size of his palm, I considered making an escape attempt.

Another glance at Declan showed that he was injecting himself in his stomach. He'd pulled up the edge of his black shirt to expose a flat, muscled abdomen, which bore a thick diagonal scar bisecting his navel.

My God. What had this horrible man been through to scar his entire body so badly? The thought turned my stomach.

"What is that?" I asked, referring to the needle. I didn't normally ask this many questions and could see how it could be annoying to the askee, but at the moment I didn't exactly give a shit.

"My serum."

He continued to answer my questions, albeit vaguely and abruptly. At least it was better than the silence from earlier. I felt somewhat assured that he wouldn't be putting a bullet into me. At least, not yet. He needed me. Or rather, he needed the poison inside of me. Maybe his father would be able to draw it out and help me. Give me a transfusion. Otherwise, why bother at all with this field trip to who knows where?

"Are you a diabetic?" I had a friend who injected regularly and had a similar case that she kept her insulin in. However, she'd taken it when she checked her blood sugar levels before meals, not when an alarm went off.

"No."

"Then what's that for?"

"It helps me control my hunger."

"You're on a diet?"

"You could say that."

What kind of diet would a hard-muscled assassin be on? Maybe it was steroids to help him pop some biceps, like vintage Arnold. He wasn't that bulky, though. And he didn't look like he was a competitive weight lifter. No, Declan's fat-free body was meant for stealth work—sneaking up behind a victim and slitting his or her throat, then dragging the corpse away to hide it.

My hand automatically went to my neck as if to protect it from an invisible blade.

"Look, Declan . . . we can work this out between us. Come to some sort of a deal for you to let me go."

"There is no deal. You're carrying something I need. End of story. Consider yourself a reluctant courier."

I turned that over in my already crowded brain. "Can your father—whoever he is—help to get this poison out of me?"

"That would be the ideal solution to this unfortunate situation, wouldn't it?"

Why couldn't he just answer yes or no? I forced myself to look at him. At this angle I only saw the strap of his eye patch. The damage was on the left side of his face. His right side was mostly unmarked. My gaze moved to his hands on the steering wheel. The imprint of my teeth was still on his scarred left forearm, although it didn't look as bad as I thought it would. However, it still looked as if it had been painful.

Good. Bastard deserved it.

He tucked his serum container away.

"I need to call my coworkers," I said. "And my roommate. They're going to be worried. There were witnesses and security cameras."

"I don't care about any of that."

"If I can call them, let them know I'm okay—"

"You're not okay." He shifted into drive and the tires screeched as he pulled back onto the road. "That poison's going to kill you. It's only a matter of time. What part of that don't you understand?"

3

I WANTED TO START SCREAMING AT HIM, START POUND-
ing on him. Maybe grab the steering wheel and crash us
into the nearest telephone pole. But I didn't.

I could still fix this. I clung to that thought like it was
the last floatation device on a doomed, sinking ship. I
grappled to maintain my grip on it as my growing despair
and panic tried to drown me.

I didn't want to die.

I'd had some hard times in the past. I wasn't Mary
Sunshine 24/7. I'd dealt with some depression that, five
years ago after my parents died, made me look long and
hard at my own continuing existence. But that was then
and this was now.

Knowledge was power. The more I knew about what
was happening to me, the better off I'd be. At least, I
hoped that was the case.

Declan hadn't beaten me unconscious for having a

tendency to ramble on and ask incessant questions. That was a good sign. He'd answered most of my questions, although I was still horribly confused.

Anderson had been developing some sort of poison for Declan's father. It sounded as if he'd had second thoughts about handing it off and Declan had been sent to take it anyway. What had Anderson said? That it was dangerous. An abomination. Something that could just as easily destroy Declan as the other—

—had he said *bloodsuckers*?

That could mean lots of things. Lawyers and tax collectors came to mind, along with mosquitoes, leeches, and vampires.

"What did Anderson mean when he said you're no better than the other bloodsuckers?" As soon as the words left my mouth, Declan glared at me. Great. The first sign of any sort of emotion from him had to be anger.

Had I insulted him? I forced myself not to turn away and cower.

"I answered your questions already."

"Why would your father be developing a poison meant for these . . . bloodsuckers? I don't understand."

"You don't have to understand. And trust me, you don't want to."

That helped a flare of anger rise up inside of me like a small, pissed-off phoenix. "Of course I don't want anything to do with this. I'd *prefer* not to understand. But that was before I got a syringe full of deadly poison injected into my jugular and had a man murdered in front of me. And now you tell me I can't go to a hospital or that will mean certain death for me. I don't know how fucking long this drive is, or where exactly you're taking me, but if you want me to stop asking questions about all this you're going to have to beat me unconscious and throw me in the trunk."

There it was. An open offer for him to pound those meat hooks of his into me and make me stop talking.

But really, I'd rather have been unconscious than sitting here for God only knew how long, waiting and wondering what was coming next. It was like torture.

"I don't hit women," he said after a long silence passed between us. "Not human ones, anyway."

"No, but you'll kill them if you're given the order, right?"

His jaw tensed. "Only if there's no other choice."

I thought about what he'd just said. "Wait. You said you don't hit human women. *Human?* Is that something you really need to clarify?"

"Sometimes." His attention was back on the road.

I licked my dry lips, wishing desperately for a bottle of water. "What women aren't human?"

"Those bloodsuckers Anderson was referring to." His lips thinned.

I gaped at him, and touched my wounded neck, grimacing as I ran my index finger over the lump where the tip of the needle had gone in. "You're not trying to tell me that they're—they're . . . *vampires*? Are you?"

It had been on my list of potential bloodsuckers.

He nodded once. "Most humans don't know of their true existence. They've kept to themselves for a very long time."

I could really use some of that water right about now. "Vampires are just fiction."

He gave me another one of those humorless twists of his lips. "Sorry to be the one to break it to you then, but they're real."

I waited for the punch line. But, of course, it didn't come. "I don't believe you."

"Doesn't really matter whether or not you believe me. I don't give a shit either way."

My stomach turned. "Well, that's good, because it's the most ridiculous thing I've ever heard."

"Is that right?"

"If vampires were real, everybody would know about them. It would be all over the news."

"I guess you have it all figured out, don't you?"

There was that sarcasm again. I was used to sarcasm with a large helping of humor when dealing with some of my friends—as well as my own liberal use of it. Declan's wasn't that pleasant. It was more mocking. Cruel.

I watched his attention shift to the rearview mirror, and whatever borderline amusement I thought I'd seen vanished from his expression.

"Most vampires choose to stay underground. There are a few rogues who come to the surface and enter larger cities and murder whomever they choose. But they're dealt with."

"Dealt with," I repeated.

"Usually hand-to-hand combat since they're hard to kill otherwise. Regular bullets don't work that well. Hunters tend to get a bit beaten up. Most don't have a long life expectancy, if you know what I mean."

Declan's scars. The ones that covered the left side of his face. That laced over his arms and the backs of his hands. The big one on his stomach.

"You're one of these hunters?" I asked, incredulously.

"Gee, how'd you guess?"

"Because you look like you've been through a meat grinder a couple of times."

"It was a rhetorical question." He touched his eye

patch. "I've taken down my share of rogues. Unfortunately, while my wounds heal fast, I scar up even worse than a human would."

That was a strange way to put it—*worse than a human.* "You're . . . not human?"

There was a wry twist to his mouth as he answered me. "Not entirely."

Okay, I'd been poisoned and kidnapped and witness to a murder, but I knew ridiculous from nonridiculous. I wasn't in the mood for Declan to yank my chain and give me half-assed answers when my life was hanging in the balance.

"Let me guess: You're a vampire?"

"If I was a vampire, I wouldn't come out during the day like this. It's one of the reasons most of them choose to live underground."

"Because sunlight turns them into dust."

"No. Because the sun fries the eyes right out of their heads, which would make them much easier to kill. They have a problem with that so they stay hidden during daylight hours. The smart ones stay hidden all the time."

The midday sun was high in the sky at the moment, glaring in through the window. Perspiration slid down my spine from the heat. Despite this, a shiver danced across my skin. "So, what are you?"

His jaw was tense and there was no humor in what little expression I could read on his scarred face. "It doesn't matter what I am."

"What are you?" I asked again. He was either lying about everything or he was completely and dangerously delusional. I was leaning toward the latter. "You said you're not human. Not *entirely* human."

He didn't reply. It only made me angrier.

"I didn't ask for this. If you want me to behave myself

so you can take me to this undisclosed location to see your father so he can get this poison out of my veins, then you need to talk to me." .

That earned me a look. "I should have gagged you and tied you up when I had the chance."

"Then why didn't you?"

"I'm not used to dealing with conscious human cargo." He glanced at the rearview mirror, then reached up and adjusted it a little. "We've still got a long way to go today."

That wasn't exactly answering my question. "How long?"

"Five hours."

I looked at the clock on the dashboard. If it was correct, it meant I'd been unconscious for about an hour. A six-hour drive from San Diego. That could mean a lot of places.

"So, are you going to tell me what you are or not?" Could I be annoying enough to make him lose his composure, his concentration? His blank-slate expression seemed to be his default. Maybe waving my hand in a lion's face would get it bitten off, but maybe it would be distraction enough to gain me the chance to escape. I'd managed to hurt him a little bit earlier. He wasn't a machine, that much I knew. I didn't know how I'd get away from him and get to a telephone, but I was going with my gut. And my gut told me to keep at him.

He said he didn't hit human women. I did hope he'd been telling the truth.

"Well?" I said.

He was silent for a moment. "I'm not usually the one answering the questions."

"You're usually the one demanding the answers, with a gun pressed to your victim's head?"

"Insightful."

"You're not a vampire and you're not entirely human. So what are you?"

"I'm a dhampyr," was his answer, which came a full minute later. He said it so quietly I had to strain to make it out.

"A damn peer?" I shook my head. "What's that?"

"Dhampyr," he repeated. "My mother was human but my father . . . my *real* father . . ." There was a tightness around his mouth. "He was a vampire."

I blinked. "So you're half-vampire."

The road ahead held Declan's entire attention again. "Yes."

There was silence in the car for a few heavy minutes.

My mouth felt very dry. "You don't have fangs."

"No." From what I'd seen when he spoke, he had straight white teeth. Totally normal and not any sharper than a regular human's.

"You're out during the day. You're not even wearing sunglasses."

"The injection I took helps dampen any vampire traits I might have, including hunger and out-of-control emotions. My father had it developed for me when I was young—"

"Your father, the vampire."

His jaw tensed even more. "No. My human father who raised me. He found my mother after she'd been raped and drained of blood nearly to the point of death. She was in a coma until I was born. They had to cut me out of her. She died shortly afterward."

My chest tightened at hearing that short, unpleasant story. "She was raped."

"Vampires are monsters with appetites for many unsavory things—sex, blood, death. And I have half of that monster inside of me. My father—my adoptive father—

had the serum developed for me. It allows me to go out during the day. It also holds back my hunger for blood . . . and other things that could hurt others."

I crossed my arms to stop them from trembling. "You're trying to tell me that you drink blood?"

"No. I eat and drink as a human does. As long as I take my injections, every part of the vampire that is inside of me will be controlled. I take an injection every three hours to dampen that behavior. My father's been developing another serum that will last a lot longer, but for now I have to deal with what I have."

Stop taking his serum and he'd turn into one of the monsters. Kind of ironic, since I already thought he was one.

"My father raised me to fight and kill vampires," Declan continued grimly. "And I do it to help save the humans who don't even know about the danger that surrounds them. That's why that poison was developed—something that can kill them easier than any other weapon."

"That's what the poison is?" I touched my neck and tried to will my heart to stop pounding so fast. Just the thought of it pushing the poison quicker through my veins made me feel sick.

"The means to destroy vampires once and for all was in that syringe. Do you see why it's so important that I get you to my father before it's too late? Why you can't go to a regular hospital? As soon as they find out that's what you're injected with they'll want to destroy it. Destroy *you*."

Before I died from that poison, he meant.

He eyed me. "You don't believe me."

I shook my head. "No. I don't."

"Then why am I wasting my fucking breath explaining

all of this to you?" He glanced again at the rearview mirror. "There they are. I wondered how long it would take them to catch up to us."

I looked over my shoulder, through the dirty back window of the car. There was another car behind us—*far* behind—in a silver sedan.

"Who?"

"The proof that everything I've told you is the truth."

I cast another look over my shoulder. "I don't understand."

"That's painfully obvious." He shook his head and then spoke under his breath. "I'm used to killing things, not protecting them. This should be interesting."

"Protecting? Who are they? What are you protecting?"

"I'm protecting that formula you have inside of you right now. And since I'm protecting the formula, that means I'm protecting you, too."

I glared at him. "The only thing I need protection from is you."

"Then you're about to add a few people to the list." He whipped out his cell phone, pressed a button, and held it to his ear. After a moment, he said, "They're on us." He went silent, listening to whomever was on the other end of the line. "Two of them. Maybe three. I can't see. I just took an injection so my vision's not as sharp as it was earlier. I'll try to lose them, but if I can't, I'll have to eliminate them."

Whatever reply he received was enough for him; without another word he ended the call and tucked it back into the pocket of his jeans. I took note of its location. If I could get my hands on that cell phone long enough to make a call, then—

Declan took the next exit so abruptly that I slammed

into him. I wasn't wearing a seat belt. I pushed away from him as quickly as I could and got back on my safer, dhampyr-free side of the car.

"What are you doing?" I demanded.

"Double-checking if my instincts are right."

"Who are they?" I put my seat belt on. I'd prefer not to go headfirst through the windshield if I could avoid it.

"Blood servants. Humans who work for vampires in various capacities. I already knew they were tipped off about what we've been working on. Anderson was going to sell the vampires the formula so they could destroy it. That's why I was sent to intervene."

"Sell it to vampires? Why would he do that?"

"Money. Carl Anderson could talk about the greater good all he wanted, but his greater good was focused on his bottom line. Stupid, though. If it hadn't been my bullet that got him, he would have become a vampire's breakfast."

"Why are they after us?"

"They must know I have the formula. So that means they also know Anderson's dead. This should be interesting."

"Why did you get off the highway?"

"Easier to lose them on the back roads."

"And if you can't lose them?" I asked, thinking of what he'd said on the phone. What he asked permission to do. "You're going to kill them?"

"That's the general idea."

I didn't want anyone else to get hurt today. It could be just a few people in a car minding their own business, but if Declan thought they were the enemy, then they'd end up dead. I'd already seen him kill. He hadn't hesitated. He hadn't listened to begging.

He didn't have to be half-vampire to be a cold-blooded murderer.

Off the highway now, Declan kept driving, even faster than before. A glance over my shoulder confirmed the silver sedan continued to follow us.

Declan looked at me and must have seen the strained look on my face. "Not your average Tuesday for a city girl like you, is it?"

"Stop this car right now," I demanded.

"I don't think you're getting that you aren't in control here."

"Oh, I'm getting that. You have the gun so you're the one in control. You're also the one who's going to get us both killed."

"So you believe that we have some blood servants on our collective ass right now?"

"No, you're going to kill us by crashing this car."

"Trust me, I'm a very good driver." His good eye flicked to the rearview mirror again. "If it makes you feel better, I'll answer a few more questions for you. Help you get your mind off things."

He took the next corner so fast I would have ended up in his lap if I wasn't wearing my seat belt. I grabbed hold of where it cut across my chest and held on tightly.

The moment I had the chance, I'd get away from him. With or without that cell phone. Escape was all I wanted right now.

Questions. I had so many of them, but where to begin? I sorted through the cluttered mess in my head and latched onto the first thought that presented itself to me.

"How did you lose your eye?"

"Noticed that, did you?"

"The eye patch gave it away."

"Figured it might." He touched it casually, as if he wasn't going a hundred miles an hour. "Lost this to a rogue who clawed it out with his fingernails. I'd dragged him into the sun. As the eyeballs were melting out of his head and he was screaming in pain, he decided to share a little of the misery with me. It was my own fault for thinking I had him beat. His mate had already scored my face up pretty bad with a knife before I managed to kill her. The blood in my eyes made it difficult to see properly." He trailed his fingertips along the spiderweb-like scars and then glanced at me. "Glad you asked me to share that fun little anecdote?"

He said it with such detachment. Such a horrible experience all around, and it was as if it was just another day at the office for him. I wasn't sure if I should feel bad for him or disgusted.

I chose disgusted. It was the easier of the two. I wiped my sweaty palms on my thighs. "Thrilled. Guess you need to be more careful now. You only have one eye left."

"Thanks for the suggestion. Two more questions and then you hold true to our bargain about shutting that pretty little fucking mouth of yours for the remainder of this trip."

He took another abrupt turn, spraying gravel out from under the tires as the car went from a paved road to a dirt one. I braced my hand against the window next to me.

"Have we lost them?" I couldn't see the silver car in the side-view mirror anymore.

"It's possible. Now you have one more question."

I glared at him. "That wasn't a question, it was a . . . an inquiry."

"One question left," he said again.

I blinked and felt the sting of tears. Frustration and fear. It was getting to me. I was trying to hold it together, but I was finding it more difficult with each passing moment.

"Would you have killed me in that alley if you'd been told to?"

"Yes," he replied without hesitating.

I'd expected that answer, but it was still enough to send an uncontrollable shiver through me. "Do you always do everything you're told?"

"You're officially out of questions." He brought the car to a lurching stop behind what looked like an abandoned gas station. We'd reached an unpopulated area a few miles off the highway. He inched the car forward until we could see a bit of road past the building covered in peeling white paint.

"Declan—"

He held a hand up. "Be quiet."

I pressed my lips together and waited. There was a churning sensation in my stomach that didn't feel right. I touched my forehead to find it damp with perspiration. My hands were now clammy as well.

"I don't feel so good," I said.

And I didn't. It was like a slow-moving wave coming for me. I saw it in the distance and knew what it meant, but there was no way for me to get out of its way in time.

When my stomach cramped, it brought with it a sensation like a knife tearing through my core.

I gasped for breath and reached for the handle. "Let me out."

"You're not going anywhere. We're waiting here until we see the servants go by. Five minutes before we get back on the road."

My heart had doubled its pace. I kept trying to open the door but it was locked. I couldn't find the strength to unlock it.

"Please." My voice was so weak that it sounded truly pathetic. I couldn't move. Couldn't brace myself against the agony that ripped through my body. It felt as if I'd ingested the poison orally. It centered on my stomach and lashed its razor-sharp claws out in all directions.

"What the hell's wrong with you?" Declan asked gruffly before he grabbed hold of my chin and moved my face so he could see me. A frown furrowed his brow as he registered that I wasn't faking. "Fuck."

The pain let up for a moment, enough for me to take a great gasp of breath. "I'm going . . . to be . . . sick."

Without further argument, he reached over me and fumbled with the lock, popping it up and pushing open the passenger door. Then he undid my seat belt. I still couldn't move. I couldn't run if my life depended on it. And, actually, it currently did.

It only took seconds before he'd exited his side and come around to mine, grabbing hold of me and pulling me out of the car and over toward a small patch of dry, dead grass.

"Then be sick," he said.

And I was. I puked everything that was in my stomach and that, too, felt like knives carving their way out of me. It tasted like acid, sour and rancid as I threw up onto the grass. I shuddered and felt my cheeks wet with tears.

I heard a ripping sound and a moment later there was a piece of black cloth at my mouth. Declan had torn off a piece of his shirt so I could mop the vomit off my lips.

What a fucking gentleman.

That was my last coherent thought before my eyes rolled back into my head and everything went dark.

The next thing I felt was the sharp sting of a slap across my face, and I gasped as I came to. Still on the grass. Still kneeling there with Declan standing next to me. How long had it been? Only seconds?

"No time for weakness. We need to get going."

He'd slapped me. Bastard. And he'd said he didn't hit women. He'd kill them if ordered to, but he didn't hit them.

I tried to punch him, but he deflected it easily.

"Really? Don't be ridiculous."

"Just kill me," I begged him. "The pain . . . it's too much."

"Life is pain, princess. If this is the worst you've ever felt before, then you're one lucky bitch."

Nice.

Before I could comment on his heartwarming philosophy, he'd grabbed me around my waist and hoisted me back up to my feet. Instead of moving toward the car, though, we moved in the opposite direction, toward a run-down shamble of a house fifty yards behind the gas station.

"Car?" I asked feebly, the taste of death mixed in my mouth with the bagel and cream cheese I'd had for breakfast.

"Last-minute change of plans. They're here. The blood servants have found us. We wouldn't make it back to the car in time."

The pain in my gut now fought with fresh panic. "What?"

He glared at me. "Like I said before, you're way too distracting for me. And that weakness is going to get us both killed."

4

I TRIED TO PULL MYSELF TOGETHER. AFTER THROWING up and passing out, the pain was finally lifting. If I had anything to be thankful for today, that would be it. Nothing like experiencing severe pain to make you appreciate *not* being in pain.

I didn't have to be told that we were being followed. Rather, *stalked* would be a better way to put it. At the house, which was as abandoned as the gas station with dirty, broken windows lining the porch and four rickety stairs leading up to the front door, Declan released me. His gun was in his right hand, held slackly at his side even though I could see the muscles flexing up and down his arm.

Two men and a woman walked past Declan's car; one of the men took out a knife and slashed the tires. Declan swore under his breath.

My stomach sank. Couldn't go too far with a car with flat tires, could we?

The blood servants slowly approached us. The man in front, sporting a shaved head and black goatee, appeared to have no weapons. He held his hands up in front of him.

"We don't want any trouble," he said.

"Oh yeah?" Declan raised his gun. "Then get back in your car and leave."

"Declan, right?" the man said. "Declan Reyes? How's the old man doing?"

He came to a stop about ten feet away, his associates five feet on either side of them. The woman was a blond, nearly as light as I was, and she wore a knee-length black leather coat despite the heat of the day—it was easily over a hundred degrees out here. The other man had cropped red hair and wore a faded gray T-shirt emblazoned with the logo of a rock band I'd never heard of.

"He's just fine," Declan replied.

"Who's your friend?" The man's eyes flicked toward me.

"She's not a friend."

"She doesn't look so good."

"The flu's going around."

"We want the formula." The man's associates remained silent but watchful, and didn't seem the least bit perturbed by the gun Declan now had raised at their leader's head.

"What formula?" Declan asked evenly. It was without humor or even challenge. It was just a question.

"You didn't have to kill him, you know. Anderson was worth more to you alive than dead."

"I get an itchy trigger finger when somebody's trying to shoot me. What can I say?"

"We know about the formula. He told us. We went there today to retrieve and destroy it. Instead, we walked in on a murder scene. Your father isn't going to be very happy about that."

"What do you know about my father?"

"We know that he likes things just so. And putting a bullet into Anderson's head isn't *just so*. Bad move, Declan."

"Like I give a fuck what you think."

"Give us the formula and we'll leave you and your little girlfriend alone."

"I'll cop to killing Anderson, but he didn't have anything on him. He was trying to flee the city, said something about mindless blood servants after his ass. Maybe I did you a favor. He wasn't very trustworthy."

The man's lips curved into a smile and he looked past Declan at me. "You sure you want to get involved with this guy, honey? He's bad news."

"I don't want anything to do with this." I swallowed hard. "I just want to leave."

"Hear that, Declan? That's got to sting, huh? A face like yours can't keep the attention of a pretty lady like that. I guess having the flu doesn't help her see past the fug."

"The flu"—Declan turned his head and snarled under his breath to me—"that you need my father's help to cure or you're not going to get better. Try to remember that."

There was a warning if ever I heard one. And I hated the fact that I believed him.

He'd told me doctors couldn't help me. That going to a hospital could only lead to my death—and possibly more blood servants like these ones coming to get me when they realized what I was poisoned with.

Only one thing stopped me from begging this stranger for help and a ride back to the city, and that was the fact he'd said they meant to destroy the formula. Being that it was inside me at the moment didn't exactly convince me that the trio would shuttle me to the nearest hospital.

Even if they did, even if Declan was wrong, he was right about one thing. A normal hospital might not know what to do with me once I got there. It wasn't as if I'd been doing shots of Drano and just needed my stomach pumped. I had a prototype poison in my blood that had been secretly developed to kill vampires. Hell, if I told a doctor that, they'd have me admitted to the psych ward.

His father had helped develop this. His father might be able to help me.

Might.

At least the wave of nausea and pain I'd felt before had nearly completely passed and I was well enough to stay on my feet, despite the shakiness and the cold sweat dripping steadily down my spine.

"Stay behind me," Declan growled.

I did as he said. For now. After all, being behind the gun was a great deal better than being in front of it.

"Why don't you give me the keys to your car?" Declan said to the bald man. "And I'll let you and your friends live."

"You'd do that for us? That's so nice of you."

"I'll give you ten seconds to comply or I have three bullets in here with each of your names on them."

"But we haven't even introduced ourselves yet."

"I'll make up names for you. Ten . . . nine . . . eight . . ."

"Matthias wants that formula. And he won't take no for an answer."

There was an almost imperceptible catch in Declan's voice before he stopped counting. "Matthias."

The blood servant nodded. "So you see why it's vital that we don't go back empty-handed."

"Right," Declan replied drily. "Wouldn't want to upset your lord and master, would you?"

The man smiled. "You've met?"

"Never had the pleasure. If I had, he'd be dead right now."

That earned a laugh from all three of the servants. To me, it hadn't sounded as if Declan was attempting to do stand-up comedy.

"If you think for a moment you could defeat Matthias, you're an idiot. He's king for a reason, you know."

I'd moved to an angle that let me see Declan's lips stretch humorlessly over his white teeth. "I heard he's only king because he keeps the real king locked away in a coffin somewhere."

The laughter faded. "You heard that, did you?"

"I did."

"From where?"

"You're not the only one with sources."

"Our sources are reliable."

"So are mine. Now, we were talking about those car keys of yours? You did slash my tires. It's the least you can do."

"Seems we're at a bit of a standoff. You want my keys and we want to know where you've stashed that formula."

"I don't have it."

The man shrugged. "I guess I just don't believe you."

Did these people know that Declan was a dhampyr? Would that make any difference to them? And what were they talking about with this Matthias person. A vampire king?

I had no idea that going out on a coffee break today would help me take a nosedive directly down the rabbit hole.

"Declan—" I wasn't even sure what I wanted to ask

him. Maybe for some assurance that everything would be okay. How insane was my day if I was now looking for assurances from somebody like him?

"Keys," Declan said to the man again, ignoring me. "Or you're going back to Matthias in a body bag."

"Thing is," the leader said with a fierce look on his face, "I embrace my death. I'm loyal to my king where others may falter. Laying my very existence on the line in order to help him destroy the poison you and your ignorant people had developed to annihilate an entire species—"

"That species doesn't deserve to live," Declan bit out through clenched teeth. "They're evil leeches who drain the life from their victims, leaving bodies in their wake."

"Sounds like a hunter to me."

"I only kill what needs to be killed."

"Everything and everyone deserves a fighting chance at life, be it predator or prey." The leader took a step closer. "And who the fuck are you to say any differently? Nice god complex there, asshole. Did you learn that from your father? I've heard things about him and the people he works for. Bad things."

"Everybody's a critic."

"Declan," I said louder, but he paid no attention to me. I had a very bad feeling about where this was going.

"I choose to give my life for Matthias," the man said, taking yet another step closer. "So he can live eternally."

The next moment, he launched himself at Declan. I jumped at the sound of the gunshot. The bullet hit the man in his chest and he staggered back a few steps, looking down with surprise at the wound before he raised his fierce gaze, bared his teeth, and surged forward again.

Declan didn't hesitate. He fired two more shots, one to the chest and one to the head. That ended it. The man dropped heavily to his knees and then hit the ground at Declan's feet, face first.

"Bad choice," Declan said to the dead man.

A strangled cry escaped my throat and Declan turned to look at me.

"Get back to the car and lock yourself in," he said. "Now."

What happened next was so quick I could barely follow it.

The woman approached Declan fearlessly and kicked the weapon away from him. Without lowering her leg she kicked again, higher, thrusting the sharp stiletto heel of her shoe deep into Declan's shoulder before he could dodge the blow.

Blood streamed down his bicep, past the short sleeve of his shirt. Declan grabbed her leg, pulling the silver heel out of his injured shoulder, and twisted it hard, forcing her to hit the ground heavily.

Then he turned and smashed his fist into the other servant's face, who had in his right hand the knife he'd used to slash Declan's tires. Blood burst from the man's mouth and he stumbled back a step.

The woman jumped back up, eyes flashing. She was adept at some kind of martial arts, like something out of a movie. She aimed her foot, lethal-heel out, toward Declan's jugular this time. He deflected it and got her fist in his face instead. He grabbed her, his arm coming around her throat, but she fought hard against him and broke free, spinning around to kick him again with her sharp heel.

I'd never seen a woman fight like this in real life. For a blond no taller than me, she was deadly.

Declan said he didn't hit human women. True to his word, he hadn't actually hit her yet, but was simply deflecting her blows.

On the ground nearby was Declan's gun from where it

had been knocked out of his grip. I reached down and grabbed it.

"Not so fast." The second man was in front of me. Before I could aim, he backhanded me and pain exploded in my face. He quickly retrieved the gun after it flew out of my grip.

I thought he was going to shoot me, but instead he turned, aimed, and shot Declan in the back.

I screamed and covered my mouth with my hand in horror.

Declan buckled and hit the ground, landing hard on his stomach. The man went over to him and ground the sole of his shoe against the bullet wound. Declan let out a harsh sound of pain, his face smashed against the gravel. It wasn't a scream and it wasn't a plea to stop. More like a growl of warning from a dangerous, injured animal.

"His name was Smith, that guy you just shot," the blood servant hissed. "His life was worth more than some stupid formula. His life was worth more than some stupid fucking hunter and his blond bitch." He pressed his heel harder against the bloody wound. "Now, that formula? Where is it?"

"Fuck you," Declan ground out.

"That's not a very polite answer."

"Fuck you, please."

"Maybe we'll see what your girlfriend has to say. A little torture works nicely on most women. Makes them squeal quicker than a scarred, brainwashed piece of shit like you would."

"Leave her alone or you'll regret it."

"Nah, don't think I will." The man removed the pressure from the bloody wound only long enough to bring his boot down hard on Declan's head several times— hard enough, in my opinion, to kill him. The woman drew close enough to kick him in his stomach, then once in his face.

Declan's form was now very still.

Then they turned toward me.

Had they killed him? I didn't know how anyone could take that much damage and live. I hated him, hated what he'd dragged me into, but the thought that he was dead scared me deeply. After all, he'd been the only thing standing between me and . . . these two.

"Sorry about that," the woman said, a smile touching her lips that turned her previously feral expression into something much more attractive. "But when you get mixed up with a hunter, especially one who works for Carson Reyes and his people, you're in for a bad time all around."

Carson Reyes. That had to be Declan's father.

The man drew closer so he could grab the back of my hair to hold me in place.

"So, when did you meet scar-face over there?" the woman asked pleasantly. Seemed a major contrast to the other one pulling my hair and gawking at me like I was his latest science project.

"T-today," I stammered. "He grabbed me . . . kidnapped me . . . after what happened with the man he killed."

I didn't have to give all the details, just enough so they'd think I was being completely helpful and ready to talk. Which I was. I'd be happy to tell them everything except what had happened to the formula.

The man looked at my injured neck with interest, but nothing passed over his expression that made me think he'd figure it out. They weren't detectives here to figure out a mystery, they were just muscle ready to kill to get what they were after.

It wasn't all that reassuring, actually.

"You don't seem like his type," the woman said. "I

would have assumed the hunter likes them way sluttier than you look. Someone he can get a blow job for a twenty without her complaining too much about his nasty looks, you know?" She slid her hand over my shoulder and grabbed the back of my long-sleeved shirt to look at the label inside. "Calvin Klein. I thought you looked like a rich bitch."

"I'm not rich. It was a gift."

"From who?"

"My roommate. She was going to get rid of it, give it to charity, but she gave it to me instead."

She grinned. "Does that make you a charity case?"

I looked at Declan, hoping to see him rise to his feet, shake it off, and come to my rescue like some sort of battle-damaged knight in shining armor. Obviously I was still reaching for that delusional silver lining when it had already rusted and chipped away.

Declan didn't move.

A bullet that possibly severed his spinal cord, a stiletto heel stab wound to the shoulder, and thirty seconds of having his head used as a soccer ball weren't exactly things that could just be shaken off. Or *lived through,* for that matter.

I was totally on my own now.

I wouldn't be taken to see his father, Carson. That had been held up as my only chance to get out of this alive—for him to somehow extract the poison from my blood. Something a regular hospital couldn't do for me.

But if Declan was dead, that wouldn't happen. I had no idea where his father was.

Then again, there was a strong possibility that these servants would do the same thing to me as they'd done to Declan. Or worse.

The poison in me right now was currently the least of my worries.

My shirt. We were talking about my blue silk shirt.

"When you don't make a lot of money, you need to go on the barter system," I said. "My friends and I trade all the time."

"We can barter, too." The man used his free hand, the one that wasn't twisted painfully into my hair, to trail down the line of buttons on the front of my secondhand designer shirt. His fingers then shifted to graze over my left breast. I repressed a shudder.

I looked at the woman, hoping to see some sort of female kinship there that she wanted to help me, but there was only a tolerant and slightly bored look on her face as she watched her friend feel me up.

She pulled a knife with an ivory handle from inside of her leather jacket and traced the tip of it lightly over my throat. "Talk to us about the formula."

"I know where it is," I said, blinking back my tears of panic.

The man's hand stilled. "You do?"

"Yes."

They exchanged a look.

"Where is it?" the woman asked.

"I give it to you and you let me go. You don't hurt me. And you tell your buddy to keep his fucking paws off me."

She appeared to mull that over. "You killed our friend."

"I didn't kill him. Besides, you killed my—" I looked over at Declan and felt my chest tighten to see how much of him was now covered in blood. "You killed *him*. Doesn't that make us even?"

"He's still breathing." She flicked a glance in his direction. "But I doubt if he'll wake up."

I cringed. "So we're even."

"You prove to us you know where it is," the woman said, stroking a piece of blond hair back from my forehead and tucking it behind my ear. "And I promise we'll let you live."

"Without torturing me. Or hurting me."

"No need to torture or hurt you if you have what we're looking for. We're not heathens."

She sounded sincere. Maybe that was only wishful thinking.

"Let her go, Davis," she said and took a step back. "Time to cut our losses and get what we came here for."

His expression soured. "Matthias won't give a shit that Smith gave his life to retrieve the formula."

She narrowed her eyes. "Let her go. *Now.*"

Davis leered at me for another moment before he finally released me. "Fine. Have it your way."

"You're going to destroy it?" I asked. "The formula?"

"Yes."

I looked at both of them warily, expecting them to hurt me, but they didn't. The woman held the knife like she knew how to use it, though. The man just stood next to her with his arms crossed, watching every move I made.

Then I walked toward Declan's unconscious form and went down on my knees next to him. His face was bloody. The eye patch had shifted so I could see the scarred, hollow socket where his eye used to be. For some reason, a flicker of sympathy went through me at that, rather than disgust. I pulled the eye patch back into its proper place.

Then I patted him down and located the case containing his serum in the left pocket of his jeans. Not too many other places for him to hide it. I looked it over to see that it had no markings, nothing that might give away what it really was.

I pressed my finger against the side of his throat and was surprised to feel a weak heartbeat. He looked like he should be dead, but he wasn't. Not yet, anyway.

I stood up again and faced the servants, holding the black case out to them. "Here."

"He actually had it on him?" the woman asked with disbelief.

"He took it from Anderson before he shot him. Didn't have enough time to hide it anywhere."

She nodded at the man and he snatched it away from me, unzipping it to look at the pen needle and unmarked vials of clear liquid inside.

I kept my face as emotionless as possible. I was sure that I looked terrified, but that wouldn't give me away as a liar.

"Well?" she asked.

"Five samples left. Anderson said what he had today was all there was."

"Give it to me." The woman held out her hand and the man gave her the case. Her gaze moved over the contents slowly before she zipped it up and tucked it into her jacket pocket. She glanced over to where Declan lay. "He took you as a hostage to get out of San Diego, right?"

I nodded shakily. They believed Declan's serum was the formula. I held my breath.

"Hunters have their own rules. This one," she nodded at Declan's still form, "I've heard things about him. He's cold-blooded, even more so than the rest of them are, and some think he's undefeatable. Doesn't look like it to me. Maybe his reputation was only something created to put fear into the hearts of vampires and their clan."

"Is that who you are? Part of the . . . vampire's clan?"

"I'm part of Matthias's clan. He takes care of me. And in return, I take care of him by eliminating any threat like this poison." Her expression soured.

"But . . . but you're human."

"That's right."

"You're not a vampire."

"Not yet. Matthias doesn't give eternal life to just anyone. We earn it by choosing to give our human lives over to him without question." She smiled and stroked the side of my face. "You don't understand, of course. But if you met him, you too would want to give him everything you have to give—your body, your blood, your very life."

I highly doubted that. "I don't want to meet him."

"Pray that you don't. He'd devour a little thing like you in minutes."

I forced myself not to look away from her. "You promised you'd let me live if I gave you the formula. Well, I gave it to you."

"You did. Thank you." She glanced down at Declan again before returning her gaze to mine. "There was a time when I was a lot like you."

"What's that supposed to mean?"

"I was an ordinary woman who couldn't defend herself. One who had to stand behind a strong man for fear of being hurt." She leaned closer to me. "Strong human men are a myth. They're all weak, selfish, and can be manipulated. Or killed." I felt something cold touch my hand. It was her ivory-hilted knife. "Take this."

"Why are you giving me this?"

"This man took you." She touched my neck, sliding her fingertips along my bruised skin. "He hurt you. That's unforgiveable. This weapon is for when you wake up. You can kill him and take your power back by spilling his blood. A symbolic gesture. One that could make you worthy of being in Matthias's presence, if you ever choose to be."

I looked at her, my eyes wide. "When I wake up? Wake up from what?"

She moved out of the way to make room for Davis who, with a leering smile, looked me up and down. I braced myself for what he was going to do and held the knife tighter in my grip as I prepared to defend myself.

However, the gun came so fast I couldn't duck it. The blow against my temple from the cold steel was more than enough to knock me out cold.

5

SON OF A BITCH.

Gravel bit painfully against the side of my face. It was the first thing I noticed when I came to. My head felt like it had spent some quality time in a tightening vise. Or, possibly, hell itself.

I'd never been hit like that before. Never. And the sharp backhand from earlier had been the first time a man had struck me in my entire life. Two in one day, from the same asshole, and that didn't even include being shoved around by Declan already. That was entirely enough abuse for a Tuesday afternoon.

I reached up to touch my mouth, expecting to feel shattered teeth, but they all seemed to be intact and not loose or in danger of falling out. I touched the rest of my face to find everything still in the right place. Pushing myself up to a sitting position, although a bout of dizziness slowed me down, I shielded my eyes and looked up. The sun seemed to be as high and bright as it had been before. However, enough time had passed that the blood servants were nowhere to be seen.

They hadn't killed me. No, instead they'd knocked me out. Anger flared inside me at the thought. It was hardly necessary. It wasn't as if I would have chased after their car like an enthusiastic golden retriever.

I looked around. Still next to the abandoned house, about fifty feet away from the useless old black car with its newly flat tires. The dirt road was beyond the gas station, although I couldn't see it from my current vantage point. To the right of me lay the body of the bald man the servants called Smith—they'd left him behind. According to the bullet wound in his head, which bore a striking resemblance to the one Anderson received earlier in the day, he wasn't getting up anytime soon.

To the left of me, Declan was sprawled in the same broken position he'd been in earlier. Still unconscious.

I crawled toward him clutching the knife Cruella de Vil had given me and checked his pulse again. It seemed even stronger than before. His shoulder was bloody from where I'd witnessed Cruella's heel going in. I ran my left hand over the pockets of his bloodstained jeans searching for his phone—there was another deep injury on his hip causing the massive blood flow there. When I located it, which probably would have been easier if I wasn't dealing with a scrambled brain, I pulled it out, only to find that it was broken.

"Fuck!" I yelled and threw the useless gadget away from me.

No phone. So much for calling in the good guys to save me.

At that moment I wanted to kill him—to do exactly what Cruella told me to do and plunge this knife right into his heart.

Suddenly, Declan's fingers wrapped around my wrist and I shrieked, looking down at him with shock. His bloodshot gray eye was barely open, but it was trained on me. His lips moved a little. I couldn't hear anything for a moment.

"My . . . serum . . ."

I tried to pull away from him, but he held on to me tightly. My hand was slippery with his blood. "What about it?"

"I need more time . . . to recover. You'll have to inject me when . . . my alarm . . . goes off. You . . . have to."

"I don't have to do anything." I clenched my shiny new knife tighter.

"You need to get me out of the sun."

"Or what? You'll melt?"

"No. It prevents me from healing. It weakens me. And . . . and I need water. A lot of it. Now."

Demanding little bastard, wasn't he?

It was on the tip of my tongue to tell him his serum was long gone, on its way back to Matthias, the goddamned vampire king of California, but his eye closed again and his grip loosened enough for me to scramble back from him and get to my feet.

I scanned the surroundings and wasn't happy with what I saw. In other words, not a hell of a lot. I half expected tumbleweed to blow by in this one-gas-station ghost town. Was it only a few miles back to the highway? I could flag someone down. We weren't that far away from civilization. My ankle was still tender from when Declan had thrown me into the front seat of his now-useless car, but it wasn't that bad. I could manage.

Without looking at Declan again, I started walking away from him and the man he'd killed.

"You can't leave me here," he called after me in a pained, raspy voice. "You can't go to a regular hospital. You need me if you want to live."

I ignored him. My head throbbed, my neck ached, and my veins still felt strange, stretched, and tender. But I was still breathing. My heart was still beating. And, despite what he said, a hospital sounded like a wonderful destination.

Poison, I'd tell them. I'd been poisoned. I didn't know with what exactly—no need to mention the vampire thing—but my life was in jeopardy. *Please help me.*

And they'd help me. Of course they would. That's what hospitals were for.

Declan had to be lying when he said that doctors couldn't help me.

My health insurance was paid up. May as well make use of it.

I got to the road. Which way had we come from? The gas station—now that I gave it a good look, didn't seem like it had been open for business for half a century—had been on our right when we'd arrived. So I turned left. The heat from the sun beat into me.

Declan was going to bleed to death.

Good. He deserved it.

I wouldn't allow myself to feel any guilt about my decision to leave him there. Still, the unwelcome emotion gnawed at my insides.

What else was I supposed to do? It was his own fault he was in this situation. If he'd given them the formula when they'd asked for it, he wouldn't have gotten the life beaten out of him.

Wait a minute.

I stopped walking for a moment. No, that wasn't right. I was confusing his serum with the formula. It wasn't the same thing.

Declan hadn't told them the poison was in me, which would have been the truthful answer. He'd told me to get behind him and then for me to get to safety just before things went downhill. He said he was going to protect me.

Protect me. Right. If it wasn't for him, I wouldn't be here in the first place.

I had no idea how long I had left to live. Weeks, days, hours.

Hell, I had no idea for sure that the poison would actually kill me. Maybe it wasn't even *poison*. Maybe Declan just said that to help keep me in line and to make me do whatever he wanted.

I grasped hold of this thought with both hands. I'd been going only on his word, and what damn good was that?

Dhampyr vampire hunter. Sure. All I'd seen was a trigger-happy, scar-faced lunatic. And three other lunatics who all believed in mythical creatures that drank blood and avoided the sun. Except for the lunatic part, I wasn't sure what I believed.

I picked up my pace. I could get to the highway in about a half an hour, I figured. Maybe a car would venture along—although it looked as if the last time it had been a well-traveled road, the gas station was in business.

The hope didn't last long.

Five minutes later, the pain returned, stopping me dead in my tracks. I collapsed at the side of the road and retched my guts out.

I would have thought my stomach had been emptied before, but when I opened my watering eyes I saw that I'd managed to throw up something that was as black as ink and the consistency of corn syrup. The sickening substance puddled on the dry ground. I wiped my mouth and saw that my hand came away smeared with blackness.

"Oh God," I murmured, then cried out as another wave of pain crashed over me.

Declan hadn't been lying—I couldn't even try to deny it any longer. That formula had poisoned my entire body and it wasn't getting better. It was getting worse.

You need me if you want to live.

Declan's father—he said he could help me. This was a poison developed to kill vampires. Hospitals, *regular* hospitals were useless. His father knew what the poison was, he valued it enough to send his mercenary adopted son out on a suicide mission to retrieve it.

If I went to a hospital, more blood servants like the ones I'd just been faced with would come to get me. To kill me. To eliminate the threat aimed at their precious vampire king and others like him.

If I had to place my bets, all my money would be on Carson Reyes as the man with the answers I needed if I wanted to live another day.

My life was in the hands of someone I'd never met before.

And if I let Declan die—or if I killed him—I'd never get the chance to meet him.

As soon as the pain and nausea passed, which took another ten torturous minutes, I forced myself to head back to where Declan lay on the ground.

Part of me—the rational and sane part—resisted what I knew I had to do. But I had to help him if I could. Declan Reyes had caused my current condition, and by God, he was going to fix it. Him and this mysterious vampire-hating father of his.

I shook Declan's shoulder, which was damp and sticky from sweat and blood. "Wake up."

It took a minute, but his eyelashes fluttered and his eye opened a millimeter.

"You said you have to get out of the sun," I said. "That means I need to get you in there."

I could see the agony on his face as he lifted his head to look at the abandoned house I nodded toward.

"Fine." The single word held deep pain.

"You said you also need water?"

He gave me a barely perceptible nod. "Yes."

Come to think of it, I was pretty damn thirsty myself, and my mouth currently tasted horrible after throwing up.

He moved his legs, which was enough indication that the bullet in his back hadn't paralyzed him. He got all the way up to his knees by himself, but hunched over on his hands, his chest heaving. He didn't make a sound. I was sure moving hurt like a son of a bitch, but he didn't cry out in pain once.

Tough bastard, wasn't he?

I helped him up to his feet, not pleased about being so close to someone I'd spent so much time and energy trying to get away from, but I'd run out of options.

Declan had to be six-four and at least 220 pounds of solid muscle. And all of that weight was braced against me as we maneuvered up the four stairs to the front door. I fumbled for the handle and wasn't surprised to find it locked. But the door looked flimsy enough.

I leaned Declan against the wall and put some shoulder into it as I bashed against the door. I wasn't exactly Ms. Olympia when it came to strength, even on a good day— which this wasn't—but the door was old and it only took a few tries before the lock splintered and it swung open.

Once we got through the door his legs gave out and he crashed to the wooden floor. Couldn't stop it if I'd tried. I hadn't really tried.

Declan's face was pasty white and he already looked half-dead to me.

And water was going to help him recover from this? I'd believe it when I saw it.

The house opened up on a bare room, dusty but luckily not rotting or smelly or infested with insects. To the left of us was a kitchen. Leaving Declan where he lay, I went into the kitchen and looked at the faucet. It reminded me of the one my grandmother had in the home she lived in her entire life—old-fashioned, utilitarian, and very practical. Definitely not courtesy of Ikea. I turned the handle. Nothing happened.

I hadn't really expected anything to happen. The house looked like it had been abandoned for decades.

Water. Where was I supposed to get some?

"Where else is there water?" I asked aloud.

"There's a . . . pump at . . . the side of the house. I noticed it when we arrived."

I looked over at him. "You're thirsty?"

"I need it to heal from the silver they used on me. Full vamps heal quickly without scarring. I heal fast . . . but I scar, obviously . . . and it takes a great deal more effort for me. Water helps speed up the process." His eye moved to the knife I held. "Where did you get that?"

"The servants swapped me for your gun before they knocked me unconscious with it and took off. I thought it was a fair trade."

Without another word, I went outside again and around to the side of the house. Sure enough, there was a pump. Rusted. More searching netted me a dirty wooden bucket. I brought it to the pump and put it underneath the nozzle.

Then I started pumping. It took a while to even loosen up the handle. Blisters formed and popped on my palms, but I gritted my teeth and kept going. A few blisters for the chance to live a long healthy life? Totally worth it.

After what felt like an eternity, but was probably no more than five minutes, water, dirty and dark, began to flow. I kept pumping and it soaked into the ground. A couple more minutes and it ran clear. I felt like I'd just struck oil.

"Finally something's going right," I mumbled, then rinsed out the bucket a few times before filling it with the clean water and carried it back inside.

I did find several old teacups in a kitchen cabinet and one that wasn't chipped. I wiped the dust off with my shirt and scooped some water from the bucket into it.

"Here. Drink." I held the cup to Declan's mouth, my hand at the back of his neck to raise him up a little.

He drank. My own mouth felt parched and rancid from throwing up that black ink, or whatever it was, but I could wait a bit longer.

"How does water help your injuries?" I asked.

"Her—her heels were made of silver. They were meant to be weapons. That material affects me as much as it would a full vampire. It leaves a . . . residue behind, preventing the wounds from healing as they normally would. Same with the bullet—it was silver. Pour water on it to purify it." A violent shudder went through him.

"Thought silver bullets were supposed to be for werewolves," I said uneasily.

He didn't reply to that. He was unconscious again.

Silver. I wondered if the knife Cruella gave me was made from silver. I'd left it on the kitchen counter for now.

I hissed out a long, shaky breath. I still wasn't completely convinced this would work. Declan needed an ambulance, not a sponge bath.

He had at least two serious wounds on his upper body. I clenched my teeth and pulled at his black T-shirt until I'd managed to remove it. Even with the covering of blood, the scars that crisscrossed his chest were visible—both long lines and small gashes. Some of the scars looked like healed bullet wounds, although I was no expert aside from watching emergency room TV shows.

I didn't like blood.

In fact, I might go so far as to say I hated it.

The raw, painful-looking wound on Declan's upper chest near his shoulder oozed blood. I couldn't see any silver residue. Since when did silver leave a residue?

And if silver harmed vampires, why would any servants working for vampires be armed with it?

I scooped another teacup full of water and poured it directly on top of where the stiletto heel had stabbed him. Declan's unconscious body jerked violently and I jumped. Steam rose from the bloody wound and there was a sound like a steak sizzling on a grill.

I gagged. The wound was welling with blood again, so I forced myself to scoop another cup of water and poured it over the damage again. No jerking this time. Less sizzle, too.

Now there was less blood. I repeated it twice more, amazed at what I was witnessing. His previously raw and bloody wound seemed to be healing in mere minutes, right in front of me. But it didn't heal back to smooth unmarked skin. After a while, it formed a raw-looking reddish mark about the diameter and shape of a stiletto heel. More water washed the surrounding blood away and I wiped it dry with Declan's black T-shirt before I actually touched the skin. Raised scar tissue. Like a wound that had been healing for weeks, not minutes.

"Holy shit," I said under my breath. A glance over his bare, muscled torso, now less bloody thanks to the water, confirmed that he'd been down this road many times before. Like his face, there were wide patches of skin that were unmarked and smooth, but they were few and far between.

There was no time to let this all register with me. I rolled Declan onto his stomach and grimaced when I saw the bullet wound there. Just to the left of his spine and under his shoulder blade. I couldn't help but gag again at the sight of it. I still had half a bucket of water, so I scooped and poured. His body jerked even more violently than before, and a scream caught in my throat.

I was very thankful he was unconscious for this. Even though there was no love lost between myself and Declan, I hated seeing anyone in pain.

After pouring cup after cup of water on the wound, nothing seemed to be happening this time. There wasn't even a sizzling sound. I even had to go outside to pump more water. There was a pile of old, dirty rags underneath the kitchen sink, which I used to mop up the water around Declan's unconscious body. Then I poured more water onto his wound and wiped with his T-shirt so I could see what I was doing.

He'd lost a lot of blood, most of it soaking into the gravel outside or into the old wooden floorboards here. I could barely believe he'd stayed alive this long.

The bullet wound wasn't healing like the stab wound had and I didn't know what to do next. After several more cupfuls, however, it finally started to sizzle and smoke so much I worried that it might catch fire, but it still wasn't healing up. Then as I wiped the jersey material of the shirt over the fresh well of blood, I saw something odd.

Silver. Just a glint of it beneath the raw, punctured flesh.

I drizzled more water on it so I could see it better and my eyes widened.

It was the bullet. Had it . . . risen to the surface?

More water coaxed it farther out, enough so that I was able to get my fingernails on the tip and pull it out completely. I stared at it for several long moments, stunned. I threw the bullet to the side and kept up with my ministrations of the water. Now that the silver had been released from the wound, it began to heal. Ten minutes later a reddish scar was all that was left of it.

I exhaled shakily. Done.

No, wait. I wasn't quite done, was I?

There was one more wound I'd noticed. I'd found it when I'd tried to take his cell phone only to find it was broken. A deep injury on his lower hip by his groin.

Terrific. I glanced at his face, which was turned to the side toward me, but his eye was still closed. His eye patch hadn't shifted from the ruin of his left eye.

I rolled him onto his back again and looked at the general area of the wound.

This might have been vaguely humorous if it wasn't totally mortifying.

"You damn well better stay unconscious for this," I growled. Then, without delaying any longer, I unbuttoned and unzipped his jeans and pulled one side down as far as I could. Unfortunately, it wasn't quite far enough to see the wound completely.

Although I did see enough to confirm that Declan Reyes went commando.

Oh boy.

"No time for modesty," I told myself, and pulled his jeans down over his hips and buttocks so I was able to clearly view the wound. And . . . everything else he had going on for that matter.

He had a pretty big cock for a scarred, one-eyed dhampyr assassin. Then again, he was the first one I'd ever met. My eyes flicked from his impressive penis up to his face and I wondered how often he'd been in a situation like this. Probably not that often.

Believe me, I wasn't enjoying myself in any way, shape, or form. Puking up gallons of poisonous ink like a dying squid had taken its toll on me. And besides, I hated the man I had undressed and been forced to splash cup after cup of water on—I didn't really care how big his unit was. He was only a means to an end. If I had any choice, I would have let him bleed to death if it meant I could escape with my life intact.

It wasn't selfish or cold. It was practical.

Silver was Declan Reyes's kryptonite. I would keep that piece of info safely filed away.

The wound three inches to the right of his groin closed up and scarred after I slowly poured six cups of water on it to help wash away the invisible silver residue.

Then I used the rags to wipe up the excess water, and tried to pull his pants back up, but that didn't go completely without incident. There was the need for significant tuckage. His T-shirt helped serve as the barrier between my hand and his—thankfully flaccid—genitals.

"You owe me for this," I said under my breath when I was done. "Big time."

He didn't reply. I might have been faking sleeping earlier in the car, but he wasn't faking at the moment. He was so still and so pale under the blood that caked his face I thought for a second he might have croaked while I'd been juggling his goods.

Holding my hand over his nose confirmed that he was still breathing. Since I couldn't stand the sight of blood another minute longer, I took a minute to wipe as much of it off his face as I could. Then I felt his scalp, locating the bump he'd received thanks to the redheaded servant's shit-kickers. The injury was smaller than expected, though, considering how hard he'd been stomped on. Dhampyr healing abilities, activate. At least bumps didn't leave scars.

I scooted away from him until my back hit the wall behind me and tossed his black shirt, bloody and wet from wiping up his waterlogged wounds. It draped over his stomach.

I finally took a moment to rinse my mouth out with the remaining water until I felt better. Then I sat there and waited impatiently for Declan to wake up, but he didn't seem to be in any hurry.

A couple hours later, the alarm on his watch went off, piercing the silence of the house. I nearly jumped right out of my skin.

The alarm indicated it had been three hours since his last injection of serum. The same serum that he wanted me to administer to him, since he was unconscious until further notice. The serum that kept his dark vampire tendencies at bay and kept him from having a thirst for blood or . . . for *other things,* as he'd said.

His father had been a rapist. A murderer. A vampire who drank blood and killed without conscience.

According to Declan, all that stopped him from truly being his father's son was taking that serum every three hours.

That serum he no longer had, thanks to me.

6

IT WAS ANOTHER FOUR HOURS UNTIL DECLAN WOKE up. He'd officially missed two doses of serum. Both times the reminder alarm sounded, I scurried to his side and shut it off as quickly as I could and tried very hard not to think about the consequences.

Since I'd had hours to wait, I'd taken the time to study him rather intently—his face and his body. Long enough to imagine him without his scars or the eye patch or that flat, emotionless expression. If you took those things out of the equation, Declan Reyes wasn't all that monstrous to look at.

I tried to guess his age. Earlier I would have guessed high—forty, maybe more. Now that his face was at rest, I'd say no more than thirty.

A good age to be fighting a war nobody knew about and showing that very battle on your skin.

I looked away, refusing to feel anything for him other

than hate and disgust. He'd caused me enough pain so that the last thing I wanted was to empathize with his.

I tried to think about something else, *anything* else. It had only been hours but my old life—the one I'd had before I'd met sleeping beauty, that is—felt like an eternity ago.

When Declan finally woke, I tensed and clutched the knife in my hand. I wasn't sure what would happen next. He was dangerous enough to start with, but add on the fact that he hadn't been given his serum . . .

I had no other options other than to wait and see. I was dead for sure if I didn't. I just thanked God that I hadn't had another squid attack since coming back to tend to Declan's wounds.

He groaned, and it sounded as though it was from the act of waking than any indication of pain. He stretched his arms over his head, arching his back. I studied him warily. He was still shirtless. I'd taken the bloody and wet T-shirt off his stomach a couple hours ago, wrung it out, and draped it over the railing of the stairway a dozen feet to my right. It would still be dirty, but it had to be mostly dry by now. His hand went to his face, touching his eye patch as if to check if it was still there. Then he turned his head toward where I sat in the shadows in the corner of the room.

If he attacked me, I wouldn't hesitate. I'd stab him.

I braced myself.

"How long . . ." he began, then tilted his watch so he could see it. It was dusk. Still light enough to see, but not very well. "Okay. *That* long."

"You were out for a while."

"It's the silver. And the healing process taps my energy. The more wounded I am, the longer I'll stay unconscious." His muscled abdomen contracted as he sat up. Then he touched his shoulder, tracing his fingertips over the new scar. "You did it."

"You sizzled."

"I'm sure that wasn't pleasant for you." His gaze moved to the knife I clutched, as if it would hold back the demons from hell.

"To say the least." I watched for any sign that he was out of control, a monster ready to suck my blood and do other horrible and violent things to me.

He reached to his back and touched the scar from the bullet wound, then nodded as if satisfied with what he found. Then he frowned as his hand slid down to the side of his groin where the third wound had been. His eye flicked to me.

I felt my checks heat up. "Just don't let it happen again. I'm no Florence Nightingale."

"Thank you," he said after a moment. Those two words surprised me. He didn't seem the grateful type. "I don't normally lose so thoroughly against blood servants."

I swallowed hard. "Don't thank me. Just get me to your father. That's the only reason I did it. You get me to him and he helps me with this poison and we're all happy."

His hand moved from his hip up to his stomach, just under the old scar there. "You stuck to the schedule?"

It took me a second to figure out what he meant. He was asking me about his serum, touching where I should have injected him if all had gone according to plan.

"Yes. I have your case safe for later." I didn't elaborate further than that. I'd deal with telling him what I'd done when the time came.

He nodded. "Good."

He believed me. Then again, why wouldn't he? He'd instilled enough fear in me about his "vampire side" that there was no way I wouldn't do anything possible to prevent it. After all, what woman in her right mind would disregard the threat of being raped and murdered?

If he believed that lie, then it might work as a placebo. His personal beliefs would keep his vampire hungers at bay.

No, that didn't make any sense. This wasn't a diet pill that gave a patient extra willpower. The serum worked as some kind of behavior modifier. And his vampire hungers wouldn't merely be for a slice of cheesecake.

Maybe every three hours was just a precaution. He'd probably built up a huge surplus of the serum. Missing a couple of doses wouldn't really do anything at all.

I clung tightly to that theory.

"I'm just surprised they didn't kill me," Declan said. "Or you. What the hell happened here?"

"They weren't interested in killing us. They just wanted the formula. When it was obvious to them that we didn't have it, they finally left." I rubbed my aching head. "The guy hit me pretty hard, though. Knocked me out."

He frowned. "Asshole deserves to die."

"He's not on the short list to join my book club, that's for sure."

"So that was it? They just left?"

"Are they here right now?"

His jaw clenched. "No. And neither are we. I've wasted enough time recovering. We're late and we have to go. Come on."

He got up from the floor so fluidly it was as if he'd never been shot or gored or unconscious for hours. It only served to remind me how tall, strong, and dangerous he was. He snatched his T-shirt and put it back on. Then he grabbed me by my upper arm and pulled me roughly with him out of the house, down the stairs, and past the dead body of the guy he'd shot.

"No need to manhandle me." I tried to wrench away from him.

"Fine. Just try to keep up." He let go of me so abruptly I nearly lost my balance, and he walked away from the house on long strides. I had to jog to catch up to him. When we'd reached the gas station, he stopped and turned to look at me. "We need to go to the main road and flag down a ride."

"Sounds like a plan."

"How are you feeling?"

"Poisoned."

"Can you walk?"

I nodded. "I haven't had any pain for a few hours."

His eye moved to the knife I held. "You should put that away. You might cut yourself."

"I'll keep it out, thanks."

"You really think that's going to protect you against me?"

"I think it's better than nothing."

"It's silver."

"I thought it was. So you'd better watch yourself or—" Before I got another word out, he came at me so quickly I barely saw him move. He pushed me against the side of the abandoned gas station, successfully knocking the breath out of me. He squeezed my wrist and I dropped the knife.

"Or what?" he asked calmly.

My heart hammered against my rib cage. That wasn't pretty. And it didn't make me feel very good about my own abilities of protecting myself. Pathetic, really.

"Or you'll be sorry," I finished.

"Right." He didn't let go of me right away. Maybe he was sick of me. Maybe he wanted to end this once and for all so he wouldn't have to cart me around. They could always find another chemist to make more of the poison. Maybe I wasn't as important as I thought I was.

"It's strange," he said.

"What?"

"Your scent." His forehead was furrowed as if he was concentrating very hard. "It's different than before."

"I probably need a shower."

"No, it's not that." He brought his face closer to mine, then to the side of my neck, so close that I felt his warm breath on my skin. My own breath hitched as I realized he was smelling me.

Panic coursed through me.

Oh God. He wanted to tear out my throat. Drain my blood. No serum meant a loss of his control. And a loss of his control meant . . . bad things.

But he didn't bite me. Instead, he pushed away from the wall and me and shook his head, scrubbing his hand over his scalp.

"That was strange," he said.

Yeah. For both of us.

I didn't move. I waited to see what would happen next. I hated feeling like a mouse cornered by a snake that might or might not be hungry.

Whatever the look on my face was, it made him snort loudly.

"I know I'm fucking scary, but I have no intention of hurting you. Let's just get that straight."

I cleared my throat. "You know you're scary?"

"Of course. I'm not stupid." He bent over and snatched up the knife I'd dropped. I looked at it warily as he hefted the weight of it in his hand. "They gave this to you?"

I just nodded.

"Why would they do that?"

"The woman, she suggested I . . ." I trailed off, thinking better of discussing something like this with him.

"She suggested you kill me while I was unconscious?" His lips curled to the side.

He hadn't smiled before—not genuinely, anyway. He seemed strangely at ease now, more expressive. Friendlier, even.

Was it because of the serum—or, rather, the *lack* of it? Taking it regularly flattened out his moods. Kept his emotions in check. Now that he wasn't on it, he was acting a bit more like a normal person would, not just a cold-blooded assassin.

"She may have mentioned something like that," I said.

"But you didn't kill me. You helped me to heal instead."

"Like I said before, I need you to take me to your father."

"If you hadn't needed me to get better, would you have been able to do it? After all, you knew what I was willing to do earlier."

Kill me in the alley if he got the okay without a moment's hesitation or guilt. I remembered it all too clearly.

I looked at him for what felt like a long time without replying, my gaze moving over his scarred face as if trying to find the answer there. Would I have been able to kill him? If he'd just kidnapped me, threatened my life, and taken me here? If I wasn't poisoned and in need of his help? Kill a man when he was unconscious. With a knife?

Yes, I could.

Just the thought of it made tears well up in my eyes, but I swallowed them down. No time for that. I could fall apart when all of this was over.

He finally turned away from me. "Forget I asked. Just put it somewhere safe."

I was ready to ask what he was talking about when he held out the knife to me, hilt first.

I frowned. "You're—"

"Just take it."

I took it. Then he turned his back and began walking again.

I walked behind him along the side of the dirt road. No big surprise, but there were no cars that just happened to come by. We walked in silence until it was fully dark. The moon was full enough tonight to help me not fall over my feet. I carried my heels since they hurt too much to walk long distances in. It still wasn't exactly ideal, but the dirt road was more dirt than rock so I didn't run the risk of cutting up my bare feet.

After forty minutes of brisk walking had passed, I had to ask.

"Why did you give me back the knife?"

He didn't slow his pace. "Because you need it more than I do."

"I *need* it?"

"It makes you feel more secure. Like you have some control over this situation."

"And I don't?"

"Afraid not."

Anger worked well to help burn off some fear. "Aren't you afraid I'm going to kill you?"

"Not really." I could hear the smile in his voice now. "Don't take it personally, though. You're untrained. You'd need a lot of practice before you could even come close to cutting me."

"Looks to me like you've been cut a lot."

"Yeah, well . . ." The smile was gone. "Every time I take a wound, I get a scar. Some of these weren't even that bad to begin with."

"They look bad."

That earned me a glance over his shoulder. "Luckily it's dark now so you don't have to look at me. People usually can't stand the sight of me. I scare the shit out of them."

"That's not what I meant."

"Doesn't matter."

"Besides, I find it hard to believe that *all* people would feel that way." I didn't know why I felt the need to say anything, but I did. "Sure, some are superficial, but not everyone."

"Like I said, it doesn't matter. It's not an issue for me."

"What's not an issue?" I was confused again. It seemed like my default setting.

"I'm not . . ." But whatever he was going to say, he stopped himself.

"Not what?"

My persistence earned me an unfriendly glare. I'd caught up to him enough that I walked next to him on his left.

"Along with curbing my lust for blood, my serum helps curb my lust for . . . anything else. So whatever anybody might think of what I look like doesn't really matter."

"Are you trying to say that you—"

"I'm trying to say that I take the serum because I refuse to be like my real father. He hurt my mother. I won't run the risk of hurting anyone like that. Ever."

I tried to piece it together. The serum didn't only flatten out his emotions, but it also flattened out any natural desire or lust he might feel. No emotion, no passion, no . . . *sex?* The man *was* a machine, even if he was made of flesh and bone.

"How long have you taken the serum?" I asked.

"A long time."

"Every three hours?"

"Yes."

"Have you ever tested it? Gone longer without a dosage?"

"No."

"But at night—"

"My alarm wakes me."

He was so dedicated to taking his serum, he never got a full night's sleep. The fact that he was obsessive-compulsive about it didn't help to relax me.

"And how long have you done this? Fight . . . uh, vampires?"

That got me another amused look. My annoying cascade of questions had launched into action again. "You still say it like you don't believe me. Are you still in denial?"

"A little," I admitted.

"You'll get over that."

"I'm not sure I want to."

"I trained from the time I was a teenager. I was active when I turned eighteen. That was ten years ago."

He was twenty-eight. "You're the same age as I am."

He'd been through a lot in his life. I felt like I'd been through practically nothing. Our lives couldn't be more different. He fought and killed vampires and had the scars to prove it. I worked for a temp agency, had never been passionate enough about a job to pursue it full-time. There was no way we ever would have met if it hadn't been for my being in the wrong place at the wrong time.

Suddenly, I felt a pain in my stomach and I stopped walking. "Oh, no."

"What?"

I hit the ground hard enough to bruise my knees, sweat breaking out on my forehead as the pain swept over me. I didn't have the strength to deal with this. I'd so quickly gotten used to being okay again, I could almost lull myself into a false sense of security that it was over.

But it wasn't.

"Just breathe." Declan pressed his hand against my back.

I didn't want to throw up again. That felt worse than anything else. The look of that black syrup and not knowing what it was or where it had come from other than an indication that my internal organs were dissolving . . .

I grabbed hold of something, anything, to keep me from falling off the edge of sanity as the pain wracked my body. Luckily, it did pass. No more than five minutes this time. And I didn't throw up.

Progress.

Only after my head cleared and I blinked my tear-filled eyes did I realize what it was that I'd grabbed hold of. It was Declan, who'd sank to his knees in front of me. I clung to him; my fingers dug into his shoulders.

"You okay now?" Instead of the flat disregard from before, I now heard concern in his voice.

I nodded and found I wasn't letting go of him quite as quickly as I should have. He felt so solid. So real. Like an anchor that could keep me from getting swept into the void.

He pulled back from me. His thumbs wiped at my tears as he held my face between his hands.

"You're okay, Jill. You're okay." It sounded like how you'd talk to a child when one stumbled and skinned her knee. Calming her down so she didn't keep crying.

I inhaled shakily as I got control of myself again and the pain and fear retreated.

Declan gently stroked his fingers over my face as he dried my tears. I inhaled sharply as his thumb slid slowly across my bottom lip, his gaze now focused there.

Suddenly it didn't feel as if he was only comforting me anymore.

His Adam's apple jumped as he swallowed. Then he shook his head and got to his feet so quickly that it nearly knocked me backward.

"What the fuck is wrong with me?" he asked.

"What do you mean?"

"I don't . . ." His expression looked strained and confused. "It's like I . . ."

His hand moved over his stomach before slipping into his pocket. He frowned. "You said you have my serum case. I need it back."

My mouth felt very dry. "What?"

"The case holding my serum. Give it back to me now."

Shit.

I got to my feet with effort. Declan didn't move to help me this time.

"I don't have it," I said.

He swore loudly. "You left it back at that house?"

"No."

"Then where is it? You said you had it." His hands were now clenched into fists at his sides.

I had nothing prepared for this discussion yet—one I'd wanted to put off for as long as possible. No more lies came readily to me. My head hurt and I felt achy and defeated and tired and angry.

"I gave it to them. The blood servants. They were looking for a formula, so I gave them the one you had. It satisfied them enough to leave without killing us."

He gaped at me. "You gave it to them. Just like that."

"Yes, I did."

"So when my alarm went off, when I was unconscious and you were supposed to inject me . . ."

"You got nothing." I looked warily at his reaction to this news, but stood my ground.

His reaction was to look at his watch, which would tell him how many doses he'd missed—two of them. Then he turned and started walking again. "I knew it. I felt that something was off, but I wasn't sure what. You should have told me."

I grabbed my shoes and the knife from where I'd dropped them. "You're fine."

"You have no fucking idea what you're talking about."

"I've been watching you closely since you woke up and you're fine. In fact, you seem better than you were before."

"Is that so?"

"Yeah, before you were horrible and emotionless. It was like you weren't even here. Now—"

"Now I'm beginning to lose my control. And you don't want to be around me when that happens."

I literally had to jog to keep up with him. "You seem fine to me."

He stopped walking and grabbed my upper arms so tightly that I gasped. "You don't know me. You don't know what fine is and how far from it I am." He looked down at his bruising grip and released me. "Damn it. It's not even your fault. I can't blame you. It was smart what you did, it's just fucking inconvenient. And I should have known it the moment I smelled you after I woke up." His gaze flicked to me. "You smelled too good to me—like food. Made my mouth water. So until we get where we're going, you need to keep your distance, got it?"

I nodded stiffly. "Got it."

"Good. And if anything happens, you take that knife of yours and do your best to sink it in me up to the hilt. The silver will slow me down so you can try to escape."

"I'm not going to try to escape."

He gave me a very unfriendly look. "Do you want to die?"

"No. I don't. Which is exactly why I'm sticking with you until we see your father."

"Fine. Your call. But I take no responsibility for anything that happens to you from this point forward."

With that, he turned and walked away from me.

I followed after him.

7

"YOU NEED TO FLAG SOMEBODY DOWN," DECLAN said when we finally reached the main road leading to the highway. He'd kept at least ten feet between us for the last twenty minutes of our brisk walk. "Driver sees me and they'll keep going. Need a pretty girl in distress to make them stop."

I could not feel less pretty at the moment if I tried. But I nodded and slipped my heels back on. Declan sank back into the shadows.

I'd hitchhiked once when I was a teenager, mostly because I'd gone through a rebellious stage and did it just to tempt danger. Instead I tempted an old married couple in a Winnebago who drove me fifty miles to my friend's house while they told me about their grandkids.

This felt different. I stood on the edge of the road, placing the knife down on the ground so when the next car passed I could wave my arms. It didn't even slow down;

the wind from its passing blew my hair back from my shoulders. I tried again. No luck. The third car that passed was a red pickup truck. It stopped ahead of me, tires screeching as it backed up.

Two guys in their twenties grinned at me out of the open passenger-side window.

"Hey there," one of them said. "What are you doing out here all alone?"

"Car broke down." I tried to seem friendly and at ease. "Can you give me a lift?"

"Be happy to, beautiful." They exchanged a look. "What are you willing to trade for it?"

"Trade?"

The one on the passenger side shrugged. "We help you out, and maybe you can help us out."

Their meaning was fairly obvious, but this wasn't a bar and I wasn't drunk. "Fuck off. I'll get someone else."

They laughed. "Oh come on, sweetheart," the driver said. "A ride back to civilization for your lips wrapped around my cock for a couple minutes. Is that so bad?"

His head swiveled when the driver's-side door opened up and a scarred hand grabbed him by his throat and threw him out of the truck. Then Declan reached across to the guy on the passenger side and dragged him out as well.

Declan got behind the wheel, then reached over and opened up the door for me.

I didn't argue. I grabbed the knife off the ground and got in, closed the door, and Declan stepped on the gas. In the rearview mirror I saw the assholes get up off the pavement and start running after the truck, shaking their fists.

"Was that the original plan?" I asked.

"Carjacking them?"

"Yeah."

"It was. But I might have done it a bit more politely if

I hadn't wanted to watch them bleed." His eye flicked to me. "An increased desire for violence is from not taking my serum."

"You didn't kill them. Or make them bleed."

"I guess it's a good thing my gun was taken away from me earlier."

I didn't feel bad that he'd taken the truck. Maybe if they'd been more helpful and not complete dicks I would have. As it was, I hoped they had to walk all the way back to the city.

"Don't you already have a desire for violence?" I asked. "Killing vampires for a living doesn't sound like doing needlepoint."

"You're still saying it like you don't believe they exist."

"Seeing is believing. And I haven't seen anyone with teeth any sharper than normal." I looked at him. "What are they like?"

"Vampires? They're fast. And strong. And a lot of them are smart, as long as they're well-fed. Those are the ones that are hardest to kill. If they're hungry, they're not as smart, but they're more vicious."

"And they look like humans? Just like in the movies?"

He nodded. "They're pale—the older they are the paler they are, and when they're hungry you can see the veins right through their skin. Their eyes are pale and color-less, too. Like mine are, but even lighter. It makes them extremely sensitive to sunlight. Even sunglasses or UV protection won't help."

"And they're immortal? That woman, the servant, gave me the impression she's trying to gain favor with this king . . . Matthias . . . so she can be turned into an im-mortal vampire."

He shrugged. "Maybe. But they can still be killed."

"With silver. Or does a wooden stake do the trick?"

"Silver. Wood's too breakable. I've never used it. For all I know, it could work."

"How about crosses? Holy water?"

"That's myth only. Besides, I'm not religious. I figure if you use a cross to fight against an evil being, you'd have to be a believer for it to work."

"You don't believe in God?"

"No," he said. No elaboration. Just a flat answer. Sounded like the serum-taking Declan again. "You?"

"I . . ." I pressed my lips together. "I don't know. I'd like to. I went to church as a kid."

"You don't anymore?"

"I stopped after my parents were killed five years ago. You might say I had a bit of a breakdown and I blamed everyone I could for their loss, especially God."

He was quiet for a moment. "How'd they die?"

"Plane crash," I said tightly. "My father got his pilot's license as a hobby when he retired. Took my mom up one afternoon. The first time she'd been up. I guess he got distracted having her there. Stupid." My throat closed and my eyes began to sting.

I didn't think I liked being on the receiving end of a Q&A. I much preferred to be the one asking the questions.

Declan didn't say anything. He didn't offer any condolences or any words of comfort. I was glad he didn't.

"How are you feeling right now?" he asked.

"Horrible."

"More specific: Do you feel another spell coming on?"

That was a pleasant way of putting it. A spell. It sounded almost magical.

I touched my stomach, which was where the pain usually began. I didn't want to think about what was going on inside me. We'd wasted a lot of time stuck at the house today. If that hadn't happened, we'd already be at our destination.

"Where are we going?" I asked.

"You didn't answer my question."

"Do I feel another spell coming on? No. Not right now, anyway. But it doesn't usually give me much warning, so be prepared to pull over at any moment."

"I will. And where we're going is a town right on the edge of Death Valley. It's called Silver Ridge."

"*Silver* Ridge?"

"I think it's a coincidence. A hundred years ago, they used to mine for silver in the area."

Death Valley. I was trying to find a way not to die in a place named for death. The irony was not lost on me.

Declan took an exit off the highway and I tensed.

"Are we being followed again?" I asked.

"No."

"Then where are we going?"

"To find some food."

"I'm not hungry."

"I am. And you need to eat, even if you have to force yourself. Keep up your strength."

I eyed him. "You're concerned for my well-being?"

"If you're dead when we arrive, my father won't be happy with me. I've already fucked enough things up today. The least I can do is make sure you're still breathing."

Such heartfelt sentiment was seriously going to go to my head.

But he was right. Despite the pain and the constant worry about my next "spell," I felt a gnawing in my gut that had very little to do with being poisoned. I hadn't eaten anything since breakfast.

The first restaurant we came upon was a small roadside diner with only a couple cars out front. Declan pulled into the parking lot.

"We'll make it quick," he said.

I nodded and opened up the truck's door, half-expecting him to stop me from getting out, but he didn't. I slipped from the seat to the ground and then ran my fingers through my hair to neaten it. The next thing I knew, Declan was at my side and he grabbed hold of my wrist.

"Don't try anything," he said.

I yanked my hand away from him. "I won't. I already told you I'm not going to try to escape."

"Maybe I don't totally believe you."

Paranoid, wasn't he? He should have been. After all, he *had* kidnapped me. Whether or not I was now along for the ride was beside the point.

We entered the diner and it did feel like a natural thing for me to call out for help. I'd wanted that for hours—to escape from Declan. It was all I could do to stay quiet. I felt Declan's hand at the base of my spine, almost too low to still be polite, a reminder that he was there and for me to behave myself.

There was a television attached to the wall on mute. Would what happened earlier at my office building have made the news? A downtown public shooting wasn't unheard of, but it didn't happen every day.

Did anyone know what happened to me? Or did everyone simply assume I'd been traumatized and gone home early that day? Somebody would have checked on me. Stacy witnessed firsthand what had happened. And my roommate, Donna, would notice when I didn't come home after work. She'd be worried. She'd call my sister. Then my sister would be worried.

Maybe they thought I was dead. That only helped guilt

to twist in my gut. I needed to get in touch with them as soon as I could.

And tell them what? I wasn't sure, but they had to know I was still alive.

We went to the counter. I couldn't help but notice that Declan received wary glances from a few people at tables. Whether it was because they might recognize him from the news or just because he was, in his own words, *fucking scary,* was another thing. At least his black clothes helped to mask the blood stains.

The waitress cast her own wary glance at the two of us. "Have a seat and I'll be with you in a second."

"We're not staying," Declan said. "Need food to go."

"Oh, well, okay. What do you want?"

His brow furrowed. "I don't know. What do you have?"

I grabbed a menu off the counter and scanned it. "Two burgers. Fries. Cokes. And two pieces of key lime pie. As fast as you can, please."

"Sure." Her gaze flicked cautiously to Declan again, before she scribbled the order down and passed it over the counter to the kitchen. "Won't be long. Take a seat."

I looked at Declan. "You can let go of me now."

He still had his hand on my back. He removed it and crossed his arms. "You ordered food for me."

"You didn't seem like you knew what you wanted."

"Key lime pie?"

"It's my favorite."

"Never had it before."

"You don't seem like a citrus-flavored pie kind of guy." Then I felt a twinge of pain in my gut. "Oh, no. Not here."

"Sit down."

I shook my head. "I need to go to the ladies' room."

"I'll come with you."

"No, wait here for the food."

Doubt skittered across his expression. "But what if you—"

"Try to escape?" I said under my breath.

"Need my help," he finished.

"I'll scream."

He studied me for a moment. "Fine. Then, go."

I made a beeline toward the short hall leading to the public washrooms. A pay phone between the men's and women's rooms caught my attention. I felt at my pockets, but remembered I had nothing. No change. Only a silver knife, the blade of which I'd wrapped in a plaid handkerchief I'd found on the stolen pickup truck's dashboard so I wouldn't accidentally stab myself.

I went into the washroom and stood at the sink, staring at myself in the mirror. Considering how I felt and what I'd been through, I didn't look half bad. Sure there was a shimmer of perspiration on my forehead, but my shirt and pants were surprisingly unmarked aside from a couple rips and scuffs. My skin was clean, pale, but unblemished and no longer showed any of the makeup I painstakingly applied that morning. My hair was a mess. I dragged my fingers through it and tucked it behind my ears, wishing for an elastic to keep it back from my face.

I gripped the sides of the sink, waiting for the next wave of pain to take me over, but nothing came and what pain there was faded away to nothing. It must have been a false alarm. It didn't make me feel much better. I knew it was there, waiting in the wings for the first opportunity to step out on stage. It seemed to prefer surprise performances. If the poison had a personality, it was one mean diva bitch.

I unbuttoned and rolled up the sleeves of my shirt, splashed some water on my face, and then made use of the toilet even though I didn't really need to go. The day had worked to dehydrate me pretty well. Except for a couple of cupfuls of water at the house, most of which I'd spat back out to cleanse my mouth of the inky black substance I'd vomited, I hadn't drank anything. Still, I didn't know when the next chance I'd get for a bathroom break would be.

When I exited the stall, there was a woman standing there. I hadn't even heard the door open.

"I know who you are," she said in a conspiratorial whisper. "I saw you on the television earlier. That man . . . the one with the eye patch, he killed somebody today. Shot them. You were a hostage and he went after you."

Somebody recognized me. But it wasn't right. This couldn't happen. I couldn't tell this stranger anything about my situation even though I desperately wanted to. Besides, she couldn't help me. Nobody could.

"I think you have me confused with someone else," I offered feebly, knowing she wouldn't believe it. After all, Declan's was a face that would be very hard to forget.

She stepped in my way as I tried to get past her.

"Just forget you saw me, okay?" I said. "For your own good."

"My God," her voice changed, it suddenly sounded awed. "What are you?"

I frowned and looked at her. That seemed like a strange thing to say. "What do you mean?"

"I mean . . . that scent. Your scent. It's overpowering."

Shit. I guess I really did need a shower.

"I shouldn't be here. It's too dangerous with the hunter outside," she murmured. "But I can't resist."

How did she know Declan was a hunter? Had they said something on the news about that?

But then the fog cleared for me and I noticed how pale

the woman's skin was. And suddenly I could see dark blue veins appear under the surface of her skin that circled her eyes and branched out across her jawline. The sight made me gasp.

Her eyes were light gray, but suddenly the pupils expanded, swallowing the lightness until they were black. Her cheeks hollowed, giving her face a skull-like appearance.

Even though she was shorter than me by a couple of inches, when I tried to get past her this time she grabbed hold of me in a tight grip.

The look in her black eyes was nearly sexual in its desire. Her lips parted and I could see the sharp tips of her fangs. It seemed like something out of a Halloween party, unreal and almost amusing. But it wasn't. This was very real.

She was a *vampire*. The realization was like a blow to my gut, knocking the breath right out of me. Declan said vampires stayed underground except for the rogues. I guess this one was a rogue.

She held me prone and I felt her cool breath as she brought her mouth closer to my throat. She moaned, a quivering sound that froze me with fear. Then her tongue snaked out and slid against my pulse there, tasting me, and I felt the graze of those razor-sharp teeth. I struggled to break free of her grip, but she was too strong.

I didn't remember screaming, but I must have let out a shriek loud enough to get attention. After all, I did tell him that I'd scream if anything went wrong.

The door to the washroom burst open and Declan grabbed the vampire by her long, dark hair, his other hand at her throat, pulling her mouth away from my skin and wrenching her back so hard if she'd been human it would easily have broken her neck. His eye flicked to me for the briefest instant before it focused on her again.

"Bad girl. Should have stayed safely in your hole."

She hissed at him. But instead of attacking, she turned and ran. He caught up to her in the hallway, grabbing her hair again to stop her in her tracks. She clawed at him and I saw a streak of red from where her fingernails gored the right side of his neck.

"I'll kill you!" she shrieked.

"Knife," he growled. It took me a moment before I realized he was speaking to me. I fumbled for the knife I had in my pocket and removed the handkerchief with trembling fingers. Declan reached out and grabbed it away from me.

The vampire came at him, grabbing his arm, lips peeled back from her sharp teeth.

Without hesitating, he slashed the vampire's throat. I clamped my hands against my mouth so I wouldn't scream.

She made a surprised sound, her hands flying up to stop the immediate spill of blood. Her eyes widened and she tried to grab for him again, but he was able to slice the blade into her chest.

The vampire looked down at the ivory hilt with surprise. The next moment the knife burst into flame and she screamed—a horrible, high-pitched keening sound.

No, it wasn't the knife that was on fire. It was the wound itself. A circle of fire from it spread out and consumed her in a few seconds flat. Then in a burst of fiery ash, she was gone.

Declan leaned over and snatched up the knife—the only thing that remained where she'd been standing.

I stood there shocked, unmoving, not breathing, not believing what I'd just seen with my own two eyes. She'd tried to bite me. To kill me. Declan had killed her instead. And vampires turned to fire and ash when they died.

I was trembling, but I felt his hand against my back again.

"We need to get out of here," he said. "Now."

Our altercation with the vampire had not gone unnoticed. Considering he'd killed her in full view of everyone, that wasn't a surprise. All four patrons of the diner gaped at us as Declan pushed me past the tables. The waitress backed up, her eyes as wide as mine probably were, her hand clutching at her chest.

"Grab the food," Declan snarled.

Our take-out order was waiting on the counter. Declan threw a couple of bills on the counter as I snatched the brown paper bag and tray of drinks.

No one tried to stop us from leaving. I couldn't say I blamed them.

8

TEARS STREAKED DOWN MY CHEEKS AS DECLAN screeched the truck out of the parking lot and headed back to the highway.

"Why the fuck are you crying?" he demanded.

"It's just a little something I do when I'm freaking out."

"I never should have let you go off by yourself. Christ. That bitch could have killed you."

It was on the tip of my tongue to say something nasty back to him, but I realized that he'd saved my life. As horrible as that had been to experience, if he hadn't intervened, I'd be dead right now.

I wiped at my face. "Thank you."

"For what?"

"Stopping her."

"So you believe in vampires now?" He eyed me sideways.

"Yes." My breath hitched. "Unfortunately."

"Let me see." He reached over and pushed at my hair. I batted his hand away. "What are you doing?"

"Checking your throat. Seeing if she did any damage to you." He roughly slid his index finger down the undamaged skin there. "Looks fine."

"It's the other side that has the puncture wound. But that wasn't from fangs." I looked at him. His neck was bleeding. "She hurt you."

"It's nothing."

"I don't have any water to throw at you for healing purposes. Will Coke work?"

He frowned. "No. It doesn't matter. I'll heal shortly."

"I was joking."

"You can joke after what just happened in there?"

"It's either that or I keep crying." I pulled out a napkin from our bag of food and pressed it up against his throat. "Here."

He took it from me and his warm fingers brushed against mine. The intense and unexpected sensation jarred me. I balled my hand up and placed it safely in my lap.

"I'm sorry you had to see that," he said after a moment. "Killing vampires isn't a pretty sight. Luckily, there was only one of her."

"You didn't hesitate. You just . . . killed her."

"She could have torn your throat out."

I didn't doubt that. And I hadn't even meant my comment as a criticism, which is how he seemed to be taking it. Had I enjoyed seeing someone—especially a woman—overpowered and murdered right in front of me? Of course not. But she hadn't been innocent and she hadn't been human. And if she was willing to attack me, who knew how many others she'd hurt in the past?

"She said something to me," I said. "Same thing you

said. About my scent. She'd seemed coherent before that. Said she saw me on the news and seemed like she wanted to help. But as soon as she caught a whiff of me, it was all over."

He nodded. "Humans have a scent that separates them from other species. Vampires hone in on that. It helps them locate the nearest food source. Your scent just seems . . . more pronounced."

"And dhampyrs?"

"Same deal. The desire is there . . ." he said, and I felt him looking at me. My heart picked up its pace at the way he said it, but I kept my eyes fixed on the road ahead of us. "But the human side helps a little in holding me back."

"Then why take the serum?"

"I said it helps a little. But there's still room for error."

"So if given the opportunity, you'd drink my blood?" It seemed like a simple question, but it was met with absolute silence.

When I finally braved a look at him, I noticed how white his knuckles were as he gripped the steering wheel. His expression was so tense it looked like it might shatter. Actually, he looked ill.

I reached over and touched his shoulder. "Are you okay?"

"You really shouldn't touch me right now."

I drew my hand back as if it had been burned. "Why not?"

"I know you're blond, but I'd prefer not to think of you as dumb. I haven't taken my serum for way too long. Longest ever. I'm feeling . . ." His jaw clenched. "A bit out of control at the moment."

A shiver went through me. "Which means you want my blood."

"No. Not blood specifically. But I am feeling a very inconvenient hunger for you."

There was a predatory look in his eye, as his gaze traveled the length of my body. I began to feel very warm, a heat that spread over my cheeks and down my neck to my breasts, stomach, groin, legs. Or, in other words, everywhere he was looking.

Hunger. *That* kind of hunger.

Okay.

I reached into the paper bag. "You're going to have to settle for a hamburger."

There was a sound like a laugh, only sharper. "I'll try my best."

He took the burger from me when I handed it to him and I avoided any chance of touching him this time.

"Bad news," I said. "She forgot to put the pie in the bag. However, there seem to be extra fries."

"A feast."

It was. I had no idea how hungry I was until I bit into the meal-to-go. That diner might have had a vampire patron, which considerably lowered their "good restaurant" rating for me, but they made some great greasy food. It helped the constant churning in the pit of my stomach subside a bit. I sincerely hoped I wouldn't soon be throwing it all up. Seemed a waste.

The food didn't help to keep my mind off Declan's problem. No serum. No control over his vampire side. If I wasn't worried about this, I'd be an idiot. I was new to this world, brand-new kicking and screaming upon being birthed into the knowledge that vampires exist. For real. And they were fucking scary.

Declan's healing ability was enough to prove to me he wasn't entirely human. I'd also witnessed how the serum affected him because there had been two Declans I'd met today: the first one, a deadly, emotionless machine who'd been willing to kill me if ordered to. And the other Declan, a bit more personable—for a killer—and focused on keeping me safe, even if it was from himself and his . . . hungers.

I was afraid of him on too many levels to count. But there was also a part of Declan Reyes—the man who'd put me in danger, threatened to kill me, kidnapped me, tossed me around and bullied me, but also saved my life and comforted me when I'd been sick—that I'd slowly begun to depend on and even . . . *like*. And that was just as scary as anything else I'd had to deal with today.

We ate in silence that began to feel uncomfortable, and I felt the overwhelming need to say something. Anything.

"Will I be able to contact my sister once we get to Silver Ridge?"

"No."

I put my Coke into the drink holder and glared at him. "Why not?"

He sighed. "Do you need an explanation for absolutely everything?"

"Yes, I do. Why can't I call my sister? Or my friends? If what happened was on the news, they're going to be worried to death about me. The least I can do is let them know I'm okay."

"Silver Ridge is not a publicly known location. If word of what it is and what's done there gets out, the sanctuary will be ruined."

"What happens in Silver Ridge, stays in Silver Ridge?"

"Something like that."

"So what happens there?"

"It's a secret."

I just looked at him.

He glanced at me, then balled up the foil that had contained his hamburger and tossed it into the empty bag. "Let's just say it's a small community of like-minded people who have pooled their resources together to figure out a way to fight against the things that go bump in the night."

"A town of vampire hunters."

"No, not exactly." His jaw tightened. "There are hunters, but it's mostly made up of researchers. The government funds it—"

"The government funds a secret anti-vampire town?"

"They fund the research program my father's a part of. They're just as interested as anybody in destroying a threat to human life, whether it has fangs or not."

"And how long has this research gone on?"

"About twenty-nine years. Around the same time Carson found my mother and learned about vampires in the first place." There was a haunted, pained look on his face whenever he mentioned his mother.

"Declan, I know you'll say I don't know you. And I don't. I'm not claiming any amazing insight on you other than a gut feeling. But . . . no matter who your real father is, I don't think it has any true bearing on who you are. You're in control of yourself, not some magical connection to an über-violent gene pool."

"Is that what you believe, or what you want to believe?" he asked tightly. "That I'm not a true threat to you?"

"That is a factor, I'll admit it. But . . . but how do you feel? Like, right now?"

"Cloudy. Like there are a million things in my mind all battling for first place. But even though my head's messed up, my senses are more acute. I can see better, sharper. My hearing is improved. My taste . . . well, that burger was the best thing I ever remember eating. Normally it's dulled for me. Food is bland. I eat because I have to, but it doesn't matter what it is. And my sense of smell is . . ." He gripped the steering wheel even tighter, ". . . *distracting*."

"Well . . ." I grappled for something to say next. He could smell me, that's what he meant. And for some reason, despite being disgusting and pukey and generally grubby, he found how I smelled appetizing on several levels. "Maybe this is how you're supposed to feel. Maybe dulling everything with a serum is doing you more harm than good."

"Is that your professional opinion, doctor?"

Welcome back, sarcasm.

"That's just my opinion." I leaned back in my seat and tried to look relaxed when I felt anything but. "A few years ago I was on some medication myself and it dulled my senses. Evened out my moods."

"What was it for?"

"It was . . . for depression." I didn't like saying it out loud. It brought back too many unpleasant memories.

"Why were you depressed?"

"It started with my parents' deaths and spiraled from there. My life wasn't going according to plan, and one thing heaped on top of another, and I just fell into a deep well and couldn't get myself back out. The problem runs in my family, so it was always lurking in the shadows, ready to jump out and grab me."

"And your doctor put you on medication?"

"It was her first and only suggestion, actually. And I know lots of people who've been on depression meds and it's worked just fine and dandy for them. But for me . . . I never felt like it was the right fit. It made me feel . . ." I thought back to my nearly five years of being on a succession of different meds. "Kind of like floating on a river with no oars in my boat. I finally went off them a few months ago. I felt kind of crazy for a couple of weeks, but then the fog cleared."

"Are you still depressed?"

"I have my moments, but I deal in other ways. Pills weren't the right solution for me. For someone else it might be different. However, it feels like the solution to any problem these days is medication." I felt at my neck for the needle wound. That was another drug developed to fight a problem. "We rely on drugs to take away any ache or pain we have. It makes it easy, but it doesn't necessarily make it right. Not all the time, anyway."

"But your depression didn't cause you to harm others," he said pointedly.

"No. But it made me think about doing harm to myself. Once. Luckily, the urge passed. I counted all the things I had to keep me here. Things I'm still counting right now that make me fight to keep living despite becoming the walking, talking petri dish for your father's little experiment."

Declan was quiet for what felt like a long time. "Your situation is not the same as mine."

"I never said it was."

"And talking isn't taking my mind off it."

"Not trying to."

"Yes, you are."

I pressed my lips together. "Maybe a little. But consider yourself one of the privileged few. I don't discuss my mental issues with just anyone. Only very close friends or men who've kidnapped me against my will."

That earned a quiet snort of laughter. "I guess I fit the bill, then."

"Can I have my knife back?"

He hesitated, then reached to his side to hand me the weapon. "Keep it out, just in case."

Just in case I needed to use it on *him,* he meant.

I examined the blade, expecting to see blood from the vampire, but there was nothing but the sharp silver surface, shiny in the moonlight. I wrapped the handkerchief around the blade again.

"Do you really think your father can help me?" I asked a little while later when silence had settled around us. "Or do you think I'm going to die?"

"I think he can help you."

I was surprised at his definitive answer. He'd hinted at it before, enough to make me believe I needed to stick with Declan in order to meet this mystery man, but he hadn't outright said that the path to Silver Ridge was the path to my bright and shiny future.

Since I liked the answer, I didn't press for details in case they would burst my optimistic balloon. I noticed that Declan was looking at my hand. Or not specifically my hand, but my wrist. He wasn't the only person who had scars.

"You just thought about it, did you?" he asked softly.

I made a move to hide the mark, but he grabbed hold of my wrist, turning it so he could see better. His thumb brushed against the faded, two-inch-long scar.

"It was a long time ago," I said.

"And now you're different."

I nodded soundlessly, fighting back against the sting of tears. Sometimes I forgot about my wrist. The scar had faded a lot. I usually covered it up with bracelets or a watch. Earlier it had been covered by the long sleeves of my shirt, but I'd rolled them back in the diner washroom. Besides, it was only my left wrist that was affected. It had hurt so much, it had knocked sense into me enough to stop before it was too late.

After all, I really hated the sight of blood. Especially my own.

"Just don't let it happen again," he said, and he sounded angry. He squeezed my wrist, the heat from his skin sinking into mine.

"Don't worry, I won't."

"Good. Because if you're not willing to fight to stay alive, then why the fuck should I worry about what happens to you?"

That surprised me, as did the fierce way he said it. "You're worried about me?"

"It's my fault this happened to you in the first place. Your life is in my hands right now until I set things right again."

"Even though you were going to kill me."

He was quiet for a moment. "Things change."

I chewed my bottom lip. "Even though you want to drink my blood now, right?"

"I don't want to drink your blood, Jill," he said, his attention on the road ahead of us again. "I want to tear off your clothes and bury my cock deep inside of you while you scream my name. There's a big difference."

For a moment I think I stopped breathing. He'd intimated that was on his mind—his *hungers*—but for him to state so bluntly that those hungers were of a sexual nature left me without any possible reply.

His words should have scared me, made me feel threatened by his dark intent, especially after being told about his vampire father. But they didn't. I was afraid of Declan, but not for the reasons he probably thought I was. And as he continued to stroke his thumb over my wrist, I didn't pull my hand away from him.

So there I was, hurtling down the highway in a stolen pickup truck toward a secret anti-vampire research town with a scarred, dangerous dhampyr on the very edge of his self-control holding my hand, comforting me about a failed suicide attempt once upon a time, and proclaiming that he wanted to screw my poisoned brains out.

It was like a fucking fairy tale.

9

SILVER RIDGE WASN'T ALL THAT SHINY FOR A TOWN named after a precious metal. It just looked like a small town. A *really* small town.

Declan pulled the truck up to a house in the middle of this small town and directed me inside. My legs ached from sitting for four hours without a break. We'd needed to stop for gas, an event that was, thankfully, without incident. I'd stayed in the truck. There were a couple of people who'd looked at him funny when he'd gotten out to pump the gas, but I wasn't sure if it was because they recognized him or just that he looked scary.

He didn't look *quite* as scary to me anymore, I had to admit. But he definitely wasn't the type of guy you'd want approaching you in a dark alley.

Conversation between us had dropped off. I'd watched

him carefully and he seemed to be concentrating very hard on not looking at me, possibly pretending I wasn't even there.

I watched as the wound on his throat slowly closed up and scarred, a light and hard-to-see mark since it hadn't been a deep wound.

So dhampyrs got the healing abilities, but they were still marked when all was said and done. A reminder of the pain that had been there instead of a nice clean slate. Kind of unfair, if you asked me.

I was nervous as we entered the house. I still had the knife tucked into my pocket, its blade wrapped in the cloth. I wouldn't say it was incredibly comfortable, but it did ease my mind a little knowing I had a weapon to help protect myself.

Again, Declan had his hand at the base of my spine as if he half-expected me to run away at my first opportunity. He'd promised to protect me, after all. Proven it, even. I'd come to rely on that more than I probably should have.

There was a man waiting for us seated in a living room that looked very normal with a couch, a coffee table, and a television. He was reading the newspaper when we entered, which he put down as he stood up.

"What took you so long?" His hair was grayish, but he wasn't as old as I'd expected. Mid-fifties, maybe. There was a deep crease between his eyebrows that looked as if it would be there even when he wasn't frowning.

"I told you about the blood servants following us," Declan said. "There were complications, but it was taken care of and now we're here. This is . . . Jillian Conrad. Jill, this is my father, Carson Reyes."

He remembered my full name. I wasn't sure if he'd been listening or not when I'd told him.

Carson's gaze brushed over me. "Come. There's no time to waste."

He left the room.

A man of few words. Like father, like son.

I must have looked at Declan with worry because he shook his head. "It's okay. He's going to help you."

I nodded. We followed Carson to a flight of stairs leading to the basement. Before I put my foot on the top step, I turned to face Declan.

"You're staying with me?" I asked.

"Do you want me to?"

"Of course."

"I would've thought you'd want to get away from me the moment you could."

"I would've thought that, too. But I guess not." I tried to smile.

He removed his hand from my back so he could stroke the hair off my forehead. Again, his touch sent that strange, jarring sensation through me. I must have inhaled sharply because he drew his hand back.

"Sorry."

"No . . . I . . ." I took his hand in mine and brought it back to my face. He watched me warily. "It's okay. Really."

I touched his face, too, and he didn't jerk away from me. I traced a scar on his cheek under his eye patch that led to his jawline. His day's growth of beard felt rough against my fingers.

"How are you feeling?" I asked.

"I'm feeling . . ." His throat shifted as he swallowed. "Too much."

"Too much?"

"Jill . . . I . . ." he began, then pulled away, breaking contact with me completely. "We have to follow him."

He thundered down the stairs as if trying to escape from me.

Downstairs consisted of a huge room and it didn't look as if it belonged to the regular home upstairs. It was modern and bright with glass and stainless-steel tables, like a laboratory. I gazed around in wonder. There was another man with Carson. He was young, no more than mid-twenties.

"That's her?" he asked eagerly. "Sorry, uh, I mean . . . she's the one you mentioned to Carson on the phone?"

"This is Jillian," Declan said. "*Jill*. And yes, she was attacked by Anderson and injected with the formula."

The guy approached curiously. "Hey, how are you feeling?"

My mouth felt dry. "I'm still breathing."

"I'm Noah Palmer." He peered at me. "You look pretty good, you know. Considering."

That didn't exactly make me feel better. "Thanks, I think."

"We need to take a sample of your blood," Carson said. He already had the syringe out and handed it to Noah. I looked at him warily.

"Don't worry. I've done this a million times before. Well, maybe not a million, but a lot. Haven't lost a patient yet." Noah grimaced. "Probably not such a good thing to say, considering the circumstances."

"Noah's my father's assistant," Declan said.

"Assistant, general errand boy. Whatever. You make a mess, I'll clean it up and analyze it. Doing what I can for the betterment of humanity. My mother would be proud if I could tell her anything about it." He grinned. He was the only person in the room wearing that particular expression at the moment.

He patted the metal table and I took a seat on it. He indicated for me to roll my sleeve up higher and then tied plastic tubing around my bicep, as if I was having blood drawn during a regular physical at the doctor's office.

"Tell me exactly what happened," Carson said.

"Anderson grabbed her when I arrived, just as he was trying to make his escape," Declan replied, arms crossed. His attention didn't leave me for a moment. "Said if we wanted it we could have it and then injected it into her. He says it's the only sample left. He destroyed the rest."

"Did you double-check or simply take him at his word?"

Declan hesitated. "I didn't have time to check."

"I'll send someone to investigate his lab tonight. You're probably right, but it's best not to leave any rock unturned."

I jumped as the needle slid into my vein at the crook of my arm.

"Just an FYI, it hurts less if you don't thrash around," Noah said dryly.

"Sorry."

I felt Carson's gaze on me, assessing. I didn't need to be a mind-reader to know he was thinking that I was an inconvenient obstacle to his plans. It's not as if I'd asked Anderson to inject me, but what happened must have ruined a great deal of research in developing this poison.

Declan stood next to me, his eye focused on the syringe as Noah took a second vial of blood from me.

"It's okay, Jill," he told me softly. He reached forward as if to touch me, then withdrew his hand as if he'd had second thoughts. "Won't take a minute."

Carson frowned and looked at him. "Is there something wrong?"

Declan's shoulders tensed. "Excuse me?"

"You don't seem yourself. When was your last injection?"

His jaw clenched. "My vials were stolen by the servants. They thought it was the formula."

"Holy shit, Dec." Noah's hand stilled on my arm. "Are you kidding? You're off the juice?"

"How long has it been?" Carson asked.

"More than twelve hours."

After what Declan had told me about his serum and how obsessive he'd been about taking it according to a superstrict schedule, I expected Carson to get upset and reprimand him. But he didn't react that way. Instead, Carson's previously harsh and businesslike expression softened with concern and he put a hand on Declan's shoulder.

"Why didn't you say something the moment you arrived?" he asked.

"I thought it could wait a while longer."

"You know that it can't. The risk is much too great." He moved to a silver cupboard and pulled out a syringe and a vial that he handed to Declan. "Here."

The hesitation before Declan took it from him was barely noticeable.

"Declan . . ." It was on the tip of my tongue to tell him not to do it. Not to take the new dose of serum. But I shut my mouth. It was none of my business. His father was the expert on this. I'd just learned about vampires a few hours ago. How was I supposed to give any advice on the subject?

While Noah switched to a third vial for my blood, I watched Declan wordlessly load the syringe with the serum vial. He pulled up the bottom of his T-shirt and injected himself in his stomach without any further hesitation.

My heart sank.

"That's better." Carson patted his arm. "Twelve hours is a long time. Too long."

Declan nodded. "I know."

As Noah finished up with me, I watched Declan's face. What had been filled with concern and distress the last few hours only took a couple of minutes to turn to stone. I had seen glimpses of warmth in his single gray eye, but it flattened out and cooled.

Whatever was in that serum helped remove a large part of Declan's personality. The uncontrollable part. The unpredictable part. The part that had looked at me with desire only five minutes ago in the hallway upstairs.

It was gone, leaving behind the assassin who'd been ready to kill me in the alley this morning.

Declan now stood like a sentry at the stairway as Noah finished with me, four vials filled with my blood laying on the table between us. Declan explained to his father the rest of what happened with us and the servants in a detached tone until Carson was fully briefed on the events of the day, including my reactions to the poison in my system.

I swallowed past the lump in my throat. "Can you fix me?"

"I'm going to try," Carson said. "The best thing for you to do right now is to settle in and get some sleep."

"I can't sleep." I wrung my hands as Noah covered the cotton ball on the crook of my arm with a Band-Aid. "Listen, what happened today . . . it's on the news. My friends and sister are going to be worried to death about me. I need to use a phone and tell them I'm all right."

"I told her she couldn't," Declan said. "But she's very persistent."

I glared at him. He had no idea how persistent I could be.

"Of course she can," Carson said and my eyebrows went up in surprise. "But not tonight. I know it's difficult, but it's important that no more alarms are raised. There's a great deal at risk right now if one more thing goes wrong. Can you understand that enough to give me two days? Then I assure you, not only will you be able to make a phone call, but you will be reunited with your friends in person."

"Two days?"

"That's what I'm asking for. I know this is all very strange to you, Jillian. It's a rare occurrence for an outsider, a civilian, to be brought into our midst. What you've already seen here in Silver Ridge is classified. Declan's already made an exception for you due to the events of the day by telling you what he has. But no one else knows of this location and I'd prefer it stays that way."

I ran my hand through my tangled hair as I thought it through.

"Fine. Two days." My throat felt thick, and guilt coursed through me again. "But I can't sleep. Not right now."

"You might be surprised. Besides, it's late. Nearly one thirty now. You've had a long day. The formula . . . Declan said it made you ill, but how exactly has it affected you?"

"When it was first injected, it felt as if my veins were on fire. I can still feel them more than I should. Also I've had crippling stomach cramps. And I've thrown up a couple of times. The last time it was black, like ink. I . . . I felt like I was going to die."

"Black ink?" Noah asked. He was writing down everything I said on a clipboard. "Even though the formula was injected into you? It wasn't taken orally, right?"

"It was injected right here." I touched my neck.

Noah raised his eyebrows. "Kind of ironic."

"What is?"

"Looks kind of like a vamp bite. If the vamp only had one fang. Like a vampire unicorn." His smile faded when he noticed no one else was joining in.

A glance at Declan's stiff shoulders and downcast gaze confirmed that he'd regressed to his previous emotion-free persona. Why did that feel like such a big loss to me? I barely knew him.

He *had* to take the serum. It wasn't as if he had a choice in the matter.

"I'm sure it's been horrible for you," Carson said. "Anderson . . . we trusted him with a very important project, one that could save countless people, one he's been working on for more than a year. I offered him space here to work, but he refused to leave the city. I gave him a chance to make a difference to the world . . ." He touched my neck, and then poured some liquid from a bottle on a cloth and rubbed it against where Anderson had injected me to cleanse it. It stung for a moment and I flinched. "And look what he did."

"Why would he do this?"

"Because he wanted to destroy it in a showy manner so it would send a message to me."

"Is the formula destroyed?"

"I don't know. As I said, I'll send someone to check his lab to see if there is any more there. If not, I'll need to try to extract it from your blood and find a way to duplicate it. Anderson was wrong in what he did to you. But he shouldn't have been shot dead for it." Carson's gaze moved to Declan and narrowed. "We needed him. You should have brought him back here even if it was against his will."

"He tried to kill me," Declan said evenly. "I reacted."

"It's done. Now we must make do with what we have. It's been over twelve hours since the incident." Carson next applied the cloth to my head where the servant had pistol-whipped me. "The formula has been in your system all that time—"

"*Poison,* you mean," I said.

"The formula was developed under the code name Nightshade to be a poison used against vampires. However, I assume you're not a vampire."

"No, but—"

"Since it was untested, we have no idea how Nightshade will react in a human's bloodstream. It has made you violently ill, but you are still alive, still conscious, still coherent."

"So you're saying it's *not* going to kill me?"

"What I'm saying is we don't know. That it was injected into you specifically is an experiment that obviously wasn't planned. But here we are."

"And where exactly is that? How many other people are here?"

"There's two dozen of us stationed in this town. More than half are hunters or investigators and don't stay here all the time. This location is remote. Rogue vampires tend to navigate toward large cities, where they can disappear and have their pick of victims."

"So why is this home base? Wouldn't it make more sense to stay in the city?"

"We're here because this is close to the heart," Carson said.

I frowned. "The heart of what?"

Carson flicked a glance at Declan. "Show her upstairs. I had the guest room prepared for her. She can rest there." He looked at me again. "We'll talk more tomorrow, once I've analyzed your blood to find out what I can do for you. Try to sleep. It will do you good."

I opened my mouth to ask more questions, but closed it. "Fine."

The rest of my questions could wait till tomorrow. But no longer than that.

It was on the tip of my tongue to say thank you, but I didn't. I wasn't ready to be grateful quite yet. I hadn't asked to be here. I hadn't asked for any of this. They were the ones who'd done me wrong when it came right down to it. I'd hold off any thanks until life got back to what I considered normal.

Declan soundlessly turned and walked out of the silver-and-white room and headed up the stairs. I followed him. Once on the main floor, he took another flight to the second floor and down a hallway. This house was larger than it appeared from the outside. Generic paintings hung on the walls, wallpapered with a stripe design. No photos. Nothing very personal.

"Is this where you grew up?" I asked.

I didn't get a reply.

"Declan," I said louder.

"What?" He turned the handle on a door near the end of the hall.

"Did you grow up in this house?"

"No. We moved here six years ago."

"Where did you live before that?"

"This is your room," he said.

Okay, so he wasn't in the mood for a walk down memory lane. I looked inside the room. Fairly utilitarian, but livable. And there was an ensuite bathroom.

"Noah will bring you breakfast in the morning."

"He really does do everything, doesn't he?"

"He does a lot."

I struggled to find something to say. "How do you feel now?"

His gaze moved to me. "Better."

"So how you were feeling before, when the serum had worn off . . ."

"I don't feel that way any longer."

"Back to normal."

"Yes."

"Completely."

"Yes."

"Well . . . good."

"If you need anything—"

"I'll just scream. Seems to be the best way of communicating if phones are off limits."

"Fine."

It was as if there was a wall between us now. Like I was talking to a machine that didn't give any elaboration on his answers. Who gave me nothing at all. He'd been asked to take me to my room and he'd done just that. End of story.

What else did I want? To commiserate over some herbal tea? To breathe a collective sigh of relief that we'd both lived to fight another day? For him to tell me more secrets about his life?

"Declan—"

"Good night, Jillian." He closed the door between us.

I pressed my hand against it.

He had to take his serum because without it he'd lose control and become more like a vampire—an out-of-control creature with a thirst for blood and sex and death. Not necessarily in that order.

I remembered what he said to me in the car, about what he wanted from me. A shiver went through me and I realized it wasn't from revulsion at the thought of his hands on me. Quite the opposite, actually.

I touched my stomach, remembering the pain I'd felt—hands down, it had been worse than anything I'd ever experienced in my life. I'd gone from being terrified of Declan to, well . . . I wasn't sure what I felt at the moment other than weariness.

Maybe I was tired after all.

But I had to talk to him. There were things I wanted to say, questions I wanted answered, and I'd given up much too quickly on the phone issue. Also, what had Carson meant about this place being close to the heart? The heart of what?

I nodded to myself, firm in my resolve to march out of this room and demand what I wanted in full.

However, there was a problem. The door handle didn't budge no matter how hard I tried. It only took a second before I realized that I wasn't going anywhere.

Declan had locked me in.

10

I PULLED AT THE HANDLE, STRAINING MY ALREADY sore muscles, and then wedged my fingernails around the door and attempted to pry it open. Nothing happened, not even when I tried to use the knife. Frankly, I was surprised Declan hadn't taken it away from me before locking me in here. Maybe he'd forgotten I had it.

The window was sealed and there was no way of opening it. I considered breaking it, but decided against it. Where would I go? I'd be back at square one, poisoned and with no idea how to solve that particular problem on my own.

I went back to the door.

Maybe Declan hadn't realized it would lock.

That thought lasted about two seconds. He knew. They all knew. And I could even see their point of view if I squinted really hard. I was the outsider here. The civilian who had only been allowed through the invisible gates of

Silver Ridge because I was, as Declan had called me earlier that day, the reluctant courier of something vital that they needed.

They didn't want me here. They didn't want their top-secret town to become public knowledge.

I didn't call out and I didn't pound my fists against the door like some sort of imprisoned damsel in distress. But just because I wasn't pitching a fit didn't mean I wasn't pissed about being caged like an animal.

I tried to breathe normally and think it through.

I wasn't in any pain at the moment.

I was safe. Relatively speaking.

I was alive. For the time being.

After taking a long shower and inspecting my various cuts and bruises in the mirror, I realized I had no clothes to wear to bed. I slipped under the covers naked, keeping my hand wrapped around the ivory hilt of the knife just in case I had any unexpected visitors that night.

I WAS AWAKE AS SOON AS IT WAS LIGHT OUTSIDE. I dressed in my clothes from yesterday. Well, it was either that or a bedsheet toga. Then I waited.

When there was a knock on the door a couple hours later, I went to it soundlessly. It creaked open. Noah stepped inside carrying a tray of food. He flinched when he saw me.

"What are you trying to do?" he asked.

I'd taken the back of the toilet off and was brandishing it like a weapon, ready to crack the porcelain lid over his head at the first sign of trouble. My arms ached from holding it steady.

"Defending myself," I said.

"You don't have to defend yourself from me. I come in peace. Bearing eggs." He indicated the tray.

I watched him warily. "The door was locked."

"So you're going to murder me with a toilet because of that? Sorry, we take precautions here. Just the way it is. Put that down. Please."

I backed away from him and put my makeshift weapon down on the bed. I'd opted for the toilet lid rather than the knife since I would rather knock somebody out than try to slit their throat or stab them. Although if it had been Declan coming through that door, it was possible that I'd choose to watch him bleed a little after locking me in here without a warning.

Noah brought the tray over to a small desk in the corner. "Eggs. Bacon. Toast. It's just Wonder bread, but there's extra nutritional grains baked into it. Says so on the label."

I looked at him skeptically. "How do I know it's not poisoned?"

"You have enough poison in you as it is. This is just food. Trust me."

"Why should I trust you?"

"Don't I have an honest face?" He grinned, but the expression faded quickly. "Look, your situation sucks, I'll be the first one to admit it. But I'm not trying to kill you."

"What about my blood sample?"

"Carson was up half the night looking at it. He's still down there."

"And?"

"And . . . I don't know. He isn't really the sharing type unless he feels like it. However, he did say someone already checked out Anderson's lab this morning and came up empty. He didn't seem all that surprised about it."

I wrung my hands. "Where's Declan?"

"Out."

"Out where?"

"Just out. He doesn't always give me a detailed itinerary. But he's supposed to be back soon. Why? Do you miss him?"

That earned him a powerful glare I hadn't even known was in my arsenal. It worked, since he visibly grimaced.

I was about to say something, try to push past the anger I felt about feeling trapped and powerless, but a wave of pain closed in on me. I buckled over and fell to my knees.

Shit. There hadn't been anything for so long I'd thought it was over. This time it was even worse than the last. I cried out and Noah rushed to my side.

"What can I do?" he asked. I hadn't needed to explain what was happening to me. He just knew.

"Bathroom," I managed, but barely.

He helped, half dragging me, to get to the bathroom just in time to make it to the toilet, where I emptied my stomach of the black inky substance that tasted like death.

"Oh my God," Noah exclaimed. "Jesus Christ."

I wasn't all that religious, but it was a good suggestion to start praying. Pain wracked through my body for a couple more minutes until it passed and I collapsed on the floor. Unfortunately I was still conscious. I wiped my mouth off with the back of my hand, tasting oily, rancid death still on my tongue. Just the thought of it made me feel sick all over again, but there was no more pain. I blinked watering eyes and looked up. Noah stood over me, his hand held to his mouth in shock.

"That shit's not right," he said.

"Tell me about it."

"That is one nasty-ass side effect."

"I know."

"Are you okay now? Can you get up?"

"I think so."

It took a minute or two, but Noah helped me back to my feet. I washed my face and rinsed out my mouth. There was a fresh toothbrush in the otherwise empty medicine cabinet, which I'd used last night and again today with a squirt of some generic toothpaste.

"What was that shit that came out of you?" he asked.

"I thought you were a scientist?"

"No. I'm a research assistant. I've dealt a bit in forensics, but never . . . I don't know. I've never seen anything like that before."

"That's not very comforting."

My stomach growled loud enough for Noah to hear. "Are you going to be sick again?"

"I don't think so." I covered my stomach with my hand. "Believe it or not, I think I'm hungry."

"That is messed up."

Messed up or not, I *was* hungry. So I ate the breakfast Noah had brought me. He stayed with me, although he still looked disturbed.

"Did you make this?" I asked.

"I did. Nothing special."

"It's good." I looked at him skeptically. "How long have you been here?"

"Almost a year."

"Fighting the vampires."

"I try to stay inside away from vampires whenever possible, actually. I leave fighting the vamps to Dec."

"You and Declan . . . are friends?" If I wasn't going to get any more answers out of the one-eyed Batman himself, I may as well grill his much more amiable Robin-like sidekick.

He pursed his lips. "Kind of hard to be friends with

somebody like Dec, but I'd say we're as close to it as you can get."

"Why's it hard?"

"He's not exactly racking up congeniality points on a daily basis, as I'm sure you're well aware. He keeps to himself mostly. Except for Molly, that is. They spend a lot of time together."

Molly? There was a woman in Declan's life? This revelation caused an immediate and very unwelcome sliver of emotion to run through me.

I think it may have been jealousy.

I really was sick. Mentally. But then again, that wasn't news to me.

"So Molly's his girlfriend?" I asked.

Noah stared at me blankly for a few long moments. "Molly's his cat. A rescue he found half-dead and nursed back to health. She's only got one eye, too, so I always figured that was the attraction since otherwise she's a flea-bitten miserable little bitch. No, Dec . . . he's not exactly somebody who would have a girlfriend."

I frowned. "What's that supposed to mean?"

Noah grimaced. "Forget it."

"You can't just say something like that and tell me to forget it. I spent all day with him yesterday and I'm trying to figure him out."

"It's probably best that you don't try too hard."

"Has he ever had a girlfriend?"

Noah looked uncomfortable with this conversation. "Not on my watch, but . . . uh, it's not easy for him, you know."

"Because of his serum?" I asked. "He said it flattens him out emotionally—when he was off it yesterday for a while he started acting . . . well, he acted differently. Then when he started up again, he changed back to normal."

"That sounds about right." He cleared his throat. "I'm surprised he told you any of this."

"We had a lot of time to chat." I blinked, thinking through it all. The serum flattened him out. No emotions. No desire, no lust, no chance of turning into his biological father. That's why he didn't have a girlfriend. The serum took away any lust he might feel.

Those moments in the truck, when he'd admitted that he desired me—no wonder he'd seemed so disturbed by that. It might have been ages since the last time he'd felt that way.

I chewed my bottom lip as I sorted through everything I'd been told. "How long has Declan been on that serum?"

"Forever. Since he was a kid, I think."

Since he was a kid? So if he'd been taking it every three hours like clockwork since then, did that mean he'd never been with anyone romantically?

"Are you feeling better now?" Noah asked after a moment of silence passed uncomfortably between us.

"A little."

"Thank God." His brows drew together with concern over what he'd witnessed. "How often does that happen to you?"

"Too often. The last time was early last night. But that was just pain. I haven't puked since yesterday afternoon."

"Noted." He glanced at my now-empty breakfast tray. "Looks like it hasn't affected your appetite, so that's a good sign, right?"

"My compliments to the chef."

"What's going on in here?" a deep voice asked and I jumped. Our backs were to the door that had been left ajar.

Declan stood there, his arms crossed over his chest.

"You're back," Noah said.

"Does Jillian need a breakfast companion?"

Jillian. Full-name usage. When I'd told him my name, I'd said my friends called me Jill.

"She wasn't feeling well," Noah replied. "To put it extremely mildly."

His gaze moved to me. "You had another spell?"

"I did." I stood up to face him.

"Are you all right?"

"Still breathing." It was going to be my answer now to that question. *Still breathing.* Because I couldn't say I was fine or a-okay. I was still breathing. At least, until I wasn't.

"Carson needs to speak with you."

I glared at him. "You locked me in here last night."

He just looked at me without saying anything for a moment. "Yes, I did."

"That wasn't necessary."

"Like I said, Carson needs to speak with you."

"Has he found something in my blood sample?"

"Yes."

"So I have your official permission to leave this room now?" I didn't try to make it sound the least bit pleasant. After everything that had happened yesterday, I couldn't help but feel betrayed that he'd treated me like nothing more than a prisoner.

"Yes."

"Then lead the way." I looked at Noah. "Thank you for breakfast."

"Anytime."

Declan led me out of the room and back down to the basement lab. I wanted to feel the same level of anger toward him as I'd felt last night, but I couldn't. This wasn't someone I could feel any emotion for anymore. It was like he wasn't even here.

And it didn't matter, anyway. Carson had looked at my blood sample and analyzed it or whatever he was supposed to do with it. He would have found a way to clean my blood of the poison by now.

There were several other people with Carson downstairs speaking with each other. When Declan and I entered the room they stopped and looked over at us. Or rather, at me.

"Jillian," Carson said and beckoned me toward him. "This is Dr. Monica Gray."

The attractive older woman had long, slate-gray hair that hung in a long ponytail down the center of her back and skin that was lined but otherwise flawless. She reached forward and took my hand in hers as she studied my face. "It's a pleasure to meet you, Jillian. You look . . . well."

"Thanks." I felt uncomfortable at her scrutiny, like I was a slide at the end of her microscope.

"Anderson must have failed," she said.

Carson looked at her. "Why do you say that?"

"I don't see any physical indication that she's been given the Nightshade. I expected something tangible."

"She was given it. Declan witnessed it himself."

"Perhaps it wasn't a viable sample. After all, it was untested."

"Who are you again?" I asked.

Her intense examination of me ended and she stepped back. "I'm so sorry. We're being rude. But it's just hard for me to believe that this could have happened to a civilian."

"Dr. Gray is the head of research for the Nightshade program," Carson said. "The others have flown in from Washington D.C. Dr. Peter Singh and Lieutenant Joseph Franklin. They'll be observing today."

The other men didn't approach, but nodded curtly at me.

It didn't put me totally at ease, but my comfort levels didn't matter that much at the moment. All that mattered were getting the results I wanted. "Did you find a way to help me?"

"We do want to help you," Carson assured me. "I need to ask you a couple more questions. I already got a full debriefing from Declan, but I'd like it in your own words, if I may."

Impatience ate away at me. After my most recent bout of pain, I didn't want to wait too much longer for some sort of relief. "What do you want to know?"

"Declan said you were attacked by a vampire at a rest stop during your journey here."

"I was."

"How did this vampire react to you?"

I forced myself to think about what had happened at the diner. "Initially she was normal. I mistook her for a human, but then again, I'd never seen a vampire before. When she caught a whiff of me, she seemed to change, lose control."

"As if she couldn't resist trying to bite you?" Dr. Gray asked.

I nodded. "That's exactly what she wanted to do. Luckily she didn't."

"So she didn't break the skin at all?" She brushed my hair back so she could inspect my neck more closely.

I stood still and didn't pull away from her. After all, she was trying to help me. "No. Declan stopped her just in time."

"He also said that he noticed your scent as well and was drawn to you, more so when he wasn't taking his serum."

I shrugged, trying not to think about how "drawn to me" Declan had been yesterday. It didn't seem to matter anymore. "I assumed that vampires or half-vampires are simply drawn to the scent of humans."

"They are. But not quite like this. Nightshade was developed to draw the vampire, to entice it, to make the kill much quicker. Almost as if the creature is choosing its own death—much like a moth to a flame."

I shook my head. "I don't really understand any of this."

"We wouldn't expect you to." Carson flipped through several pages on a clipboard. Then he set it aside and looked at me. Tension etched his features. "The Nightshade formula has been in development for over a year. It's cost a great deal of money."

His comment made me feel defensive. Was I supposed to feel bad about the money lost? "I didn't ask him to inject me."

"I'm not saying that you did. But"—he sighed with frustration—"since being administered to you, its properties are no longer evident. Such a result is both the strength and weakness of using parachemistry."

"Parachemistry?" I repeated.

He just looked at me patiently. "It's the study and application of drugs, toxins, and potions in combating preternatural creatures such as vampires. Bottom line, there is no way for me to duplicate the formula. The only way would be to have Anderson's notes, his computer files. Or Anderson himself. He was the expert on the subject. But now that he's dead, that's not an option."

I didn't know what Carson wanted me to say. The formula was ruined. While I was sorry to hear this, I couldn't do anything about it.

He looked over his shoulder at the two men and woman. "Monica, please take the others and wait for me in the observation room."

She nodded. "Very well."

Without another word, they departed.

I glanced nervously over my shoulder to see Declan standing near the stairwell leading to the main house. He'd remained so quiet I thought he'd already left.

"Jillian experienced more side effects this morning," Declan said. "I wasn't there, but Noah was."

Carson's brow furrowed. "I'm sorry you've been inconvenienced like this, Jillian. I realize it isn't very fair to you."

"I just want you to fix me," I said, ignoring the lump in my throat. I could hold it together. I could.

"I wish it were that easy."

My breath caught. "Are you saying you can't help me?"

"It's possible we have a drug that could help you. One that could work as an antidote."

"Only possible?"

"Yes."

"If it's just a possibility, then what am I doing here? I need to go somewhere they can *definitely* help me. The poison is in my blood. It's killing me, right?"

His mouth thinned. "I believe so."

I'd wanted him to say something, anything else. But he hadn't.

Hope faded away, leaving behind only a dull ache in my chest. It had been there since the beginning, but I'd thought there might be a possibility, even if it was a slight one, that this could still turn out all right.

I'd wanted to wake up this morning, come downstairs, and have him all ready with a magic pill that would heal me. So I could go back to my regular life and visit with my sister and her kids, and go back to my job that had bored me to death before, but now I remembered fondly.

A life when my biggest trouble was a dark mood ruining a day or two.

Finding a solution had only been a pipe dream from the very beginning. I had poison in my veins and it had now been there for an entire day. There was no going back.

My life was over. I felt the truth of this deep inside me.

Declan's expression gave nothing away. He'd promised his father could help me. Had that been a lie to make me behave? Or had he really believed it was possible?

Carson's gaze flicked to Declan's before returning to mine. "Jillian, I want to show you something. It's very important that you come with me. Will you do that?"

"Fine," I said dully. I didn't particularly care where he took me or what he wanted to show me. If it wouldn't help, then what difference did it make?

Death was coming for me. And I knew without a doubt it would come in the form of one of those attacks that made me spew out that darkness inside. I might not survive the next one.

Carson's hand pressed against my shoulder as he directed me out of the room and through a silver door leading to a long, brightly lit hallway.

We passed through a door requiring a security code. Beyond the door came the sound of pounding and muffled screeching that made my skin crawl. There was a small window on the door, but it was dark inside.

"What the hell is that?" I asked, tensing up automatically.

Carson looked at the door with distaste. "Some of Dr. Gray's research has included crossbreeding between vampires and humans."

"Dhampyrs. Like Declan."

"Not all dhampyrs created are like Declan. In fact, his type of dhampyr is very rare. There are others that are much more common."

I shivered. "Are you trying to tell me that's another dhampyr in there?"

"It is. However, while Declan is more human than monster, that is more monster than human. More monster than even *vampire*. Very dangerous."

"And that's what you wanted to show me?"

He shook his head. "No. You don't have to worry about what's in that room, trust me."

I staggered along after him, trying to imagine just what was making those horrible sounds that made me shudder. A monster. A *literal* monster.

I looked over my shoulder at Declan but nothing in his expression belied his thoughts. Or even *if* he was having any thoughts.

Was he afraid that he'd become like the creature in that room if he didn't take his serum right on schedule? Or why he'd mentioned another serum being developed that would last much longer than only three hours?

Of course that's what he was afraid of. And that he was desperate not to let the monster inside of him off its leash so he wouldn't hurt anyone, even at the detriment to his own quality of life . . . well, that was admirable, I guess.

Frustrating, but admirable.

"I want you to meet somebody, Jillian," Carson said.

"You really think this is necessary?" Declan asked.

Carson turned sharply. "Yes, I do."

"Who am I meeting?" I asked without much interest.

"Someone who might help give specific insight to your current condition." Carson pushed open a door leading into a room with a table and two chairs in the middle of it. A man sat there and looked over at us.

"Tobias, this is Jillian," Carson said. "Please, Jillian, if you will . . ."

I stepped into the room at his urging. The man looked a little like my tenth-grade English teacher: slight in stature, balding blond hair, otherwise pleasant in appearance. He wore a tan-colored suit that looked a bit wrinkled.

"She's the one you said would help me get out of here?" Tobias asked.

"That's right."

"But I thought you said—" I began, but Carson shut the door. It felt like a replay of last night with Declan locking me into the bedroom. So much so that I tried the handle of the door.

And just like last night, it was locked.

"What the hell?" I said out loud, then looked at Tobias. "What's going on here?"

"I'm not sure." He stood and crossed his arms, looking nervously around the room.

"Who are you?"

"Just somebody minding my own damn business when this guy . . . he came out of nowhere and grabbed me. Beat me. Tied me up. The next thing I know, here I am and nobody's giving me any damn answers."

I didn't like this one bit.

"You don't look like you've been beaten up," I said.

He touched his face. "You should have been there. The guy was scary. He didn't have to lay a finger on me; I would have done whatever he said. But he liked to use his fists."

"What did he look like?" I asked, although I had a feeling I already knew the answer.

"Tall, big. Lots of scars. Wore an eye patch."

What the hell was going on here? Why was Declan kidnapping more innocent people and dragging them here against their will?

Feeling tense, I scanned the room. Other than the table and chairs, it was empty. Smooth white walls. Along the wall to the right of the door was a long mirror. I stared at my reflection and saw the worry in my eyes.

This didn't feel right.

I mean, a lot hadn't felt right since yesterday morning, but there was something about this that was really . . . off. I glanced at the reflection of Tobias. He looked just as worried as I did.

"Meet me in the observation room," Carson had told the others.

The mirror, it was like the ones I'd seen on television. A mirror on one side, a window on the other. Meant for observing without being seen.

"You really think this is necessary?" Declan had asked just a minute ago. He'd said it with no inflection, nothing to give me a clue what he was talking about. He could have been discussing anything—or nothing at all. Was it necessary to keep me here? Was it necessary to keep trying to find an antidote when it was obvious I was going to die? Was it necessary for him to still be in my presence when there were other innocent civilians he needed to beat up and drag back here?

"Why is the door locked?" I asked the man.

"No idea."

I looked at him. "Who are you, really?"

He shrugged. "My name's Tobias Lawson."

"I already got your name. But . . . but why did he bring you here and lock you in a room? And why make me come in here with you? And"—I pointed at the mirror—"why are they watching us?"

"I don't know." He met my gaze unflinchingly, almost defiantly. His eyes were a spooky pale gray color that triggered a bit of familiarity in me.

I'd seen eyes like that. Declan's were gray, too, but not quite this light.

Wait. It was the woman in the diner. Her eyes had been the same color.

A breath caught in my chest.

I was locked in a room with a vampire.

—— 11

I THOUGHT FOR A MOMENT I WAS BEING PARANOID and imagining things. How could I make an assumption like this based solely on someone's eye color? Maybe it was just a coincidence. Or maybe . . .

"How did the man with the eye patch get you here?" I asked warily.

"He threw me in the trunk of a car."

"Before or after sunrise?"

He looked at me steadily. "Before."

I walked to the mirror and banged my fist on it. "Let me out of here right now."

"Hey, relax," Tobias said, taking a few steps toward me.

I turned and held my hand up. "Don't get any closer."

He frowned, then cocked his head to the side, a quizzical look on his face. "Why not?"

"You're a vampire."

His expression shadowed, but he drew closer still. "You don't have to be afraid of me. I mean you no harm."

I pointed at the mirror. "Why do you have a reflection?"

"That's just a myth. A lot of what is said about vampires is myth. You have to believe me."

"Seriously, just stay the hell away from me."

But he'd drawn too close already. Close enough to smell me. His eyes widened and his nostrils flared. "What are you?"

That was the exact same thing the vampire in the diner had said.

I looked back at the mirror that I was certain looked into an observation room. "What are you doing in there? Get me out of here!"

Then I felt the vampire's hand on my shoulder and he turned me around to face him.

"Your scent . . . I've never smelled anything like it." He drew his tongue over his bottom lip.

His pupils spread out to cover the pale gray of his entire iris, as though they had dilated completely. The flesh of his cheeks and jaw sunk in. Dark blue veins now could readily be seen on his forehead and they branched down to his jaw through the transparent parchment of his skin.

His top lip drew back from sharp fangs. In a few seconds flat he'd gone from looking like my memory of a high school teacher to a predatory monster. His fingers dug into my shoulder painfully. A thin line of drool escaped the corner of his mouth and drizzled down to his chin.

"Let go of me," I managed.

Whatever he'd smelled on me, whatever he'd sensed, he was no longer thinking like a reasonable being. His dead black eyes moved to my throat. He pushed my face roughly back, forcing my head against the mirror. I fought against him, clawing at his arms, but it was like fighting against a tank. He was strong and his body felt like steel; unbreakable, inescapable.

I'd nearly given up hope before, nearly ready to accept my fate. This poison inside of me was going to kill me and there was nothing I could do to stop that. It hurt to think about it, it hurt to hope for a solution when I knew that there wouldn't be one. I'd nearly accepted that death was coming for me. Fast.

But not like this. I didn't accept this.

Declan had burst into the washroom at the diner to pull the vampire away from me just in time. Where was he now? He said he'd protect me, but maybe that offer had expired when we reached Silver Ridge.

What the hell were they doing? They'd locked me in a bedroom all night only to hand me over as breakfast for a hungry vampire.

I felt it then—that spark and determination to not give up. I'd fight until my last breath even if it wouldn't do any damned good.

I didn't want to die.

This was not how it was supposed to end for me. Not here. Not now.

But then I felt the vampire's mouth on my throat. He'd dragged me to the table, forcing me back until I had no choice but to lie on it, and he held my head at an awkward and painful angle so he could have full access to my neck. I felt his erection press into me and his hand roughly kneaded my breast through my shirt before it slid down between my legs.

Terror coursed through me.

But it was only the beginning. After inhaling my scent and sliding his cool, wet tongue over my throat for a few seconds, seconds during which I whimpered and clawed at him and tried to break free, I felt the sharp tips of his fangs press against my skin.

Declan, please . . . help me . . . I wasn't sure if I said it aloud or only thought it. Either way, he didn't help. He didn't burst into the room to save me.

And then I felt the pain.

I screamed and kicked as the vampire pierced my skin and sank his fangs deep into my throat. The next moment it felt as if I'd been paralyzed. I couldn't move anymore, couldn't fight against him. But I could still feel everything.

The pain was acute; deep and searing, like twin blades digging into my flesh. Then there was the equally horrible sound of slurping as he began to drink my blood. His hand, which had been stroking between my legs quickly moved to undo the top button of my pants and greedily slip inside.

And I couldn't move. I couldn't beg for him to stop. At that moment, I couldn't even scream.

Please, no . . .

"So good," he murmured thickly. "You taste so good. Smell so good. Feel so good."

And nothing happened. No one rushed in to save me. They were going to let him feed from me, let him rape me, let him kill me . . .

All while they watched safely from behind the mirror.

But then the vampire froze. He pulled away from my neck and crotch and staggered away from me. I couldn't move for a couple of seconds, but then I did. I slid off the table to the floor and scrambled back, my hand against my neck—the same side that had been injected yesterday.

My blood was on the vampire's lips and under the fluorescent lights it looked darker than regular blood—a dark crimson. He touched it, wiping his lips and then looking at his fingers.

"What—?" Then his black eyes went wide and he convulsed and collapsed to his knees on the floor. I thought he was going to crawl toward me, but he didn't. He stayed where he was, his hands over his stomach. "No. Oh fuck. No . . . please . . ."

It sounded like he was in agony. He looked as if he was experiencing the same pain I did when I had an attack from the formula. What the hell was happening to him?

Then he screamed and fire poured from his mouth. It rippled out like liquid, coating his entire body until he was a column of flames. A moment later, Tobias exploded in a burst of fire and ash, some of which came close to me. I batted it away like a swarm of bees, desperate not to get stung.

The vampire was gone. Dead. Destroyed.

My blood—dark, unnatural blood—it had poisoned him. Killed him. There was no other explanation for what had just happened.

I was hyperventilating. My throat hurt so bad from the vampire's bite. The panic and fear and shock built up in my chest to a point that I had to let it all out or I might explode as surely as Tobias just had.

I started to scream.

A few moments later the door opened and Carson entered the room, followed by Declan and Dr. Gray.

I watched their approach, shaking, still in survivor mode. I scurried back into the corner until I had nowhere else I could go.

"I'm sorry we had to do that, Jillian," Carson said in a soothing tone. "But it had to be done. We had to see if I was right—that your blood is now poisonous to vampires or if the Nightshade formula had been completely compromised when it was administered to you."

"He . . . he almost killed me." My words were slurred and nearly incoherent.

"But he didn't. And we wouldn't have let him. It would have taken much longer for him to have drained you. We would have intervened before that happened, I assure you."

"He was going to . . . rape me." My tears felt hot sliding down my cheeks.

"A vampire's lust for blood usually drives them to satisfy their sexual needs as well. It's true. But again, we wouldn't have compromised you in that manner. We would have stopped him before it was too late." Carson crouched down next to me and put a hand on my shoulder. Through the blur of my tears, I could see he was actually smiling at me. "The experiment was a success, don't you see that?"

"Fuck you." I pushed away from him and did up the front of my pants with trembling fingers.

"Carson," Dr. Gray said sharply. "She's right. We should have come in sooner. There was no reason she had to be traumatized to this extent."

He turned to look at her. "It's done. Whether we could have done it differently is beside the point."

She glared at him, her arms crossed over her chest before her gaze moved to me and softened. "I apologize, Jillian. Truly. You've been through a great deal already and this didn't help at all."

"It was worth it," Carson insisted. "It's an incredible breakthrough. We now know that the Nightshade formula works just as Anderson claimed it would. It draws out a vampire's hunger and lust and destroys him or her when they follow that uncontrollable drive. It's a wonderful thing that happened here this morning."

"Just stay the fuck away from me," I snapped.

His lips thinned. "I know our methods may seem extreme to you, Jillian, but you have no idea what we're up against here or how long we've worked to find the perfect weapon to use against these monsters. They're nothing if not enduring. A few minutes of your discomfort or stress was a very small price to pay to come a step closer to ridding the world of the threat of vampires once and for all." He glanced at Dr. Gray. "Do you agree, or don't you?"

"The experiment was successful," she allowed.

"You had no right to throw me in here without telling me anything." My fury grew with every word I spoke.

"And would you have agreed if I'd told you?" he asked.

"No. Of course not."

"There's a first-aid kit in the medicine cabinet of your bathroom," Dr. Gray said, "although the bite doesn't look very bad. Vampires do very little damage with their bite. Ironic, really, that it can lead to death so easily. There is a component in a vampire's saliva that, along with temporarily paralyzing its victim, will allow for quicker healing of the bite. You should heal up nicely in no more than a day or two."

Carson glanced at Declan, who stood with his arms straight like a soldier's at his sides, his gaze blank. "Please accompany Ms. Conrad back to her room now."

No apologies, no "Sorry we threw you in the pit with a hungry monster with sharp teeth."

Just a "Clean yourself up, put on a Band-Aid, and stop your damn blubbering."

Carson Reyes may be a very smart man with his eyes on the prize of destroying bloodthirsty vampires, but he was also a grade-A heartless asshole.

Declan helped me to my feet, then directed me out of the room without another word. I was still breathing hard, my heart racing, my chest tight.

He said nothing as we took the two flights of stairs back up to my room. He opened the door and went directly to the bathroom, taking the first-aid kit from the medicine cabinet just as Dr. Gray had mentioned. After holding a facecloth under the tap, he then brought it to me.

"The wound might not be that bad, but it should be properly cleaned." He held the cloth as if he meant to apply it to my neck.

I pushed his hand away and then slapped him as hard as I could across his ugly, scarred face.

"You son of a bitch," I snarled. "How could you let him do that to me?"

I hit him again and again with open palms and closed fists—on his face, his chest, anywhere I could land a direct strike. He didn't try to stop me for a moment. He just stood there and took it, let me get a few good hits in until my hands started to hurt. Then he grabbed my wrists.

"Enough," he said.

I'd never felt this level of fury before. Sure, I'd been angry, I'd been depressed, I'd experienced the gamut of emotions. But this? This seething hatred that made me see red, made me want to make Declan bleed so he might feel badly instead of feeling nothing at all? I'd never experienced anything like this.

"He was going to kill me!" I yelled.

"I wouldn't have let that happen."

"He bit me. He drank from me. Do you know what that felt like? Were you watching?"

His jaw tensed, but his single eye remained emotionless. "I was in the observation room. Yes, I was watching."

I went to strike him again, but he caught my arm before I made contact.

"So you saw what else he was trying to do, right?" My voice trembled now. "It would have only taken a few seconds for him to start raping me. And you sick fucks were just standing there and watching that? I hate you!"

"That wouldn't have happened." His voice grew louder, although it still sounded frustratingly calm. "I wouldn't have let him hurt you."

"But he *was* hurting me. His hand was between my legs. His teeth were in my neck."

"And your blood killed him, just as my father suspected it would."

"You father," I bit out, "is a cold, heartless bastard."

"His methods may seem extreme to an outsider—"

"*Extreme?* Are you blind?" A ragged breath caught in my chest. "Oh, God. I guess you are, aren't you? And here I thought you still had one good eye left. I should have stuck with my first impression of you. You're just a cold-blooded killer. You're no better than a fucking vampire."

He didn't speak for a moment. "I am better."

"No, you're not. You take that serum thinking that it makes you into a better man. Well, it doesn't make you into a man at all. You're a robot built to do whatever your father programs you to do. Of course he developed it for you and has forced you to take it all these years. Without it, you'd have a mind of your own. You'd have a personality. You'd have a life. And when you're on it, you have none of those things."

"You have no idea what you're saying."

"He's brainwashed you from the very beginning. Made you take a drug that turns you into a perfect weapon he can use to destroy things with. An impotent flesh-and-blood machine that follows orders to the letter. One who's never even touched a woman because that might compete with Daddy's ultimate goal. After all, you might choose the woman over him."

Declan's gaze narrowed a fraction. "You don't know him."

"I don't want to know him. He's destroyed you."

"He gave me a chance to live as a dhampyr child when others wanted to kill me. That thing downstairs he has locked away—you heard it trying to break free from its cell. That could be me."

A chill coursed down my spine at the memory of the dhampyr—the hybrid experiment as Carson had referred to it. "You call this living? There's more to living than following orders. More to living than killing vampires and getting scarred and maimed in the process. More to living than standing by and watching someone be attacked just to prove a theory."

"Without my serum, I would become one of the monsters."

I glared at him. "You're more of a monster right now taking the serum than you were yesterday not taking it."

"If I don't take the serum, I would become like that other dhampyr. Or at the very least . . . like Tobias." His gaze hardened. "I would try to hurt you just like he did. Or like my real father hurt my mother."

"You don't know that for sure. From what I've heard, you've never bothered to test the theory; you've just gone on what Carson tells you to do."

"It's better this way," he said. "Safer."

I shook my head, feeling sickened by this entire conversation. "For somebody who's supposed to be some sort of badass assassin, you're one big fucking coward."

I supposed I should have been more careful about what I said around him. I'd seen him murder three people already. I didn't know how he'd react to such a blatant insult. Since he was like stone, there was no flare of anger. Someone else might backhand me for insolence. Declan, however, didn't react at all.

"Be sure to cleanse and bandage your wound. I'll have Noah bring you some food later." Then Declan turned and left the room, closing and locking the door behind him.

12

I COULD HAVE GLOATED THAT I'D GOTTEN A GREAT jab in and that I may have even put a chink in Declan's tarnished armor, but I didn't. I went to the bed, curled up on top of the covers, and cried my sorry ass to sleep like a little girl afraid of the monsters hiding in the closet.

When I woke, there was a tray of food on the desk on the other side of the room as well as a pile of new clothes, along with a note.

Didn't want to wake you. Declan asked me to pick up a few things for you this morning. Hope you approve.

—Noah

Hope I approved. Being that I was trapped in this room again, I sure as hell approved of nothing. Fresh anger over what had happened with the vampire continued to burn before I finally looked at what he'd brought me. Fresh clothes. He'd even picked up underwear for me, brave boy. No bra, though. I chose a green tank top that was loose enough for it not to matter. The clothes weren't the very height of style. They were simple. Jogging and yoga pants. T-shirts. Generic cotton panties.

Noah had even picked me up a half-dozen paperback novels including a story about a Greek tycoon obsessed with revenge, brought to his knees by the love of the woman he was determined to make his mistress. They were the type of books I'd read in the past when I'd been on vacation and having a good time.

My old life.

I picked at the food—a chicken sandwich and potato salad. A bottle of water. A peeled orange.

And I waited, pacing the room until my anger flared again at the morning's events.

I'd bandaged my throat. Just as Dr. Gray had said, the wound from the vampire's bite felt a lot worse than it looked. A bit of cleaning, an application of ointment, and a simple bandage was enough.

I picked up one of the books and tried to read. Anything to take my mind off things. Needless to say, it didn't work very well.

That afternoon, I had another attack, which left me weakened and defeated and crying on the bathroom floor. But it didn't kill me.

I hated Declan. It took me a while to figure out just why I hated him so much more than I hated his father. After all, Carson was the mastermind behind throwing me in with the vampire to test his theory about the formula. So why did my hate for Declan trump that? What had I expected from him? He was a killer, I'd known that from the very beginning. He was a horrible, scarred bastard who had kidnapped me and taken me away from my normal life. If it wasn't for him I wouldn't be in this situation in the first place.

I wish he'd stayed on his serum the entire time I'd known him. It was those hours he was off it that I'd begun to feel a strange connection with him, despite what he was. When he'd protected me from the blood servants and almost died. When he'd shown a glimpse of his true personality underneath the stony exterior. When he'd told me he wanted me on an entirely inappropriate level.

He'd said it to scare me, but it hadn't worked. I realized now I'd wanted him to give in to that dark lust he felt—because I'd felt it, too. While I would have fought Tobias until my last breath if I'd been able to move after his paralyzing bite, I wouldn't have fought Declan. I would have welcomed his hands on me.

This realization didn't help matters at all.

But that was gone now. The Declan I'd begun to feel something for had disappeared when he'd taken the serum again, and I hated him for that. It was as if he'd murdered someone I'd started to care for—taken him away so I'd never have the chance to see him again.

Noah returned at dusk with a tray of dinner for me. He nudged the door open with his shoulder and entered the room.

"Hey," he greeted me.

I glared at him.

He placed the tray down next to the picked-over lunch. "Not a big fan of potato salad?"

"I'm not a big fan of being held prisoner," I snarled, surprised by how angry I still sounded after all these hours.

His shoulders stiffened and he turned to face me. "Look, I heard what happened this morning."

"My near-death experience?"

He grimaced. "Carson doesn't have the greatest bed-side manner, I'll admit."

"That's putting it mildly." I'd gathered enough control over myself that I didn't try to claw Noah's eyes out so I could escape. "Don't kill the messenger," as the saying went. "Do they hold a lot of innocent women here against their will whom you have to cook and shop for?"

He gave me an awkward grin. "You're the first. Congrats."

"It's not right, Noah. You know that, don't you?" I sat down heavily on the edge of my bed.

His grin faded. "I know."

"How the hell did you get involved in all of this?"

He crossed his arms. "I volunteered."

"For *this*." I couldn't help but sound skeptical.

He nodded. "When I heard rumors about a program dedicated to killing vampires, how could I resist? It's a lot more interesting than pushing papers around a desk."

"Was that your only other option?"

"I didn't explore any other options. I knew what I wanted to do. Carson met with me, he liked my style—not that I blame him—he offered me the position here, and I took it. I haven't looked back since. The location's a bit remote, but I feel like I'm doing the best I can here."

I studied him for a moment. "You seem like a good guy. You deserve better than this."

"You haven't tried your dinner yet," he said. "Lasagna. Not exactly my specialty, I'll warn you now."

"How can you just stand by and let them do this? You saw me yesterday. I'm sick."

His expression shadowed. "I know. I'm sorry."

"It happened again today. I—I'm sure it's going to kill me. That is, if they don't manage to kill me first."

"Jill, if there was anything I could do to help you I would, but . . ." He trailed off.

"But—?"

"But you're being kept here not to hurt you but to help you. Seriously. I know how it must look from your point of view, but you have to understand—we're the good guys. Sure, our methods may be a bit extreme and a lot of the time—hell, *most* of the time, lately—I don't agree with Carson and Dr. Gray's grand plan. But . . . they're trying to do the right thing."

"Killing vampires."

"Yeah."

My stomach twisted. "I've seen two vampires who seemed fine and reasonable until they smelled my blood."

"You're the Nightshade cover girl now."

I clenched my hands at my sides, feeling utterly power-less. "I'm going to die."

"No, you're not." Noah paced to the window, glancing at the broken chair laying nearby. I'd already tried to escape only to find that it was impossible to break the glass. He wisely chose not to mention it.

"How do you know that?"

"Because Carson and Dr. Gray won't let you. You're too important to their mission."

"The mission to kill all vampires."

"No, just the king. Strike at their heart—the decision maker, the big boss. Dr. Gray's convinced that once he's taken out of the game, then the rest will be easier to pick off. It'll be like mopping up a spill after the bottle is corked." He scrunched his nose. "I'm no good at metaphors."

"The king." I thought back to yesterday with the blood servants. "You mean, Matthias?"

"That's the one."

"The heart," I said. "Carson used that term before. He said that this town is close to the heart."

Noah nodded. "Silver Ridge is only a few miles away from the heart of Matthias's vampire clan."

"So all of this is to find a way to assassinate him."

"Essentially. Or at least that's the big-ass goal at the top of Dr. Gray's to-do list. Vampires aren't easy to kill to begin with, unless you have skills like Declan. Even then it's difficult. When it comes to the king himself, it's a whole other ball of wax." He frowned. "Which is another really substandard metaphor, but I think I'm getting my point across. Ball of wax, though? What does that even mean? Did people actually collect balls of wax at some point in history?"

"And you agree with all of this?"

Noah hesitated. "My beliefs change from day to day. Like right now? I think throwing you in with that vamp was really wrong on too many levels to count."

"That makes two of us."

"Dr. Gray thinks what's in your veins is the only way to defeat Matthias."

"You're making it sound like Dr. Gray is in charge around here."

"She is."

That surprised me so much I didn't speak for a moment. "I thought Carson was the boss."

"He is when she's not around. She's been in Washington D.C. for a couple of months, but she definitely thought you were worth the trip. I heard her and Carson talking earlier."

"What did they say about me?"

He hesitated. "I really shouldn't say any more."

Noah was a font of information that I really didn't want to dry up. Where Declan wasn't willing to answer any of my questions anymore, Noah seemed ready, willing, and able.

If you asked me, he seemed kind of lonely. Not many people around here who want to chat.

"Come on," I said, pushing the closest thing I could get to a friendly smile on my face. "I have a right to know, don't I?"

"*I* think so." He rubbed his lips together as he considered the situation. "According to Carson, the reason you've been sick and have experienced all that pain is because your body is attempting to reject the formula."

I shivered. "So what am I supposed to do?"

"Carson's sent for a drug they've been developing that will help—it purifies blood from the inside out. It's supposed to be a catch-all cure for blood poisoning like this. If that doesn't work, then the next step would probably be good old-fashioned hemodialysis."

Finally something I understood. "Why wouldn't that be the first choice?"

"Because the Nightshade, well, it's not entirely . . . stable."

"Because it's based in parachemistry?" I used the term Carson used earlier.

"Bingo. It's the *para* part that is messing everything up. What we're dealing with here is based on preternatural science. A regular doctor wouldn't know what to do with this, trust me on that."

At least he was confirming for me what I already knew—a normal hospital wouldn't be much help to me.

A thousand more questions bubbled up in my mind. "So Nightshade was developed, in all its unstable glory, to kill Matthias. Why now?"

Noah paced the room, his arms tightly crossed over his chest. "Dr. Gray believes Matthias is sick of living underground and is about ready to poke his head up and say hello to the world."

"And what happens then?"

"Do the words *vampire apocalypse* mean anything to you?"

That sent a chill down my spine imagining a world gone crazy when what I'd only just discovered yesterday went public. Even if I did get this Nightshade poison out of my body and everything turned out okay, I knew my world had been changed forever.

"And she wants to stop him before that happens."

"She does. Her research is pointed in that direction."

"What about that other dhampyr downstairs? How long's it been here?"

His pleasant expression disappeared completely, replaced with worry. "Actually, there's two babies—and one on the way, thanks to Dr. Gray's other pet project."

My eyes widened. "That was a baby?"

"Baby dhampyrs are different than human babies. They grow *really* fast."

"But Declan—"

"Declan's different. But the other kind of dhamps—they're . . . unique. She's trying to figure out what makes one dhamp like Declan and another . . . not."

"A fluke of nature?"

"Maybe. I have a theory, although Dr. Gray never gives me the time of day to hear it."

"What is it?"

"Vamp women can't get pregnant; it has to be a human mother. That means the wild card is the father. The dhamp we have locked up was from a regular vamp daddy. So a human mother and a regular vampire father create a monster dhampyr."

"And Declan?"

"Normal human mother, but his father was no normal vamp. He was powerful. And seriously ancient. More so than your average, run-of-the-mill vampire."

I eyed him with surprise. "You know who his father is?"

"Of course I do." Noah nodded grimly. "It's in the files. Sometimes I read the ones I'm not supposed to read."

"Who is Declan's father?"

"The one and only." Noah shrugged. "Matthias."

13

MATTHIAS. THE KING.

The vampire that Declan said raped and left his mother in a coma before she died giving birth to him was Matthias.

"Does . . . does Declan know this?" I asked. "That Matthias is his father?"

"He does."

No wonder the mention of his name yesterday with the blood servants seemed to throw him. It made sense now. They worked for the vampire he hated more than any other.

"I have to go," Noah said, glancing at his watch. "I've stayed too long already." He stood and walked toward the door before looking back at me. "I'll be back tomorrow with your three squares a day. If you need more trashy novels, just let me know then."

When he opened the door, a small tabby cat slipped in and made a beeline for the bed.

"Molly," Noah said. "What are you doing in here?"

I lifted the comforter up off the side of the bed and got down on my knees, reaching under to gather the small animal into my arms. She didn't weigh more than six or seven pounds. When I rose to my feet, I saw that Declan now stood at the doorway.

"You can go," he said, his head turned toward Noah.

"Sure thing. Later, Jill." Noah disappeared through the open door before Declan's attention returned to me.

The anger I'd misplaced during Noah and my conversation returned in full force. "This yours?"

"She is."

"Molly, right?" My jaw was clenched so tightly it was difficult to form words.

His eye narrowed. "How do you know that?"

I shrugged, glad I'd caught him off guard. "Noah told me."

"Noah talks too much." He hadn't stepped all the way in my room, instead staying near the door.

She was not the prettiest feline I'd ever seen. She was missing patches of fur, there was a chunk that looked as if it had been bitten out of one of her ears, and as Noah had already told me, she only had one eye.

It was an ugly cat, really.

"When the hell am I going to be released from here, Declan?" I demanded.

"Soon."

"How soon?"

"Can't you be patient?"

"No, I guess I can't. Carson said two days max."

"It hasn't been two days yet."

"That was before he served me up on a platter to your vampire guest this morning."

"So now your patience has worn out?"

"I want out of here. Now."

"That isn't going to happen."

That anger inside me burned so bright it made me want to lash out. I couldn't seem to fake friendliness as easily with Declan as I could with Noah. I guessed it helped that I actually liked Noah.

"Then take your fucking one-eyed cat and leave me the hell alone." Just as I said it, the cat tensed and scrambled to leap out of my arms, managing to swipe its sharp claws over my forearm. It brushed against Declan's leg, an affectionate motion considering its previous violent turn, then ran out of the room. I eyed the door. He hadn't bothered closing it. I figured he knew there was no way I could escape with him currently blocking my way.

I held my hand against my arm, but blood had already welled up. Declan had closed the distance between us.

"Let me see." He took my arm in his grip and turned it over, then hissed out a breath at the sight of my blood.

I tried to wrench my arm away from him, but he held me firmly in place and looked down at my brand-new wound. Just as I'd seen on the vampire's lips this morning, my blood was a different color than it used to be. Whereas before it had been bright red—just as any blood was—the blood that oozed from the scratch was darker, almost burgundy. It was as if my normal blood had been blended with the black substance that I kept puking up on a semi-regular basis.

Declan's grip on my arm increased.

"What?" I asked.

His breathing had increased its pace. "You need to clean and bandage this immediately."

"Then you're going to have to let go of me."

"Right." But his grip didn't loosen. "It's . . . surprisingly hard for me to resist. I shouldn't have approached you right now. For a moment I wasn't thinking."

He was tempted by my strange, unnatural-looking blood. He'd said before that my scent was difficult to resist—but that had been when he was off the serum. Maybe it didn't matter this close up. I didn't smell anything, but I wasn't a dhampyr.

The scratch wasn't even that bad, but it was enough to appeal to his vampire half. For a moment, I wanted him to bend down for a taste. He'd destroyed my life, why shouldn't I destroy his?

"Get control of yourself," I snapped after a few more seconds went by. "You disgust me, you ugly bastard."

His gray eye flicked from my arm back to my face in a heartbeat. My sharp tone had worked as well as a slap.

He let go of me so abruptly I nearly fell backward since I'd been tugging to get my arm away from his grasp. "Good night, Jillian."

He turned and left my room. I didn't cry this time— total progress, I thought. Instead, I spent the rest of my night brainstorming how the hell I was going to escape.

FOR BREAKFAST AND LUNCH THE NEXT DAY, NOAH AR-rived right on schedule with a tray of food. He even added a flower in a vase at lunch. He stuck around for a few minutes talking to me, but had no more information about the antidote or what was going on downstairs, although he did mention that there had been many closed-door meetings since my date with the vampire yesterday.

When I told him I'd had two more attacks since last night, he visibly flinched. The kid wasn't without empathy, I'd give him that. I could probably talk him into helping me out if I had enough time to work on him.

Unfortunately, time didn't appear to be on my side. The last attack had left me weaker than ever and honestly praying for a death that didn't come. It wasn't an uplifting moment.

During our friendly chats, I'd established that Noah had car keys in his pocket. He played with them nervously when we spoke. I turned the conversation toward cars— a favorite subject of many men, I'd found. Noah was no exception to that rule. He told me about his brand-new red Mustang, which was a bit too flashy for his grocery and general supplies runs in a populated town twenty miles west of Silver Ridge.

All important pieces of information.

I hadn't seen Declan yet today, although the look in his eye when he had studied my cat scratch stayed with me. Well, he *was* half-vampire. Maybe I'd been wrong. Maybe he should definitely stay on his serum.

I figured Carson wouldn't want to help me anymore if I reduced his perfectly behaved, emotionless, eunuch weapon into a pile of ash because he couldn't keep his mouth off me.

Emotionless. He was supposed to be, wasn't he? But his reaction to the insult I'd thrown at him stayed with me. I'd called him an ugly bastard, and at the time I'd meant it. But the look on his scarred face made me think for a moment that I'd hurt his feelings.

Sure. Because *that* made sense.

Sticks and stones—and knives and bullets—might truly hurt him. But I didn't think names ever could.

So I spent Thursday waiting. Waiting for news about the antidote. Waiting for someone to tell me what the hell was really going on. Waiting for Declan to make another appearance. And finally, when that waiting didn't lead to any new answers, waiting for the arrival of my next meal.

Noah pushed the door open with his shoulder since his hands were occupied holding my dinner tray. A quick whiff told me it was macaroni and cheese. One of my favorites, actually. He took a couple steps inside then glanced around for me.

I'd been waiting behind the door so he didn't see me.

"Jill?" he asked.

"I'm sorry, Noah."

"What?"

When he turned I hit him with the seat from the wooden chair I'd used to try to break the window. Clobbered him right across the side of his head. The tray crashed to the floor a split second before Noah followed it.

"Oh my God." I swallowed a cry that welled up in my chest. I hadn't wanted to hurt him, but there was no other way. Luckily I didn't have to hit him again since he seemed to be out like a light. For a moment, I worried that I'd killed him so I checked his pulse. He still had one. That was a good sign.

I grabbed his keys from his pocket and some money from his wallet and turned toward the door that remained ajar, slipping outside and closing it behind me. I didn't know how long Noah would stay unconscious, but I figured I didn't have much time to get out of the house and find where he parked his car. Then I'd drive back to San Diego and check myself into the hospital for dialysis treatments. Declan said that wouldn't be a good idea and would cause trouble for me and, besides, they wouldn't be able to do anything for me when I got there. Well, fuck him. I didn't care what I had to do, I was going to solve this myself. I was finished with waiting for someone else to save me. I'd damn well save myself.

I flew down the stairs so fast I had to hang on to the railing so I wouldn't fall. After fumbling to unlock the front door, I emerged into the warm air outside. Keeping to the shadows—and since it was dusk there were a lot of shadows—I swiftly made my way to the back of the house, where there was a small parking lot.

Noah's Mustang was there. This was going to work. I'd drive out of here as fast as I could and never look back.

My hands shook as I fumbled for the keys, searching through the six on the key chain for the one for the car. When I found it, the keys slipped out of my sweaty hands and fell to the ground. I swore and got on my knees, feeling for them in the darkness. When I curled my hand around them again, I quickly scrambled back up to my feet and slid the key into the lock.

I was about to get in the car when I felt a hand grip my upper arm and lurch me backward.

— 14

"WHAT THE FUCK DO YOU THINK YOU'RE DOING?" Declan growled.

I reacted by fighting against him, or at least trying to, but he wasn't about to let me get a few good punches in this time. He grabbed my wrists so tightly I thought they might snap. I cried out in pain.

"Let go of me!"

"Do you know how dangerous it is out here all by yourself?"

"I think I have an idea."

"You have no idea. None." Holding both my wrists tightly in his grip, he pulled me, nearly yanking me right off my feet, back toward the house.

"No! You have to let me go!" I tried to get away from him, but his hold on me was unbreakable.

"Wrong."

And just as I'd been on the brink of escaping this house

in which I'd been kept prisoner for nearly two days, I was back in it. Declan wordlessly dragged me back up the stairs toward my room.

Noah was coming to and he pushed himself off the floor, touching his head gingerly. He looked groggily up at us.

"What the hell happened?" he asked.

"I told you not to let your defenses down around her," Declan snapped, tossing the keys, which he'd taken from me, back at Noah. "Looks like you weren't paying attention. She nearly escaped in your car."

"*My* car?" Noah looked confused and his attention shifted to me. "You hit me?"

I hated that I felt the least bit of guilt for clobbering Noah, but I did. I chose not to answer him.

"Look at this mess." Noah glanced at the broken plates from my untouched dinner. He began to clean it up.

"Forget it," Declan said. "Leave us."

"But—"

"Just go. Jillian and I need to have a little talk."

I really didn't like the sound of that.

Noah looked at me again and instead of accusation in his gaze I could see a bit of pity. Frankly, I'd prefer him being pissed at me for trying to escape than feeling sorry for me for being brought back. I could feel sorry enough for myself without anyone's help.

After Noah left, Declan closed the door behind him and turned to me. He looked pissed. Which was strange, considering that I was used to him having no expression at all.

"What are you trying to do?" he demanded.

I swallowed. "I'm trying to live to see another day."

"And leaving protective custody here where you're safe

and going out there where you might be attacked or worse is a good idea?"

"I *was* attacked out there. By you."

He hissed out a breath. "I'd feel sorry for your ignorance if your actions didn't show such stupidity."

"Stupidity," I repeated, "because I'm ready to do what it takes to save my own life? Because I'm sick and tired of waiting?"

He came closer to me so I could see the fire behind the normally cool gray glare. "We're trying to help you, don't you see that?"

I actually laughed at that. Right in his face. "Fuck you, Declan. If this is help, I think I'd be better off dead."

"My father is searching for a way right now to help you."

"Maybe I'm not willing to put all my faith in your *father*." I said the word like it was another F-word.

"This isn't all about you, Jill. It's unfortunate you've been swept up in the current, but there are more important issues at stake here."

"Like killing your *real* father, you mean."

Declan visibly flinched and took a step back from me. Confusion slid through his gaze before a hardened resolve took over. "Noah told you."

I didn't reply.

"Noah has a big fucking mouth. One that will get him in trouble someday."

"From you?"

He started to pace the room, obviously agitated. "That's very likely."

"I guess I am a little unclear on a few things." I eyed him uneasily. His current mood was confusing to me. "The Nightshade formula was developed specifically to be used on Matthias, right?"

"He's the main target, but it was meant to work on all vampires equally."

"You're okay with that? If he's really your father, I mean?"

He stopped pacing and his eye narrowed on me. "Yes. I'm more than okay with it. Destroying Matthias is my goal. Even if he wasn't the vampire I hold responsible for my mother's death, he's a direct and growing threat to human life. He needs to die."

Well, that was definitive.

"What's going on with you?" I asked.

That question received a glare. "Pardon me?"

"You're . . . acting strangely."

"Am I?"

"Have you been taking your serum regularly?"

He cocked his head and the left side of his mouth curled up in a sardonic smile. "Well, Jill, if I wasn't, you'd probably be in much deeper trouble than you already are trapped in this room with me all alone, wouldn't you?"

I inhaled sharply. "Was that a yes or a no?"

As if the fates were in perfect alignment, the next moment the alarm on his watch sounded. It beeped loudly in the silence of the room before Declan turned it off. He didn't make an immediate move to grab his vials of serum and a syringe.

"Oh my God," I whispered after another moment passed. "You stopped taking it, haven't you?"

He was silent before giving me a very unpleasant smile. "You're so insightful, Jill. Really impressive how well you seem to know me after such a short time."

His sarcasm was sharp enough to cut.

"How long has it been?" I suddenly found it difficult to speak without my voice trembling.

"I took my last injection shortly before you were introduced to Tobias."

I did the math in my head. "That was almost thirty-six hours ago."

"Yes, it was."

"Why did you stop?"

He didn't reply for so long that I began to feel more uncomfortable than I already was. "An experiment. One I never thought I'd participate in, especially not by choice. But what you said to me yesterday morning about the serum . . . well, it registered with me. And here we are. It's the longest I've ever gone without it."

"And?"

"The drug's entirely out of my system now."

"Does Carson know?"

"No. But I haven't seen much of him in the last day for him to notice any changes. He's been occupied."

"So why do you still have your alarm going off every three hours?"

"It's a reminder that I should be taking my serum. A reminder of what a dangerous thing I'm doing."

"How do you feel?" I asked cautiously.

"I feel . . . *everything*."

"You don't look happy about that."

"I'm not." His expression tensed.

I felt a flash of concern for him. "Are you in pain right now?"

His gaze snapped back to my face. "In a manner of speaking."

"Can I help?" This was incredibly scary, but also encouraging. He was off his serum because of what I'd said to him. I searched my memory for what might have been the trigger, but couldn't really remember anything clearly.

I'd been furious with him, that he'd allowed his father to use me like that and throw me in with a hungry vampire as an experiment. I'd said some cruel things afterward that I was sure I wouldn't want repeated.

"Can you help?" he repeated dryly. "No, I think you can only do further harm. I've been trying to avoid you as much as possible. Being around you is . . . painful for me."

"Painful?"

He nodded, his gaze never leaving mine for a moment. "Probably as painful as is it is for you to have to look at my ugly face right now."

I remembered then what I'd said to him yesterday. I'd called him an ugly bastard. "Declan . . . I didn't mean—"

"I have no illusions of how I'd look to a woman like you. And you've made it very clear that you find me disgusting. It's not a problem, as long as I stay clear of you. But yesterday, when you were bleeding . . ." He swallowed. "Well, that was a big problem for me. And tonight . . . it only proves to me why I need to stay away from you, especially now that I can't protect you anymore."

"Protect me? From the vampires? Noah said they were close to this town."

"No, not from the vampires." Declan drew closer and grabbed my wrist again, tightly. "Protect you from me."

I tried to break free from him but he reacted by grabbing my other wrist to help hold me in place.

"I'm not afraid of you," I said firmly.

"You should be."

"You're not like your father."

"I wish that were true, but I'm not so sure. The serum kept my hungers at bay, kept my behavior and thoughts controlled. But now . . . there's no control left, Jill. And being near you is dangerous for the both of us."

"My blood is poisonous to vampires," I managed. My

heart pounded in my chest as panic grew inside me. "You're half-vampire. If you bite me, it could kill you."

"No, Jill." He drew me closer, his expression strained. "It's not blood I want from you tonight."

He crushed his mouth against mine, letting go of my wrist so he could tangle his hand in the length of my hair. His other hand reached down to my ass and he pulled me tightly against him, tight enough that I could feel the hard length of his erection press against my stomach.

This is what the serum helped prevent. This dark lust he'd warned me about during our drive here. The one he said stopped him from tearing my clothes off and burying himself deep inside me.

The kiss may have been hard and rough and deep, but it wasn't long before I returned it, feeling desire ignite inside me, the same desire that I'd begun to feel for him during our journey here.

I tried to pull back from him a little. "Declan . . . wait . . ."

"You see?" he snarled. "This is what I am. Just like my father."

"No—"

I couldn't finish what I was going to say because his mouth was on mine again. I wasn't going to say no and that he should stop. I didn't want him to stop. I wanted to tell him he wasn't his father. His mother had been a victim, but I wasn't.

I wanted Declan, too. So much. But he was out of control, beyond reason—that was obvious to me as he tore at my clothes, roughly pulling at them to bare my skin underneath. If I was right about Declan's sexual history, well, that meant he didn't have one, thanks to the serum. It was even more evident in his clumsy attempts to undress me.

But when he slid his hand under the edge of my loose

jogging pants and down between my legs, I stopped thinking quite so logically. I think I cried out softly as his fingers brushed against me, a sound Declan seemed to take as a cry of protest.

"Does this finally prove it to you?" he whispered harshly against my ear as he boldly stroked me and I dug my fingers into his arms. "Without the serum, I'm a monster."

If I could speak I'd tell him he was wrong. That I wanted him so badly. That his hand on me was enough to render me speechless and very, very willing to let him do whatever he wanted.

Also, the fact I was kissing him back should have been a big clue to how I felt.

But I couldn't speak, and even if I could I would have been interrupted. A siren began to blare, sharply cutting through the otherwise silent room. Declan's hand between my legs froze and his gaze shot to mine. It was as if someone had thrown a cold glass of water in his face as clarity returned to his gray eye.

"Fuck . . ." he said. "Jill."

Well, yes. That was the general idea. But unfortunately it seemed as if he'd stopped. He pulled completely away from me.

"I'm so sorry," he continued, now averting his gaze.

"What is that?" I asked, breathlessly, referring to the siren.

The guilt in his expression was severe and soul crushing. "Something's wrong. I have to go."

I adjusted my clothing. Since I was still fully dressed it didn't take long to put everything back in place; I rolled down my T-shirt over my stomach and pulled up my jogging pants, retying them at my waist. My body felt like it had been lit on fire and left to slowly extinguish all by itself. There was an ache now inside of me, a needy emptiness that desperately wanted to be filled.

I heard a sound then other than the loud siren. A ringing. Declan reached into the pocket of his jeans and withdrew a new cell phone, placing it to his ear.

"What?" His raised voice was shaky. But then his back straightened. "Just now?" A short pause. "I'll be there as soon as I can." He closed the phone and put it away. Without looking at me he said, "The dhampyr has broken free and killed two guards. You need to come with me so I can get you somewhere safe."

The dhampyr had broken free? "But . . . isn't it safe here?"

"This room is mostly to keep you in, not to keep something like that out. Carson worries that it may scent you and come after you."

Fear slithered through me. "But if it got a taste of my blood, wouldn't that kill it?"

"Trust me, Jill. You don't want this thing's teeth anywhere near you. It would tear your throat out before it even started to feed on you."

"Jesus." I shuddered. "Okay, where do we go?"

He went to the door and opened it, moving so quickly that he seemed more than human. Which he was, of course. He grabbed my hand and pulled me behind him.

"I need to get you next door. There's an iron cell there, similar to the one the dhampyr was being held in."

"But it escaped that."

"True. But it won't be able to smell your blood if you're in there."

"And then what happens?"

"Then I come back and I kill it."

"You don't think you can capture it?"

He looked at me, his expression tense. "Carson wants

it killed. It can't be reasoned with. It's not even remotely human."

"But part of it is. It's half-human, just like you."

We were outside now and he pulled me alongside him so fast I nearly tripped.

A horrible screeching sound filled the warm night air. Declan froze in his tracks.

"Fuck," he said under his breath, craning his neck from side to side. "How the hell did it get outside? Carson said they'd contained it downstairs, but it must have slipped free."

"Have they escaped before?"

"Not often, but it happens. There just aren't enough guards to deal with them here. Dhampyrs are unpredictable. When the door opens, you don't know what's going to happen. I wish Dr. Gray would stop these fucking experiments once and for all. How many people have to die for her to see it's not worth it?"

The screeching sounded out again.

"It's close," I managed.

He let go of my hand and reached for the knife at his belt. "Just stay behind me."

"But what if we—"

"There's no time."

He was right. We had no time to get next door because suddenly there it was. The dhampyr.

It slowly moved out from behind the edge of the house.

Noah had told me it was only a baby, but it had grown rapidly. I hadn't known what to expect. Maybe a small child with sharp teeth and red eyes.

I'd been wrong. It didn't look like a child. It didn't look human. Large black eyes stared at us. Its completely hairless skin was so white, it seemed to glow in the darkness. At most, it was five feet tall with a hump on its back. It wasn't wearing any clothes, but I couldn't tell if it was male or female, as pockets of loose skin hung down over its genitals—if it even had any. Its stomach was concave, its ribs easily seen through the pale skin. Dark blue veins just under the skin appeared as if they were a spiderweb over its entire body. Its thin top lip curled back from sharp teeth. The dhampyr didn't have fangs per se, but every one of its teeth was razor sharp. Its arms and fingers were thin and long, its legs short.

It looked like something from a horror movie. Inhuman and hideous.

It was a monster. A dhampyr.

Like Declan.

No, it wasn't like Declan. This thing was nothing like him.

The dhampyr hissed and stepped closer, appearing to smell the air. It could smell me. Carson was right. It was drawn to the scent of my Nightshade-infused blood—like a moth to a flame. I dug my fingernails into Declan's arm.

"Stay back," Declan hissed. He was talking to me.

I eyed his knife. "No gun?"

"Didn't think I'd need to carry one tonight. An oversight that won't happen again."

Translucent white eyelids slid over those big black eyes and the creature cocked its head as if listening to our voices.

"Deccclannn," it said, its voice sharp-edged and nearly incoherent. It raised a bony arm in our direction.

"It knows your name," I said shakily.

"Looks like."

"It spoke. It said something. Maybe . . . maybe Carson's wrong. Maybe it *can* be reasoned with."

"It can't. You think this is the first dhampyr like this we've studied?"

"What happened to the others?"

"What do you think?" He pushed me back and switched the knife to his right hand.

"Noah said there's another one downstairs."

"And a pregnant victim in observation right now about ready to give birth to another one of these monstrosities. It's like a nursery from hell down there. Dr. Gray's positive her research on vamp/human hybrids will help kill vampires. I'm not as convinced."

The dhampyr kept its gaze fixed on me, raising both its arms now as if it was reaching out to me.

"It's just a baby," I said, pity for this strange, ugly thing incomprehensibly welling up inside of me.

"A baby that's killed two guards already and has the taste of human blood on its tongue. It's in feeding mode now. Go back inside the house and find Carson. I'll hold it off."

My empathy for the strange creature didn't last long. The next moment it launched itself through the air as if it could fly, knocking Declan aside. I screamed as it grabbed me by my shoulders, pushing me off my feet and I landed hard on my back with it on top of me. I felt a couple of its talons press painfully against the skin on my arms.

White lips peeled back from those horrific teeth, saliva dripping from its black tongue as it dove toward my throat.

— 15

DECLAN GRABBED THE MONSTER BEFORE IT HAD A chance to sink its teeth or talons into me and pulled it backward. It seemed frail, but in reality it was fast and strong. It screeched, an earsplitting sound, as I scrambled crablike back from them.

I was worried Declan might be hurt by it, that it might get the upper hand, but it only took a moment before I saw the arc of silver move through the air and Declan pierced the blade through the dhampyr's chest. The creature screamed, a sharp, horrific sound like nails on a chalkboard, and then it was silent. It didn't burst into fiery ash as a vampire did, but there was no doubt in my mind that it was dead.

Other people suddenly approached us, accompanied by Carson.

"Well done," he told Declan in a frustratingly calm

voice. His gaze flicked to me for a moment. "Take her back inside. We'll clean this up."

Declan nodded and stood up from where he was crouched over the dhampyr. He left his knife where it was in the creature's chest. Then, taking me by my arm, he directed me back into the house, along the hallway, and up the stairs toward my room.

"Are you okay?" I asked him shakily.

He didn't answer me, but his breathing was labored as if he'd run a marathon. Considering how in shape he was, I found it difficult to believe he'd been winded by killing the dhampyr. I pulled him around so I could see his face. His eye was focused on the ground.

"I need to go," he said. There was pain in his voice.

"Declan, what is it?"

His brow wrinkled and he raised his gaze to mine. "I don't like feeling like this."

"Like what?"

"That thing. I killed it. I killed it without a second thought, even though it was a dhampyr like me."

"You said yourself it was nothing like you."

"A few degrees of difference. Human mother, vampire father. Same as me. Only that creature ended up on the end of my blade, and it wasn't the first time I had to do something like that. And I hate that I'm doubting myself now."

"It had to be done."

"A mindless creature that only wanted to feed, driven by its dangerous hungers. Sounds exactly like what I'm turning into." He shook his head. "Carson warned me. I never should have stopped taking my serum. If it makes me feel like *this,* I have to agree with him."

"You mean, makes you feel guilty for killing something like that dhampyr?"

"That's only part of it."

"You prefer to feel like a robot programmed to kill and not feel any remorse?"

"Yeah, I think I do."

"Only because you're used to it. But that doesn't make it right."

"Carson wouldn't have given me a drug that wasn't necessary."

"Carson reacted to what you are by medication overkill. It's good that you're off the serum. It gives you a chance to actually live instead of only existing."

He shook his head. "You're wrong. I have to fix this while I still have the chance."

He dug into his pocket and pulled out a case identical to the one the blood servants took the other day. I snatched it away from him and he looked at me with surprise.

"Give that back to me."

"No."

"Jill—"

"Do you know you were calling me Jillian before?"

He glared at me. "What does that have to do with anything?"

"I told you shortly after our unusual meeting that my friends called me Jill. You called me Jill until you went back on your serum."

"What's your point?"

"My point is . . ." I clenched my jaw. Was I trying to tell him I wanted him to think of me as a friend? Despite everything that had happened? "Damn it. I don't know what my point is. But I don't think you should start up with this serum again. I think you should give yourself a chance."

"A chance to turn into a monster like the one that nearly just killed you?"

"You're nothing like that thing," I said firmly.

"An ugly, bloodthirsty dhampyr that wants to devour you. Actually, I think that thing and me are a lot alike."

"You're not ugly. And we can deal with the devouring issue."

His eye narrowed and he held out his hand. "Give me back the case. Now."

"No."

"I can take it from you easily."

"I'm sure you can. That's why you have to agree not to take this medication all by yourself."

"Stop it, Jill. I have no patience for these games."

"This isn't a game to me."

But he wasn't listening to anything I had to say. He grabbed hold of me and took the case away like taking candy from a baby. He had all the upper body strength, after all.

"If I take this I won't try to hurt you again," he said.

"Hurt me?" I frowned. "Are you talking about what happened before the siren went off?"

His expression shadowed. "It's only more proof that what I'm saying is true."

I shook my head. "Honestly. You don't give yourself any credit at all, do you?"

"What the hell are you talking about?"

I stepped closer to him and placed my hands flat against his chest. It made him tense up and take a step back until the closed door pressed against his back.

"You are a very frustrating man, Declan Reyes," I said. "Do you know that?"

"Jillian . . ."

"It's Jill. Okay?"

"Touching me is dangerous."

"For you or for me?"

"For you."

"Then why are you the one who looks scared right now?"

"You know what I tried to do to you earlier. If I hadn't been interrupted by the siren . . ."

"Right. That." I could feel his heartbeat speed up through the thin material of his T-shirt. It was going almost as fast as my own. I put the image of the dhampyr from outside out of my mind and focused on the frustrating but much more appealing one right in front of me. "Is it true you've never been with a woman before?"

His Adam's apple shifted as he swallowed. "It's too dangerous. My serum—"

"Your serum is a great excuse for keeping your distance from other people. So I'm taking that as a confirmation?"

He looked pained. "Noah has a big fucking mouth."

"Already established."

For a split second, I thought I saw a blush come to his cheeks. "There are more important things to deal with at the moment, Jill. I need to take my serum now."

"Fuck your serum." I took the case out of his hand again and tossed it to the side. "And I agree, there are more important things to deal with, like what you mentioned the other night in the car." I cast any doubts I had aside, and slid my hand down the muscled planes of his chest and abdomen and over the substantial bulge at the front of his jeans. "I think you mentioned something about burying your cock inside of me?"

He hissed out a breath. "Jill, please . . ."

"You really shouldn't say something like that to a lady when she's feeling vulnerable, you know. We tend to obsess about things like that, especially when we're locked in a room for a couple of days all alone."

"You don't have to feel sorry for me, if that's what this

is. You don't have to do charity work and let the ugly bastard touch you."

"*Ugly bastard*," I repeated. "I said that, didn't I? When I first saw you, yeah, you scared the shit out of me. You don't exactly look like the boy next door, do you? But let's just say, your looks have definitely grown on me. Your scars are marks of bravery and courage. They're heroic. And that makes them very beautiful. It makes you beautiful."

I pulled the edge of his T-shirt up to bare his flat stomach, which bore the thick scar from a vampire that had tried to gut him. I trailed my fingertips over it before leaning over and running my lips lightly along the length of it.

He exhaled shakily. "Jill . . . we can't do this."

"I disagree. Rather strongly, in fact."

"You don't know me. You only met me a few days ago."

"You're right. But I know you better than you think I do. You went off the serum so you could feel something, even though the thought of it scares you. Am I right?"

He frowned as if he were in pain, then nodded once without speaking.

"Then feel something." I pressed my lips against his, my hands on either side of his face.

He raised his arms so I could take off his T-shirt, baring his scarred but lean and muscled torso, and looked down at me cautiously as I began kissing everywhere he'd been hurt in the past—as if I could take away his pain with the power of my lips.

His hand tangled into my hair as I explored his chest, sliding my tongue over his nipples and down to his stomach.

Declan thought I didn't know him, but I did. He was a good man who'd been through a great deal of pain in his life—both physical and mental—without being given any choice in the matter. Pain he'd have to relive every time he looked in a mirror. I wanted to take that pain away, if only for a few minutes.

This wasn't a completely selfless act, though. I wanted him badly. I'd wanted him since shortly after leaving the diner, the desire eating away at me until I couldn't deny what I felt for him any longer.

In a sea of uncertainty that had become my life, it was really nice to have a goal.

I traced my lips lightly over his mouth before tasting him deeper. He hesitated for another moment before kissing me back; a moan escaped from the back of his throat. His hands were on my waist now, digging his fingers into my flesh as our tongues slid slowly against each other and an aching need built deep in my belly.

I worked to unbutton and unzip his jeans so by the time I moved down his body again I was able to take him into my mouth. It was definitely enough to coax a dark groan from him, and, granted, it did not sound entirely human, but I'd cut him some slack just this once.

"Jill," he managed. "Please . . . you're . . . you're making me lose my mind."

Along with the lust in his voice I could hear concern. He was afraid of losing control and hurting me.

"Trust yourself," I murmured to him as I slowly got back to my feet. "I'm not afraid of you. And I want you so badly right now that I think I'm going to lose *my* mind."

I directed him over to my bed and pushed him back on top of it. I pulled his jeans off the rest of the way, taking off his boots as well until he was hard and naked and beautiful lying there before me.

"Do you want me?" I asked. "Or do you want a shot of your serum?"

He looked up at me with deep need. "I want you."

I pulled my loose tank top off over my head and stepped out of my jogging pants and cotton panties. Then I crawled up on the bed to straddle his body, rubbing myself over the head of his erection.

"I want you, too," I whispered. "So much . . . you have no idea . . ."

I began to ease myself down on him an inch at a time until he was fully sheathed inside me. He was big, so there was a moment of discomfort as my body adjusted and stretched to accommodate his size. Then I brought his hands up so he could cup my breasts.

"See?" I breathed. "Not so bad after all, is it?"

He groaned as I began to move on top of him. "Oh my God . . . Jill . . . you feel . . . so good . . ."

I smiled, but it was shaky now. I could barely concentrate with the intense feel of him inside of me—this dhampyr.

My kidnapper. My protector. My enemy. My friend. He wasn't a monster like he thought he was. A monster could never make me feel this way. In fact, no man before Declan had ever made me feel this way.

"You weren't out of control before, you see that?" I dipped my head so I could whisper in his ear. My hard nipples brushed against his chest. "You just wanted this."

"You," he corrected. "I wanted you."

My lips found his and I kissed him, losing myself to the incredible sensation of his body against mine, his body inside of mine.

Then his hands were on my back and he rolled us over so he was now on top. In this position he was able to thrust deeper inside of me.

Damn, he was a very fast learner.

I gripped his shoulders as a wave of pleasure crashed

through me and I cried out. I scored him with my fingernails, desperately hoping I wasn't causing any more scars.

"I never thought . . ." he began, but he didn't finish
whatever he was going to say. The next moment he swore,
then groaned my name as his thrusts became faster and
harder. I held on to him tightly until I felt him shudder his
climax inside of me.

He was so still for a few moments that I thought he
might have passed out, but then his mouth was on me
again in a deep kiss that left me breathless and panting
and wanting him again.

"What were you going to say?" I asked, stroking his
face, my fingers trailing over the edge of his black eye
patch.

"What?" he breathed against my lips.

"You said 'I never thought,' but then you didn't finish."

"I never thought it could be like this for me." Then he
frowned. "Did I hurt you?"

"No." I smiled up at him. "Did I hurt *you*?"

His lips twitched. "Not too bad."

There was the sound of his cell phone then and the
momentarily open expression he'd had shuttered. "That'll
be Carson wondering where the hell I am."

"And will you tell him you've been banging the very
cooperative prisoner?"

I got an amusingly stern look for that suggestion. He
leaned over the side of the bed and retrieved his phone
then pressed it to his ear. "Yes?"

I ran my hand over his back. How could I ever think he
was ugly? There was nothing about Declan Reyes that was
remotely unattractive to me anymore.

Wow. I'd just deflowered a twenty-eight-year-old dhampyr assassin. This was not a claim I could make every day.

His back tensed as he sat straight up. "Yes, sir. We'll be right there."

He hung up.

"What?" I asked.

He looked at me over his shoulder. "Carson wants to meet with us. Both of us. Now."

"What about?"

"He didn't say. Sounded important, though."

"Are you going to tell him you've stopped taking the serum?"

"I'm still not entirely certain I should have stopped."

"Declan . . ."

"I'm keeping it on me just in case." He leaned over the side of the bed and grabbed his jeans and started putting them back on.

"Fine." If he didn't inject, it didn't matter if he kept it on him like a security blanket or a teddy bear. I slid my hands over his broad shoulders and down his bare chest. "Are you sure we have to go right now? Can't it wait just a little bit?"

A smile tugged at the corner of his mouth. "Probably not a good idea to keep him waiting."

"Kiss me one more time and I'll come with you without any further argument."

He turned, his gaze searching mine as if he was waiting for the other shoe to drop, for me to pull away from him and call him a monster. What he would have seen was a very naked woman who wanted exactly what she asked for. He pulled me to him and brushed his lips against mine.

"Am I getting better at this?" he asked after a moment.

"Much," I agreed. "But there is still a great deal of work to be done."

"I am a hard worker."

"I'm counting on it."

After another heated kiss, he pulled away from me, then grabbed my clothes, such as they were, and brought them to me on the bed. His gaze turned concerned. "When was the last time you felt ill from the Nightshade formula?"

"This afternoon."

"And you've felt okay since then?"

"Relatively speaking, yes."

"I know you don't like Carson, but he's trying to find a solution to fix what's inside of you. And I believe he can do it. You don't have to try to escape again."

"I'll keep that in mind. But the jury's out until we find out what he wants right now." I pulled on the jogging pants and tank top as Declan retrieved his own shirt from near the door. Declan had such faith in Carson, it was amazing to me. I didn't like the man, didn't trust him, yet I was supposed to wait for him to make some proclamation about how to save my life.

I was tired of waiting.

"Jill, I don't think we should say anything to Carson about what just happened between us," he said.

I raised an eyebrow. "Are you embarrassed?"

"No, of course not. But he wouldn't understand. Any slipups to do with the serum will worry him. You're optimistic about the outcome of this experiment of mine, but he's more of a pessimist."

"And if he found out we'd been together . . ."

"That would tell him all he needs to know. Being on the serum full-time would prevent that."

"Fine. I won't say anything," I agreed. "It's your business what goes on between you and your adoptive father, not mine. My main concern is what he wants to do about me."

It was very simple. I'd get the answers I wanted or I'd

demand to be released, no questions asked. And I wanted that phone call I'd been promised when we got here two nights ago. I felt confident that the solution to my problem wasn't far off now. I needed this poison out of my veins.

I'd waited damn well long enough.

— 16

"PLEASE SIT," CARSON SAID AFTER DECLAN AND I took the stairs to the downstairs lab where I'd been examined two days ago. Several file folders sat on top of a long silver table there.

I didn't sit.

Dr. Gray was also there. "How are you feeling, Jillian?"

"Right now? I feel okay. Considering the fact that you threw me in with a hungry vampire yesterday and I just escaped having my throat torn out by one of your adorable little dhampyr babies, I'm still breathing."

Obviously I wasn't trying to win friends and influence people anymore.

She flinched and her smile vanished. "I'm very sorry for everything, Jillian. I mean that."

I wondered if they could see my afterglow or smell Declan on me. I almost wished they could. Carson had kept him on that serum for so long without even testing how he'd react if he was weaned off such a powerful, behavior-modifying drug. Did he really look at Declan as a son or just as a hard-edged tool that took orders without any argument?

Declan had claimed he was going to protect me, but now I felt protective toward him in return. However, I had to keep reminding myself that I was the newbie here. A civilian. I didn't know what kind of setup they had or just how valuable it was to the future of mankind. My personal grudges were meaningless in the shadow of, as Noah had put it yesterday, *a vampire apocalypse.*

I stood close to Declan, almost close enough to touch. I respected his wish to not let on that anything had happened between us even though I could still feel the imprint of his hands on my body like a brand.

I still couldn't believe how quickly I'd gone from hating him to wanting him in my bed. It was not usual for me to be that forward, but he'd seriously given me no choice. And when you wanted something you should take it, especially if the object of your desire was ready, willing, and able to be taken.

What I didn't know was how Declan would fit into my life when I was cured and went back to my normal life. I didn't want to think about it at the moment, mostly because I knew he didn't fit at all. And he never would.

The thought made a hard, painful lump form in my throat.

"Have you had any more side effects from the Nightshade?" Carson asked.

"Not in the last few hours."

"But you've experienced signs of your body trying to reject the formula today?"

"Yeah. Twice. Each time I felt like I was going to die."

I narrowed my eyes. "And I don't appreciate being locked in a room like a criminal or being thrown in front of a vampire as bait to prove a theory."

"Do you want an apology from me?" he asked evenly.

I really didn't like this guy. "For starters. And then I want some real fucking answers. That would be a nice change."

I nearly jumped when I felt Dr. Gray's hand come over mine and squeeze it.

"Carson's manners toward you have been less than exemplary." She glanced at him. "I won't let anything like that happen again without Jillian's express permission. Do you understand?"

He leveled his gaze with hers for a moment before he nodded. "Fine."

The boss lady laid down the law and the men obeyed. I kind of liked that.

"Please, Jillian, have a seat," Dr. Gray said.

I looked at Declan, who nodded to me almost imperceptibly. I sat down in a chair at the table next to the one Dr. Gray chose.

"How did your little dhampyr experiment get loose?" I asked unpleasantly.

Dr. Gray and Carson exchanged a glance.

"I have the right to know." I felt deeply shaken by the entire experience. "It almost killed me."

Dr. Gray folded her hands in front of her. "I'm afraid there's no reason behind it except incompetence. The guard positioned in the holding area this evening took food to it. It attacked the guard, and once it tasted blood it became uncontrollable. Another guard got in its way and also was killed. It was a very strong reminder of how we can't underestimate a dhampyr."

I shuddered at the knowledge that two men had been killed tonight. "Declan's a dhampyr. Do you underestimate him?"

"Declan is different." She glanced coolly at him. "A very rare and very important example of what can be created between a vampire and human if all elements fall perfectly into place. All the strength and power of a vampire, but with humanity and reasoning. We value him deeply."

"If you say so."

"Don't you believe me?" she asked.

"What I believe doesn't matter."

"You're wrong. Your opinion is important to us, Jillian."

"Why? You don't even know me."

"I know you're a very brave woman. You have an inner strength that has helped you get through this unfortunate situation."

"I'm not brave or strong."

"You are. More than you know. Which is why we need to speak with you now." She glanced again at Carson, who had his hands clasped in front of him, his mouth set in a thin line. He looked tense.

Declan was watching our conversation intently, his brow slightly furrowed.

"You need to speak with me about what?" I asked. "I'm really hoping you're going to tell me that you have that antidote to the Nightshade formula you promised me."

"We do."

I let out a gasp of surprise at her quick answer. "You do?"

She nodded. "Yes. We had it couriered directly from a lab in New York. It arrived only an hour ago. It's a specially developed serum used to cleanse and purify blood after it's come in contact with a parachemistry-created toxin. It's been used successfully in the past and I'm confident that it will work in your case as well."

Relief washed over me with every word she spoke. This was my answer, finally. I couldn't believe she was actually confirming what I'd been hoping for. "Thank you. You don't know what this means to me."

Her warm hand closed over mine again. "Before I give it to you, there are things you must know. Decisions you must make."

Declan looked confused. "What kind of decisions?" he asked.

Dr. Gray pulled one of the file folders closer to her. "Jillian, what do you know about the situation with the vampires right now?"

"I know that they look human until they get hungry. They're drawn to me because of my blood. Then they change and look more like monsters." I shivered at the memory of the woman in the diner and Tobias in the locked room. "I also know that the research program is stationed here in Silver Ridge because it's close to the heart of Matthias's vampire clan."

"Where did you get this information from?" Carson asked sharply. "Did Declan tell you this?"

"No, it wasn't him." I bit my bottom lip. I didn't want to reveal my source of info since I wasn't sure if he'd get in trouble.

"I told her," Noah said, entering the room carrying a clipboard. "Sorry. I was shamelessly eavesdropping. Figured now was a good time to make my presence known before my ears started to burn."

There was a red mark on the side of his forehead from where I'd hit him with the chair earlier. I felt a sharp jab of remorse about that.

"You weren't authorized to tell her anything, Noah," Carson said sternly.

"She had a right to know."

"It doesn't matter," Dr. Gray said. "If you hadn't given Jillian the basics, I'd be giving them to her right now."

Noah immediately looked relieved that his penchant for curiosity hadn't killed the cat this time. He glanced at me and smiled as he rubbed his head. "You know, you'd be a great baseball player. You nearly knocked me right out of the park earlier."

I bit my bottom lip. "I'm really sorry about that, Noah."

He shook his head. "I probably would have done the exact same thing in your position, so forget it. I already have. Then again, I may have a slight touch of amnesia."

I smiled back at him, but my lips trembled. I felt nervous sitting here. Why didn't Dr. Gray just give me a shot of whatever this blood cleanser was and we could be done with this once and for all?

"The horror stories about vampires can wait until later," I said. "After my blood's normal again I'd be more than happy to hear anything you want to tell me."

"Not just yet," Dr. Gray smoothed her hand over the top of the file folder. "First, you need to know about Kristoff. The previous king."

I looked at her skeptically. "Why do I need to know about him?"

"When he ruled, vampires were a well-behaved and controlled species. Because of their aversion to sunlight and need for human blood, they can't blend well with human society. But they were able to survive in small numbers for many years."

I tried to be patient. "How long?"

"Centuries, at the very least. No one knows exactly how the first vampire was created or when. What we do know is that they can deliberately and selectively spread a virus to a human with their venom in order to create a new vampire. This is how they multiply, since vampire females are barren. Male vampires can only mate with a human female."

"And that's why you have your . . . *research* . . . here?" I couldn't think of a better word other than *freak show* to describe her experiments with dhampyr babies.

She nodded. "A female vampire's body can't sustain a growing fetus for enough time to allow it to be born. Vampire males, on the other hand, don't need to sustain life for nine months. However, the percentage of recorded dhampyr births is so low it doesn't even register. A vampire's main choice for reproduction is to use its venom to turn a human victim into a vampire."

I tried to ignore the goose bumps that had formed on my arms from this little monstrous lecture. Carson was staying quiet now, letting the boss do the talking. "I still don't understand why you're telling me any of this."

I kept Declan in my peripheral vision. It made me feel a little bit better.

Dr. Gray stood up and wrung her hands, beginning to pace in front of the table. Noah had to step back to accommodate her. "For a very long time, vampires existed in small, controllable numbers and stayed away from humans because they were led by Kristoff. He valued human life."

"This is why the true existence of vampires hasn't widely been known by humans," Carson explained. "We're very lucky to have Dr. Gray heading the Nightshade project. She knows more about this subject than anyone else."

I frowned. "So, if the Nightshade project exists, that means something changed. Matthias is the king now, right?"

"Yes," Dr. Gray said. "Around thirty years ago, Matthias

grew tired of Kristoff's strict rules that governed his life and behavior, and was successfully able to overthrow Kristoff's reign. It's rumored that he imprisoned Kristoff in a sealed vault."

"Wouldn't that kill him?"

"Vampires are immortal. They don't require food or water to survive. Without drinking blood for so long, it's possible he's now been reduced to a catatonic state as his body attempts to sustain his life force. The rumor is that Matthias soon plans to leave his underground kingdom and enter the human world. And that's only the beginning. Matthias wants to change as many humans as he can to become vampires. When the balance in numbers shifts enough . . . I fear that human life as we know it will end forever. Humans would be kept around as a food source only. No freedom, only slavery."

"Holy shit," I murmured.

Noah met my gaze with an expression that clearly said "See? I told you so."

Vampire apocalypse. I now understood what he'd meant. The thought made my blood run cold.

"So you've been developing the Nightshade formula to stop him," I said.

"That's right. As king, he's wary of any potential assassination attempts and only keeps a few trusted servants— both human and vampire—by his side. He hasn't come aboveground in years. He's very dangerous, very strong, and has the ability to manipulate human thought and behavior through mind control. It makes it nearly impossible to get to him."

"*Nearly* impossible."

"We have someone working for us that has successfully infiltrated Matthias's clan. This is whom we'd chosen to help destroy him using the Nightshade. Unfortunately, the formula was compromised when Anderson injected it into you." Dr. Gray's brows drew together. "I'd hoped to defeat him before he sets his plans into action."

"But . . . why can't you take some of my blood and use it anyway?"

"I'm afraid that's not an option. The formula ceases to work as well after exposure to oxygen. We used your blood samples to test this theory."

After witnessing one of their experiments firsthand yesterday, I didn't want to know how they'd chosen to test it. "Then how was your agent supposed to use the Nightshade?"

"Through Matthias's Achilles' heel, if you will," Carson cut in. "He's strong and powerful and ruthless. He'll kill without a second thought. However, he does have one known weakness."

"What?" Noah asked. Then he cleared his throat. "Sorry, I'm curious."

"We know," Carson said wearily. "Your enthusiasm is both your strongest and weakest point."

"What's Matthias's weakness?" I asked.

Dr. Gray came back to sit next to me. "The same weakness as many men: women. Specifically, human women. Since he chooses to remain underground, his exposure is limited to the women brought directly to him. He's been known to take these humans as lovers and blood servants—either willingly or unwillingly."

I couldn't help but look at Declan only to see that his face had paled and his hands were now clenched into fists at his sides. I knew all too well what Matthias had done to his mother. It did seem like the king had a problem when it came to the fairer sex.

Cruella—or whatever her real name was—the servant from the other day had been just the opposite. Her eyes were filled with stars when she spoke of him. Looked to me like she'd chosen to sign up in the "willing" column.

Dr. Gray continued, "The Nightshade formula was supposed to be injected into our agent who's been living underground in Matthias's clan for nearly a year. When he would have drank from her, it would have ended him quickly and efficiently."

It took a couple of moments for me to realize what she was saying. "So the Nightshade was going to be injected into somebody all along?"

"Yes."

Anger lit up brightly inside me. "Why didn't anyone tell me that? All this time I'd thought I had the equivalent of rat poison in my veins, but it was always meant to be injected into somebody? I thought it would be sprayed on a weapon or . . . or its scent used to lure the vampire into some kind of a trap."

Dr. Gray's expression showed distress. "You should have been told all of this earlier. It was an oversight. I apologize for any extra worry this caused you."

I looked at Declan. "Did you know this?"

He shook his head. "I only knew it was a poisonous toxin to be used against vampires. I didn't know any more about it than that at the time."

I searched his face, trying to figure out if he was lying to me. After all, he was the one in the beginning who'd told me I was poisoned and that I'd die because of it. It was the main reason I'd been so terrified—terrified enough to come here looking for a solution.

"So it's not really a poison?" I asked.

"It is," Dr. Gray confirmed. "And it's a dangerous and unstable one. What happened to you was unexpected. The formula was supposed to be administered in a controlled environment where we could monitor any complications."

Someone else was going to be injected with this shit. If it wasn't me, someone else would be going through this torture right now.

It didn't make me feel any better. In fact, it made me feel worse.

It hadn't been tested. I was being used as a unwilling guinea pig.

I touched my neck. I'd removed the bandage earlier and the bruises were already fading. Also, the bite marks from Tobias's attack had begun healing rapidly.

Poison. They weren't denying that for a moment. I'd be more concerned if I didn't know they now had the blood cleanser on hand.

Carson stood up and his chair skidded backward. "Unfortunately, our original plans were destroyed when Anderson stupidly grabbed you and pulled you into this highly volatile situation. He single-handedly sabotaged years of work and our chance to destroy Matthias once and for all."

"His actions didn't *completely* sabotage things," Dr. Gray corrected. "It would have been a setback, yes, but the fact that he was murdered is the real problem. If he was still alive, he could have re-created the formula. But now that's not even an option, is it?"

It was silent for a moment and the tension level ratcheted up another notch.

"I did what I had to do," Declan said with an unpleasant edge to his voice. "Anderson pulled a gun—"

"And, yes, you should have shot him," Dr. Gray said sharply. "But not to kill. It was an ignorant and irresponsible action to take. However, I can't say I'm surprised, given your history of violence."

Where before, Declan might have taken this reprimand with a bland look and a neutral attitude, today he looked livid. His jaw was tense and his gaze flashed angrily at her, but he didn't say anything else.

"Declan has been trained to kill," Carson said. "His actions were not out of line."

"I disagree." She pursed her lips. "This failure, however, is not the issue on the table at the moment."

This argument and history lesson was all just delaying the inevitable, and my patience was growing seriously thin.

"Look," I said. "I'm really sorry your plans have all gone to hell, but I don't really understand what this all has to do with me. The Nightshade is killing me. That's what it feels like."

She was quiet for a moment. "We don't know how the formula will react when it's inside a human body for a prolonged amount of time. It wasn't ready to be put into use yet. There was no prior testing because Anderson worked in secrecy. His eccentricities were well known, but his betrayal . . ." She shook her head. "I still don't understand how this happened, but it doesn't change anything that must happen now."

I crossed my arms. "One of your agents volunteered to be injected with poison so Matthias would drink her blood and that would kill him, therefore stopping any threat to human life in its tracks."

"Yes, that's right."

Just the thought of it made me feel weak inside. "That sounds like a dangerous job."

"It would have worked." Dr. Gray stood up again. "It *still* could work."

"Oh my God," Noah exclaimed from my left. "You want to get Jill to do it, don't you?"

I looked over at him. "What the hell are you talking about?"

"I . . ." He closed his mouth. "It . . . it sounds like . . ."

His wide-eyed gaze flicked to Carson. "She's just a civilian, you know."

"Noah, please leave us now," Carson said harshly. "This has nothing to do with you."

With a worried look cast in my direction, Noah looked as if he was on the verge of saying something else, but instead he turned and walked out of the room.

"Is that really what you're thinking?" Declan asked quietly, his voice now as calm as it had been when he'd been on his serum full time. He seemed to have recovered from his moment of anger. "To ask Jill to volunteer for the job of being Matthias's assassin?"

I looked at Dr. Gray with shock.

Her hands were clasped in front of her, her expression pinched. "It is."

"You're insane," was the first thing out of my mouth.

She shook her head. "We've been working toward one goal here and that is to eliminate Matthias. When he's dead, other vampires will be easier to destroy. Humanity will never need to know how close we all are right now to total devastation."

My throat felt thick as I listened to her making it difficult to breathe. "I can't help you."

"You can," she said firmly. "Our agent can introduce you as a potential blood servant to Matthias. You'll be able to gain access to the king, who hasn't been seen aboveground in three decades. Doing this, Jillian, will help save countless lives."

I couldn't speak. This was the last thing I'd expected her to ask of me. I thought they'd brought me down here to give me an antidote, not to ask me to help assassinate a vampire king.

"I—I don't know," were the first words out of my mouth, cutting through the silence in the room.

"This assignment takes no training," Carson spoke up. "You're already the perfect weapon to tempt a monster like Matthias to his ultimate doom."

Dr. Gray smiled. "You'd be a hero, Jillian. And you'd be well rewarded for your efforts."

My eyes flicked to hers at that. "You're going to pay me to get Matthias to drink my blood?"

"It's only fair. Payment for the pain and stress you've gone through so far and payment for working for us now. You won't have to worry about money another day in your life."

"No," Declan said and Dr. Gray's attention moved to him.

"Excuse me?"

His arms were crossed over his chest and the glare he was giving her was sharp enough to cut glass. "You want her to be taken deep into Matthias's lair where there's no easy escape. She's to put her trust in a woman she doesn't know who's been living with and likely fucking Matthias for more than a year. And if Matthias does succumb to the lure of Jill's blood, she's expected to get out of there alive? No. It's too dangerous."

"You don't know what you're talking about, Declan," Dr. Gray said.

"I know enough."

"Declan," Carson said cautiously, sharing a glance with Dr. Gray. "Perhaps you should leave the room as well. The way you're speaking, it's very . . . unlike you."

Declan didn't leave. Instead, he drew closer to where I was seated. "I'm staying."

"I know very well what Matthias did to your mother," Dr. Gray said. "But that has nothing to do with this plan."

"I disagree. It shows who Matthias is and what he's

capable of." His cheeks twitched with barely restrained anger. "Jill's blood is difficult for even me to resist and I'm only half-vampire. But what else would he do before sinking his fangs into her? Also, we saw the other day that there's a small window of opportunity between the blood flowing and the vampire's death. That's more than enough time for Matthias to tear out her throat in vengeance for ending his life."

"It is dangerous," Carson said. "But the reward outweighs any potential risk there is. Dr. Gray would never suggest something like this if it wasn't absolutely necessary."

This felt so completely surreal. I half-expected them all to start laughing and tell me it was all a big practical joke before giving me the antidote and planning a celebration party.

But no one was laughing.

Dr. Gray leaned against the edge of the table. "Declan's not entirely wrong, Jillian. There is a possibility that you'd be giving your life to stop a true monster." Tears welled in her eyes and she quickly swept her fingers over her cheek when one escaped. "We know you didn't ask for any part of this, but here you are. You represent the hope that we can defeat Matthias once and for all. However, the choice is entirely in your hands."

"I have a choice?" I asked shakily.

"Of course. You can agree to be taken to Matthias by our agent—"

"When would this happen?"

"A few days from now. No more than a week. We'd need to be sure you could be taken in without raising anyone's suspicions."

A week to live. I swallowed down my fear as best as I could. "And my other choice?"

"We can give you the blood cleanser and you can go back to your home."

I was quiet for a long moment before I spoke. "And what happens to Matthias then?"

She shook her head. "We'll find a new parachemist to help us develop another formula, and I know, if given enough time, we'll find an answer. But we don't know if it will be too late."

The knowledge that I was basically their last hope fell on me like a lead curtain. Give my life to help kill Matthias or walk away from it all and risk being the reason humans lost the fight against the vampires.

"I . . . I need to think about this," I said shakily.

"Of course. We'll give you time to make your decision." Carson leaned over the table, his face lined with worry and stress. "However, if you had to give us an answer now, what would it be?"

It didn't take me long to think of a reply. "It would be no. I don't want to die. And I'm not hearing that it's an absolute definite that my death would mean Matthias's death. I'm not willing to give up my life for uncertainties. I'm not even sure I'm willing to die for something that *is* certain." Tears spilled onto my cheeks.

I expected them to be angry with that answer, but they weren't. Carson leaned back in his chair, nodding his head as if he'd expected me to say that. Dr. Gray simply looked pale and sad and defeated. They'd been at this for nearly thirty years, after all. To be so close to an answer, only to have to rely on somebody like me? I didn't envy them.

"I do understand." Dr. Gray walked across the room to a briefcase from which she pulled out a small black leather case like Declan had for his serum. She gave it to me and I unzipped it to see that it held one vial of dark amber liquid and a syringe. "This is the blood cleanser. Take this if you're certain your decision is no and do so with a clear conscience that none of this is your fault."

"Thank you." My words were choked and barely audible.

"Declan," Carson said. "Please take Jillian back to her room so she can have some time to think."

Declan nodded and I felt him brush against me, taking me gently by my arm and directing me out of the lab and back up the stairs. Back to my room where I could decide between living with the guilt of my selfishness on my conscience or dying in the clutches of a vampire king.

17

"WHAT DO YOU THINK I SHOULD DO?" I ASKED Declan once we'd returned to my room.

His expression was tight. "You have to take the blood cleanser."

I paced over to the unbreakable window I'd spent a half an hour throwing a chair against yesterday and looked outside into the darkness. "But what if I—"

"Jill, please. Don't even think about it." He came toward me and turned me around to face him. "This isn't your fight."

"Maybe it's fate I was injected with the Nightshade."

"Dr. Gray—she's single-minded when it comes to her goal of killing Matthias. But even she can see how wrong it is to ask something like this of you."

"And Carson?"

"He's also focused on the goal here. It's his primary reason for living." He shook his head. "The mission has taken over his life, if there was even any life to begin with."

"Not his biggest fan at the moment?"

"Carson means well. He does. But he sees the world in black-and-white terms only. Just like I did, until very recently."

I couldn't help but hear the twist of pain in his voice and wished I could take it away. But as much as I wanted to I couldn't exactly help with a lifetime of emotional neglect. Hell, I was surprised Declan had turned out as well as he had.

Then again, he did kill people for a living.

I put the antidote case down on the edge of the bed. The hopelessness I'd felt downstairs started to sink in further. "I honestly don't know what to do."

"Then let me make the decision for you," he said fiercely. "Let me inject you with the cleanser right now and you go back to the life I stole you away from. Forget about all of this."

"Forget about you?" I asked, my throat tight.

He nodded. "It's better this way. And it's what you want. For this all to go away. For you to wake up from this nightmare. And the solution is right here." He picked up the case and unzipped it.

"But Matthias—"

"Matthias will be dealt with. Don't believe for one moment that the Nightshade formula is the only solution to this problem. We'll figure out another way that doesn't result in you getting killed." His expression hardened. "I said I'd protect you, and that's exactly what I'm going to do, even if it means I'll never see you again."

I met his gaze and I saw pain there. It was probably the same pain reflected in my own eyes. "I don't know."

"Then know this: They're wrong about you. You're a

civilian. Completely untrained. I've seen courage in you and a hell of a lot of tenacity and stubbornness, but faced with a vampire king and a trip down to the bowels of his lair with no way out?" He shook his head. "You'd crumble under the pressure. He'd see you as a plant and order your death before he even came close to tasting your blood. Then this would all be for nothing. You see?"

I frowned at that. "You don't think I could do it?"

"No, I don't," he said firmly.

I didn't even take offense at his lack of confidence in my Mata Hari abilities since he was absolutely right. Whatever qualms I had about taking the antidote faded away.

I would fail. Matthias would still be alive and I'd be dead.

Declan must have seen the change in my eyes because his tense, worried expression relaxed a fraction. "Good. Then it's settled."

"So I'm just supposed to go back to my old life and pretend none of this ever happened to me? Knowing about the looming threat of Matthias?"

"You'll forget. It's only been three days, after all."

"I won't forget you."

He turned away so he wasn't looking at me directly. "So you agree with me. You'll take the cleanser now."

"Yes, I agree."

He didn't wait to see if I'd change my mind again. He immediately got the vial of amber liquid out of the case and filled the syringe with it.

"You look like you've done this before," I said.

"Only thousands of times."

I looked down at myself. "Where's the best place?"

"Stomach. It hurts less there." His lips twitched a little. "Or your ass. Lady's choice."

"Let's go with the stomach."

"Just relax."

"That's not exactly a word that's in my vocabulary this week."

"Pull up your shirt."

"Yes, sir." I rolled up the edge of my tank top to bare my abdomen. Declan stroked his fingers over the skin just beneath my belly button and, despite my anxiety, a ripple of heat moved through me at his touch. It was a reminder of what had happened between us only an hour ago.

"Here's good. I was told earlier it doesn't have to be directly into a vein. It'll find its way." He didn't hesitate, perhaps thinking I was going to have second thoughts and want to be sent to Matthias on the next shuttle to the underground. The needle pinched as it slid into my flesh and I held my breath as Declan released the blood cleanser into me.

The difference between life and death took no time at all.

"Thank you." I touched his face and then hugged him against me. His body was so hard, all angles. There was no fat, no softness to him. He stroked my hair and held me gently against him as if he was afraid of breaking me.

"When the drug's finished working and you've had some time to rest, I'll drive you back to San Diego," he whispered.

"What about the police? Won't they be looking for you?"

He shook his head. "We have people all over the place including with the police. Our work here is sanctioned by the government. They like to keep it quiet and cover up any incidents. This isn't the first time I've had to take somebody out in a public place. It's usually quickly swept under the carpet. Though, I do wish I blended in a bit better. Sometimes I get recognized by people with good memories, but it hasn't been a big problem in the past. People tend to forget the things they want to." He straightened up. "You should go to bed."

I grinned despite myself and slid my hands over his broad shoulders. "Is that a suggestion or a proposition?"

He smiled faintly back at me. "A suggestion. The cleanser will make you very tired for at least twenty-four hours. I spoke with Dr. Gray about the side effects when it was delivered earlier."

He was right. I already felt weary right down to my bones. "I need to have a shower first."

He nodded. "I'll stay close in case you need me."

I was about to say I did need him. That I wouldn't forget him. That maybe I didn't want to simply leave and go back to my old life when the poison was out of my system. But I didn't say it. Things were complicated enough without me adding to the mix.

After brushing his lips softly and chastely against my forehead again, Declan left me in the room alone.

My head felt cloudy and the deepening weariness quickly spread through me. I felt like sleeping for about three days straight. But first, I really did want that shower.

I stepped under the hot jet of water and washed my hair. Noah had bought me shampoo and conditioner from his Walmart trip, as well as shower gel. He even had good enough taste not to go generic. The warmth beat into me and I willed the anxiety to leave my body. However, it seemed to be in no hurry to depart.

I tried to let the memories of everything that had happened to me over the last few days wash away. From being grabbed by Anderson and injected, to Declan kidnapping me, to the blood servants at the gas station and abandoned house, the vampire at the diner, the arrival here, Tobias's death when he bit me, my escape attempt, the monster dhampyr lunging at me, and finally how good it had felt to be with Declan in my temporary bed only a short time ago.

There were definitely some low points and some high points in the mix.

I turned off the taps and wrung the water out of my hair. Then I grabbed a bath towel and wrapped it around myself. The mirror was fogged up so I used my forearm to clear it. I looked tired and gaunt. I ran my fingertips along my cheekbone, then down my neck—which still bore the bruises from Anderson's brutal attack with the syringe—and the fading bite marks.

"Back to normal soon," I told my reflection. "Promise."

Then I cocked my head to the side and drew a little closer to the mirror. Strange, my eyes looked darker than normal. They were normally blue like my mother's had been—cornflower blue, she'd always called them. But at the moment, they looked almost . . . black.

A wave of pain suddenly crashed into me with absolutely no warning. It felt as if I'd been slit right through my center. I braced myself against the counter.

"What the hell . . . ?" I began, before I was hit again, even harder than before and I cried out.

Agony. My chest felt as if it was going to explode, my heart rate tripled in seconds, every beat helping to radiate the searing pain through my core. A primal scream tore from my throat.

Only a few seconds later, I felt hands on me just as my legs gave out. Declan was there and he turned me around, holding me up on my feet or else I'd collapse to the ground.

"What's wrong?" he demanded.

"I . . . I don't know."

His once emotionless face was now etched in concern. "Another spell? Maybe this is what happens as the poison is getting out of your body. Maybe this is how the blood cleanser works."

I gasped for breath. "No . . . this is different. It feels different. Worse."

I cried out again and clung to him as the pain made it impossible for me to speak.

It wasn't a blood cleanser. The thought came to me in the middle of the white-hot agony. Dr. Gray said it had been used before successfully. She'd told Declan about the side effects. She would have warned me it would make me feel as if my body was literally turning inside out.

"Look at me," Declan said harshly. "Look at me, Jill."

I tried. I wasn't entirely sure I was successful since the world blurred in front of my eyes.

Declan held my face between his hands. "Fuck. Your eyes are . . . I . . . I need to get help."

"Don't . . . please, Declan. Don't leave me."

He didn't leave. Instead, he yelled for help. Yelled for Carson or Noah or somebody to come here and help us. I didn't know how they'd help, though. I was going to die from this. No one could possibly live through this much pain.

Declan's blurred expression changed. His eye widened and he swore again, softly as if he was seeing something that scared even him—scared someone who killed vampires on a regular basis.

That wasn't a very good sign.

I turned as much as I could toward the mirror. My eyes were black now, not even an illusion of them being blue anymore. Tears, black like tar, slipped down my cheeks from the corners of my eyes. And my hair . . .

My hair.

There was a darkness oozing from my scalp. I reached up but Declan caught my wrist.

"Don't touch it," he said.

Don't touch it? But it was already on me. Already *in* me. This darkness slid through my blond hair as if it was inside the shaft itself. My hair slowly turned black from root to tip. Black like my eyes. Black like the substance I'd been vomiting for three days that I didn't know what it was. Black like the tears I was shedding right now.

Nightshade.

The next thing I knew, I was in the shower and the water running hot enough for me to notice through my pain. Declan was trying to wash the Nightshade off me. I saw the facecloth he held, previously white, and now streaked with black. The bath towel I'd wrapped around me fell to the base of the shower stall.

"What the hell?" Noah had run into the bathroom, alerted by Declan's call. "What the fuck are you doing to her?"

He sounded furious, as if he'd walked in on something horrible. Well, he had. I could only imagine what it looked like from Noah's perspective. Declan, fully dressed, holding my limp naked body in the shower as he attempted to wash the blackness out of my hair and off my face.

Unfortunately I couldn't speak or move at the moment. The pain continued to tear at me with its sharp teeth and claws. It felt as if I was being devoured from the inside by something invisible. Something that hated me.

"The cleanser," Declan snapped. "This is what it did to her."

Noah held his hand to his mouth, his eyes wide with shock. "The cleanser wouldn't have done that. What did she take? What did it look like?"

"It was yellow. A dark yellow color. One vial in a case. Dr. Gray gave it to her and told her it was the cleanser."

"No," Noah said, panicky. "The cleanser serum was clear—I saw it. The yellow serum . . . that was the fusing potion."

"What the fuck are you talking about?"

"Fusing potion . . . it was being developed for the original agent who was supposed to be injected with the Nightshade. I went through the files tonight—although, as usual, I wasn't exactly supposed to. But top-secret files really should be locked away somewhere as far as I'm concerned. I'm very nosy!"

The pain finally began to ease off just a little. I was trembling despite the hot water. Declan pulled his fingers through my drenched hair. He had me against him tightly, my front against his chest. My head rested limply against his shoulder and I forced myself to listen to Noah to help figure out what was going on.

"What did the file say?" Declan demanded.

"The side effects associated with the Nightshade—they're caused because it doesn't bond properly with the blood. So the body . . . it attempts to reject it, sort of like if she got a new organ. The fusing potion was created to help fast-forward the body's acceptance of the formula."

"I don't understand what you're talking about."

"Okay, okay." Noah wrung his hands. "The fuser bonds her blood to the Nightshade so that her blood cells are literally infused with the poison instead of existing side by side. And holy hell, I bet that hurt like a bastard. Parachemistry is not the gentlest science in the universe."

My blood. Changed. Bonded with poison.

"What are the complications?"

"Is she unconscious?" Noah asked.

"What the fuck are the complications?" Declan repeated, louder. "What did you read?"

"Well," Noah swallowed nervously. "The big one is death, of course. Nightshade is a new formula, but fusing potions have been used before to help merge foreign compounds to human blood."

A short pause before Declan barked, "And what else?"

"It's always been tested on nonhuman subjects—and . . . and never successfully. So . . . shit. I don't know what to tell you, Dec. It doesn't look good."

Never been used successfully before. And never on a human subject. I was a walking, talking lab rat. Currently without the walking and talking.

"Dr. Gray did this to her." Declan pushed the wet hair back from my face. My eyes were open but rolled back into my head. "She lied to us, made us believe this was the cleanser."

I think I was in shock. But the pain was finally subsiding like a malevolent tide.

"Maybe she had the formulas mixed up," Noah reasoned.

"You really think so?"

"No. But I don't want to believe she'd be this heartless."

"She wants Jill to go to Matthias's lair to kill him. And when Jill said no, Dr. Gray took it into her own hands to make sure she didn't have a choice in the matter. Fucking bitch." Declan reached past me to the faucet. The hot water quickly turned cold. I gasped out loud. "Good. You have to snap out of it, Jill. Now. There's no time."

"B-bully." My teeth were chattering.

He looked relieved I was vaguely coherent. His gaze flicked to Noah. "I'm taking her out of here."

"You think that's a good idea?"

"A real hospital might be able to help her. I never gave the thought a chance before, but now . . ."

"There's no reversal. They can't treat her with dialysis. It's too late for that. The fuser worked. I mean, fuck me. Look at her hair. And her eyes. But if she made it this far without croaking . . . that's a good sign, right?"

Declan lifted me in his arms. "Go get her clothes."

Noah didn't argue. He disappeared into the bedroom.

Declan set me on my feet. My legs felt like Jell-O. He ran a fresh towel over me to dry me. "Jill, can you hear me?"

I nodded shakily. "Y-yes."

"Did you hear what Noah said?"

I nodded again.

"And you're okay with that? With my taking you out of here?"

"B-better . . . late than n-never." My teeth chattered. Now that the pain had faded, it felt as if ice water slid through my veins, numbing me.

Noah returned with some clothes, black yoga pants and a light blue tank, and Declan hurriedly dressed me. I caught a glimpse of myself in the mirror. My skin was pale white. And my long hair, previously blond with a bit of help from the salon every other month, was now jet black. Ditto the irises of my eyes.

"Oh my God," was all I was able to say about that disturbing sight.

"Where are Carson and Dr. Gray?" Declan asked.

"Downstairs still. Waiting a bit before they check on Jill. I don't think they expected her to take the so-called cleanser quite this quickly."

"When they come looking for her, you can tell them I overpowered you."

"Not hard to believe. Uh, will you be back?"

"Yes," Declan hissed. "And then me and my father are going to have a talk about Dr. Gray."

He didn't make it sound like a friendly father/son discussion over a couple of beers.

"Good luck," Noah said, casting a worried glance at me.

Declan carried me in his arms out of the bedroom and down the stairs without another word to Noah. Before I knew it, I felt the hot night air on my face. Even though it was dark out it had to be close to ninety degrees outside. I heard a car door open and then he gently placed me inside on the passenger seat.

"Whose car is this?" I asked, my voice barely audible.

"Carson's. Lending me his car is the least he can do tonight."

"Where are we going?"

"There's a town twenty miles from here. They have a hospital. We'll figure this out, Jill. Just hold on."

Was Noah right? Was I going to die? It had been my biggest fear since the moment I'd been grabbed in my office building's lobby. *Death.* I still hadn't had enough time to adjust to that possibility. There had been a time in my life when I'd wanted to die. Life seemed too difficult to handle—I had the scar on my wrist to prove it. But I'd battled through that depression. I'd just really started getting better when this happened.

And at the moment, I felt weak and exhausted from whatever that fusing potion had done to my body. As far as I knew, I'd be having another wave of pain any minute, and I honestly didn't think I'd live through it. I wasn't even sure I *wanted* to live through it. Compared to what I'd just experienced in the bathroom, a quick death was my preference by far.

No one stopped us as Declan drove out of the tiny town.

"I'm not in pain anymore." I was too weak to move. My body felt as if it had just participated in a triathlon from hell.

"Good." Declan glanced at me and there was determination in his gaze. "I'm sorry, Jill. I'm sorry for all of this. What Dr. Gray did to you is wrong." His jaw clenched. "And I'm the one who injected that shit into you."

"You thought it was the cleanser."

"I was too trusting. I should have made sure."

"My blood. It's different now. I can feel it." I licked my dry lips. "There's no going back now. I'm either going to die or—"

"You're not going to die. I won't let that happen." He reached over and squeezed my cold hand in his. "Do you hear me?"

"I hear you." Silence filled the car for a few moments as I tried to focus on the feel of his warm hand on mine.

"And I know your blood is different now," he said, accelerating the car through an intersection. "I can smell it. It's even more potent than it was before. Dr. Gray knew that. She knew exactly what she was—"

"Declan!" I screamed as terror tore through me.

Another car was barreling toward us at the crossroads. It slammed into Declan's side, spinning us around and flipping our car over and over. I heard the screech of twisting metal as my head smashed against the passenger-side window.

Just before everything went black, I saw fire ignite all around us.

18

DEATH WAS QUIET AND DARK AND COOL. THERE WAS no pain here, only relief and peace.

I should have known it was only a dream.

"Wake up," a voice said harshly. "You've slept long enough."

When I didn't open my eyes, I felt the sharp sting of a slap.

That did it.

I'd already half-recognized the voice, but as my eyes flew open I fully recognized the face. It was the blood servant I'd dubbed Cruella de Vil. The one with the dangerous silver stiletto heels who'd given me the knife I'd left back in my room at Carson's house. The one she'd wanted me to use on Declan.

"Finally," she said. "Here. I was about to throw it in your face, but you may as well drink it."

She handed me a glass of water. I took it from her and looked at it suspiciously.

"It's not poisoned," she said. "If that's what you're thinking."

That was exactly what I was thinking.

"How long was I unconscious?" My voice sounded scratchy and broken.

"You were out for almost twenty-four hours."

The last terrifying moments of consciousness came back to me. "There was an accident."

"Yeah. Caused by a couple of fuck-ups who like the sound cars make when they grind into each other. Damn fools should have broken their necks, as far as I'm concerned."

"They planned to crash into us?"

"They were sent to bring you here. They accomplished their objective." She cocked her head. "Not sure I like the dye job. Blond suited you better."

My arm ached as I reached up to touch my previous light locks, now the cheery color of death incarnate.

She wore black leather pants that fit her slim legs like they were painted on. Her shiny, low-cut silver lamé spaghetti-strap top looked as if it would be better suited for a nightclub. Her long wavy blond hair was loose and draped over her right shoulder, and her blue eyes were thickly outlined in smoky black liner.

I sat up in the bed I'd been laying in. It was a canopied bed draped in dark blue silk linens. "Where am I?" A memory of the hot fire beginning to lick at me came back to me and fingers of panic gripped my throat. "Where's Declan?"

"My how things change, huh? And not only your hair." She smiled and stood up from the side of the bed where she'd been perched and walked over toward a large dark wooden door. "One day you hate someone and the next . . . it's true love? Are you the beauty to his beast?"

My eyes narrowed. "Where is he? What did you do with him?"

"Don't worry about him. You have enough to worry about now that you're here."

A thought came to me that I didn't want to utter out loud. Was it possible? Was Cruella the agent Dr. Gray had mentioned to me? It made sense. She was strong and capable and very believable as one of Matthias's willing blood servants. Maybe it *was* her. And if so, I might still have a chance to get out of this alive.

I drank some of the water. My throat was raw and sore and it helped a little. My head ached from when I'd bashed it against the window. I put the glass down on the bedside table and forced myself to sit up, pushing away the dark blue sheets only to find myself naked underneath. I pulled the sheets back up to cover my bare skin.

Cruella looked amused. "I suppose you'd like to get dressed." She moved to the end of the bed, grabbed something, and threw it at me. "Here."

It was a white dress made from a thin silky material, one that wrapped and tied at the waist, low cut, with long flowing sleeves. Looked fancier than I felt like wearing, but it was better than nothing. Despite the thin material it didn't seem to be see-through. I put it on quickly.

Where was Declan? Was hc okay? Were they keeping him in a room like this nearby? How soon would I be able to see him?

"Get up," Cruella said.

I forced myself out of the bed on sore, shaky legs. I looked down at myself to check for any bruises. There were a few, likely from the car crash, but not as bad as I'd expected. I felt achy and stiff, but nothing felt broken.

"What's your name?" I asked. Now was a good time for Cruella to come clean and tell me she was the agent and that she was on my side. That everything was going to be okay.

Even after everything, I still had a sliver of optimism in me.

"That's right, we haven't been formally introduced, have we? I'm Karen. And you're Jillian."

"You know my name?" That was a good sign. Maybe she'd been briefed about me since I first met her.

"Among other things."

I wasn't exactly sure what she meant by that. "And where the hell am I, Karen?"

She cocked her head, her expression revealing nothing that might help me. "Where do you think you are?"

Despite the drink of water, my mouth felt very dry. "I don't know."

"Come on. I'm sure you can figure it out. He's very interested in meeting you, you know. Even though you're a new player in this game, your reputation precedes you."

"Who's *he*?" Just like with the location, I didn't want to hazard a guess just in case I was right. Although, I knew denial wouldn't help me for much longer.

She sighed. "You really should have been honest with me about the formula the other day. You've caused me a great deal of trouble since then."

Again, hope fluttered in my chest that she was the undercover agent Dr. Gray mentioned. "Listen, Karen, I need to find Declan. I need to get out of—"

She smacked me so hard across my face that my ears rang. I gasped and tears sprang to my eyes, more from shock and anger than from fear or pain. I glared at her as I held my hand to my burning cheek.

"What the hell was that for?" I snapped.

"You stupid bitch." Her glossy red lips thinned and anger sparked in her gaze. "Do you have any idea what he does to blood servants who disappoint him? I brought him that formula and it was a dud."

"Matthias." That was who she was talking about, of course.

She looked at me like I was an idiot. "Of course."

I was having second thoughts about her being the agent. Yes, in fact, I was now certain she wasn't. It was disappointing to say the least.

"Where the fuck is Declan?" I snarled at her.

"He's dead."

I reacted as if she'd hit me again. I even staggered back a step. "What?"

"A piece of glass from the accident carved open his throat. He bled to death in minutes."

My breath left me in a rush. I searched her face for any sign of deception, but I couldn't tell for sure.

"You're lying." My throat closed off and cold, clawing hands of panic and grief at this news wrapped themselves around me and wouldn't let go.

"Matthias wants to see you." She grabbed my upper arm. "He's waited long enough. Let's go."

I was ready to fight, even though I knew I was no match for her, but when she opened the door, two other men were there. I recognized one of them from the other day. Davis, I thought his name was. The redheaded servant who'd groped me while Karen stood by passively.

Was Declan really dead? He couldn't be. No, he had to be here. Somewhere. I held on to that thought. I refused to believe he'd died in the crash like she'd said, but a mental image of him bleeding now haunted me, his good eye glassy and unblinking next to the darkness of his eye patch.

The knowledge of where I was slithered through me. I'd already figured it out, but I wanted to believe it wasn't true. However, pretending didn't change the situation in the slightest.

Declan had to be here somewhere. But if he was, that meant he was a dhampyr assassin in the heart of Matthias's clan. Based on the reception he'd received from Karen and her friends the other day, Declan was a known vampire hunter. They wouldn't welcome him with open arms. If he wasn't already dead, he wouldn't have much longer to live.

A sob rose in my throat but I swallowed it down. I willed myself not to feel despair, but it was impossible. Even if Declan was still alive, he wasn't here with me. I was on my own.

If I'd lost him forever after just finding him, I didn't know what I'd do.

Did Karen know why my hair and eyes had changed color? Did anyone here know the Nightshade was inside me? That it had fused with my blood? Or were they going to torture me until I told them where it was and how to get their greedy hands on it?

I tried to pull away from her, but she held on firmly. Davis grabbed my long black hair in his grip, so tightly that it felt like he might yank it out by the roots.

"Behave yourself, little girl," he growled. "Or I'm going to have to punish you."

I really didn't want to know how Davis would punish me.

They forced me down a hallway. I found it difficult to believe we were underground. I would have expected cold, carved stone. Something medieval. But this was all smooth, painted walls and warmly lit corridors. It felt more like the hallways in a hotel. There were no windows anywhere so I couldn't tell for certain that this was Matthias's lair. I was still hoping it wasn't and that this was somewhere I could escape from easily.

I clung tightly to my denial, but it didn't help much anymore.

I wanted to ask how far underground we were, but I didn't say anything. I assumed they weren't open to questions at the moment, and I might only earn myself another smack for asking—or worse.

Finally we reached a room with a large wooden door, which Karen opened and went inside. It was darker in there. Candles flickered. Much like the hallways had hinted, the interior gave the impression of an expensive hotel suite or a large luxury condo—richly furnished and very comfortable.

Through a living room—with a long sofa, Persian carpeting, and expensive-looking oil paintings—and down another hallway, we entered a large chamber that had many plush seats and sofas strewn about. A man sat behind a large ebony desk in a high-backed leather chair. The desk bore a laptop computer to the side. Behind the man there was a wall of books with worn leather spines and gold lettering.

The man's pale hands rested on the table in front of him, fingertips pressed together. He seemed as if he'd been waiting for us to arrive.

I knew it was him.

His hair was a color that reminded me fleetingly of the fusing potion—a dark gold I now associated with pain. It was long, not enough to brush his shoulders, but it fell past the nape of his neck, one long, thick piece resting against his cheek, partially covering his left eye. His face was pale white except for his lips, which were tinged with red. His light gray eyes framed with dark lashes were spooky in the partial darkness of the room. Candlelight flickered against his smooth, ivory-colored skin.

"Jillian," Matthias said in a deep, rich voice that filled me with cold fear. "I'm glad you're finally awake."

This was Declan's real father. Matthias had raped and nearly murdered his mother nearly thirty years ago, and yet the vampire king looked no more than thirty himself.

"Bring her closer," he said.

"Matthias," Karen began, "I don't think that's a good idea."

"Bring her closer," he said again. *"Now."*

She didn't argue again. Although frightened—to put it mildly—I kept my attention fully on Matthias as Karen pulled me deeper into the large room.

When we drew within ten feet of him, his nostrils flared and his eyes widened almost imperceptibly.

"Oh," he said softly. "So it's true."

"You can tell already?" Karen asked.

"Yes. Bring her closer."

A few more steps had Matthias leaning back in his chair, his already pale knuckles whitening further as he gripped the edge of his black desk.

"That's close enough." He blinked and the gray of his eyes disappeared, replaced by an inky black. His cheeks hollowed and a spiderweb of dark blue veins appeared around his mouth and eyes. His jaw clenched and he inhaled sharply.

So much for me keeping my secret to myself.

"Matthias . . ." Karen's grip on me tightened and she yanked me back a step.

He shook his head. "I'm fine. It was . . . just surprising. It's one thing to hear a rumor and another to have it proven without a shadow of a doubt."

He exhaled slowly through his mouth. After a moment,

the veins disappeared and his eyes returned to their light shade.

"It's proven, then," Karen pulled me against her and I gasped as the cold, sharp edge of a blade pressed against my throat. "I'll kill her now and have it done with."

Matthias's cheeks stretched to accommodate a smile that left no part of his sharp fangs hidden. "You would do that here? Spill blood in my office? You do know the value of the rug you're standing on, don't you? It's worth more to me than you are."

I wasn't sure if he was trying to be humorous.

The blade eased up and Karen let go of me completely.

Matthias stood up from behind his desk and slowly walked around it toward me. It took him a few stops, during which the physical manifestation of his hunger—his black eyes and the spiderlike veins that turned his handsome face monstrous—appeared and disappeared, before he walked the seven steps it took to bring him directly in front of me.

What would Declan do if he stood before this vampire right now? Would he have a chance to kill him? More of a chance than I had.

Then again, Declan's blood wasn't poisoned. I didn't need muscles and combat training in order to kill.

"Karen tells me your hair was blond when you first met," he said.

I struggled not to stagger back from him. I raised my chin and held his gaze defiantly. Or, what I hoped seemed like defiance. Anything to cover up the bone-shaking fear I felt. Still, there was nothing I could do to cover up the trembling of my lips as I spoke.

"It was."

He looked pained as if being this close to me was difficult for him. "I like blonds."

"They do allegedly have more fun."

His smile returned. "Your hair, though. It's . . ." He closed his eyes and inhaled. "Only another effective trap. The scent is much more alluring to me than the color."

"If you say so."

"As a human, you wouldn't be able to sense it, but I can. And the nearer I am, and the longer I can withstand it, it only increases my ability to deal with this new weapon." He brought his face close to mine, bending over a little in order to do so since he was at least six feet tall. "So you are who they chose to try to destroy me with your blood, are you?"

I shook my head. "They didn't choose me. It was an accident."

"Oh? How so?"

"It was a mistake that I got involved in any of this."

"There is Nightshade in your veins." He smiled at my surprised look. "Of course I know what it's called. I have many people who work for me, some closer to the project than you might think."

"Anderson, the chemist who created it. He switched sides."

"Among others." He shook his head. "Yes, something like this—delivered it in the form of a woman they assume I would desire on sight. I suppose my own reputation precedes me as well, doesn't it?"

His reputation as a rapist addicted to dominating and abusing women? That pretty much summed it up.

I wasn't going to survive this—I saw it in Matthias's eyes. I'd felt it at the sharp edge of Karen's blade. It didn't matter that I'd come to play a part in this by accident or not. I was here now and my involvement was imprinted on me right down to my red blood cells. I hadn't wanted this to happen, but it was happening anyway.

And if I was going to die, I resolved at that moment to take Matthias with me.

"Do you want to taste my blood?" I asked him. I could end this right here, right now. I pulled the shoulder of the dress down so it bared more of my skin. "Go ahead."

His gaze moved to my throat and his eyes blackened again as a hiss escaped his lips.

"Matthias," Karen warned. "Don't."

His eyes flicked to her. "Get him now so we can finally get to the real truth here."

She nodded and turned to leave the room without another word.

Get him? Get who? Was he talking about Declan? My stomach twisted.

I watched the path she took to leave the office before I felt the stroke of Matthias's cool fingertips on my skin. I jerked away from him.

My reaction to his touch made him smile. "They're very good, you know. I'd heard about the formula, although only recently. I didn't believe it, but it's like being a starving man presented with a feast. So very easy to give in to temptation, even knowing what it might do. Anderson's skills as a parachemist were formidable. I only wish I'd learned of this sooner. And I'm still not convinced it is as much of a threat as everyone would like to believe."

My skin crawled from where he'd touched me.

"Disgust?" he said. "Is that what I see in your eyes, Jillian? But you don't even know me."

"I know enough."

"For you to so willingly risk your life in order to kill me, you must feel that you have a strong sense of who I am. What did they promise you? Riches? Prestige? Did they really think I'd be so stupid as to not know what they planned?"

"You knew because of Anderson, right?" I said.

"I knew before I even contacted Anderson. And now he's dead and won't be able to make any more of the formula. Your scarred, vampire-hunting bodyguard saw to that, didn't he?"

Vampire-hunting bodyguard. Matthias had no idea that Declan was his half-vampire son. What would he say if he found out?

"Where is he?" I demanded. "Declan. Karen told me he was dead."

"He *is* dead." He cocked his head at the pain that flooded my expression. "You cared for him, did you?"

I couldn't speak for a moment. Grief at having his death confirmed had taken my voice. I desperately struggled not to cry. Not here. Not now.

"I'm sorry for your loss." Matthias moved as if to touch me again.

"Don't touch me, you heartless bastard."

He tsked his tongue. "Again, Jillian, you presume to know me when we've only just met. But your caution is not unwise. I don't take kindly to assassination attempts— not by my own subjects or humans who think they know it all, even if their attempts are carried out by attractive women."

"I'd say you should probably get used to it."

A flash of anger went through his gaze. "I've ruled here for nearly three decades and faced many difficulties. My own people even conspire to destroy me, but it's nothing new. You, however, are a first." He reached forward to twist a piece of my black hair around his finger. "So much taxpayer money wasted by this little government program. Sad, really. As you can see, I am able to resist your particular charms."

"Not without effort."

"No. You're right. Had I not already known about you, I may not have been able to resist." He hissed out a labored breath. "But here we are, finally getting to the bottom of this little mystery you've presented for me."

Confusion pushed past my fear and grief. "How did you know about me? Anderson was killed before I even became a real part of this."

"I have eyes and ears on most of what Dr. Monica Gray and her team have up their sleeves. Not everything, unfortunately, but enough. I was alerted to your situation. The testing. Your pain from being exposed to the Nightshade. And finally, your flight from Silver Ridge last night."

"Who told you?" I asked breathlessly. I didn't really expect him to tell me.

His lips twisted. "Someone who is more on my side of this battle than Carson or Monica would ever suspect. Someone even you trusted enough to confide in. His reports have been given to me on a near daily basis."

"Noah," I breathed. The blood rushed out of my head so quickly that I nearly passed out right then and there.

Noah was Matthias's inside man? How could it be? He'd seemed so genuine. So nice. Someone I could trust. He'd even told me about Matthias and the threat to human life.

Lying scumbag.

That little bastard was the reason Declan was dead. The reason I was going to be joining him after Matthias had finished playing with me like a cat with a poisoned mouse.

"Just kill me." My voice broke on the words.

"Is that what you want?" Matthias's gaze moved down the front of me, then he grabbed my left wrist so he could study the scar from my failed suicide attempt. "Noah made one request for his information—he had me promise I wouldn't kill you, that you were an innocent pawn in this war. However, first I'll see how my experiment goes and then I will decide what to do with you."

"What experiment?"

"Despite what I've been told, I'm having difficulties believing such a formula could exist. The claims of its potency could have been exaggerated. Noah could be lying to me, for all I know."

Karen had reentered the room with someone else. A man with dark hair and pale gray eyes.

"You wanted to see me?" he asked.

"Yes, Colin. Please, come here and meet Jillian."

Colin approached. When he got closer, his expression changed. "Matthias, what on earth? Her scent. Who is she?"

"A gift. For you. I know it's been some time since you last fed."

Colin exhaled shakily and his eyes darkened. "She's extraordinary."

"You may taste her to see if she's to your liking."

I looked at him panicked. "Wait . . . no . . ."

"Thank you, Your Majesty." He'd closed the distance between us in a heartbeat and was close enough that I could feel his cool breath on my throat.

I'd backed away from him until I hit the edge of Matthias's desk, and tried to fight. But like it had been with Tobias, it was in vain. He captured my wrists effortlessly in his.

"You don't know what you're doing," I managed. "You can't bite me."

"Look at me," Colin said. My wide eyes snapped to his and I found I couldn't look away.

Then, suddenly, it was as if I was no longer afraid of anything. My body relaxed. My panic slid away, leaving a strange and warm sense of peace behind when before there had only been cold fear.

"It's kind of you to make it easier on her," Matthias said.

"I don't want her to fear me."

"Fear is a tool."

"Not one I want to use. Not for a creature such as her."

It looked like it was love at first smell for Colin the vampire. I almost felt bad for him. But whatever he'd done to me had made it impossible for me to speak. I couldn't warn him of what would happen if he drank my blood.

He was part of Matthias's experiment. And he was going to die.

19

WHEN COLIN'S FANGS PIERCED MY SKIN, IT DIDN'T bring the pain I'd experienced from Tobias's bite. This was different—almost pleasurable.

Again the paralyzing component of a vampire's bite immobilized me so I couldn't fight against him. My fear still beat its wings inside me like a trapped hummingbird, but it was far enough away that I could choose to ignore it if I wished and instead wrap myself in this nice, warm feeling.

"You taste divine," Colin whispered, his hands at my waist, pulling me against him. While he wasn't as grabby as Tobias had been, I felt his unmistakable arousal against me.

Blood and sex. More proof that vampires were unable to feed without getting turned on.

My head felt cloudy. I couldn't keep a thought for long.

It was disturbing how good this felt, knowing exactly what he was doing to me. A dark longing filled me for a man I'd never even met before—a monster with sharp teeth and a hunger for my blood. He was making me feel this way. It was as if he'd hypnotized me to not be afraid even though his teeth were in my neck.

Suddenly, Colin gasped against my throat and pulled back from me as if the taste of my blood had turned from ambrosia to acid.

"What—?"

"My apologies, Colin," Matthias said. "But I'd heard you were one who'd been conspiring against me. Consider this your punishment for that."

Colin staggered back and screamed and the flames I'd seen before with Tobias poured out of his mouth. He looked terrified and confused, his gray eyes wide as the inferno engulfed him and his body burst into a cloud of fiery ash.

The spell was broken and I was no longer under his influence. I held a trembling hand to my mouth and another to my neck where he'd bitten me.

Matthias stared down at the ground, his jaw tight. There was a black patch burned into his expensive rug where Colin had stood a moment ago. Ashes fell to the ground like snow. His eyes flicked to me and widened a fraction.

He now had his proof that what I carried in my veins could kill him.

"Your blood is death." His voice was barely audible.

"Matthias—" Karen sounded upset. "It's true. It's all true. We need to kill her now so she can't hurt you."

Davis stepped forward. "Keeping her alive even a moment longer is too dangerous."

"No, not yet. Take her from here. I need to think." He glared at Karen. "And put the knife away. She remains unharmed until I decide how to deal with this."

"But Matthias—"

"Do as I say or you'll be joining Colin in his grave."

Frankly, I didn't really think there was enough of Colin left to bury, but I chose not to add to the discussion. Davis grabbed me hard enough to bruise and pushed me out of the room. Karen followed soundlessly behind us.

Once we'd gotten back to the room I'd woken up in, Davis roughly pushed me inside and I almost went over on my ankle.

"This is wrong," I told them. "You're both human. You can't let him do this. You have to help me get out of here."

"Shut up." Karen went to backhand me again, but I saw it coming this time and grabbed her arm, digging my fingernails in as hard as I could.

"Don't hit me again, you bitch," I snarled at her. The adrenaline coursing through my body was giving me a bit of extra courage and strength. I was tired of being abused.

"You should know, your lover didn't die right away," she said evenly. "He suffered for nearly twelve hours calling for you, but you never came to him. It was pathetic."

Hot tears streaked down my cheeks.

"We need to kill her," Davis said.

"Matthias said no," she hissed. "And his word stands." He glared at her. "For now."

Karen gave me a withering, almost pitying glare before she wrenched her arm out of my grip and left the room, slamming the door behind her and Davis.

I didn't even have to check it to know it was locked. It was a given.

I checked it anyway.

Then I screamed and threw things. I had lots of energy to burn off before I let myself feel anything but rage and grief.

THE IRONY WAS THAT THIS PRISON OF A ROOM WAS A near-mirror image of where I'd been kept in Carson's house. Different furnishings, of course, but it was the same size, equivalent to a standard hotel room with an attached bathroom.

No one brought me food. There was water to drink in the bathroom, at least. After I'd worked up a sweat with a tantrum that only served to exhaust me, I took a quick shower. Under the spray of hot water I let myself cry as if masking this act from the universe would make any damned difference.

Declan was dead.

Noah had been an informant for Matthias.

If I got another chance, I would kill Matthias. And I wouldn't feel as sorry as I did for Colin. He'd had no warning of what would happen to him. Not even a hint that biting me might be bad for his health, let alone his very life.

I shouldn't feel any sympathy for a vampire. Especially one who hadn't hesitated in sinking his fangs into me.

However, he had taken my fear and pain into consideration. That confused me deeply. Why would he have bothered?

I wasn't sure how long it was before someone came for me. Maybe six hours. There were no clocks in my room nor any windows to see if it was dark or light outside.

All I could do was wait. And think.

My thoughts were mostly with Declan as I remembered my time with him. From trying to escape from an emotionless assassin I hated to seducing the man I'd grown to care deeply for.

When the loss of him became too painful, I tried to think of my life before any of this had happened. Visiting with my sister and nieces. Trying to find my way in the city. The years had disappeared since college. Every day felt similar after I started working full time. I lived for my vacations. The years I'd been on the depression meds after my parents died were a blur. No excitement, or very little. No passion.

All I knew was the moment I became interested in living again, my life was in danger of ending. It was a good example of use it or lose it.

I was losing it. Any hope I'd had vanished little by little, every hour I was trapped here.

So I focused on my only goal now: Matthias's death.

I clung to it—the only thing that could still give my life meaning. Maybe this was fate. Maybe I was meant to be injected with Nightshade. I was meant to come here, because I might be able to stop Matthias.

My sister, my friends—they'd never have to know what I'd done. They'd never have to know there was even a threat.

And that would be a good thing.

The resolve that came from this line of thinking helped calm me. The tight black knot of panic and fear in my chest remained, but I was able to think around it.

When they came for me I knew this much—it was time to act.

Karen, without saying a word to me, directed the two men with her to take me down the hall again to Matthias's chambers. They roughly pushed me inside and left me there, closing the door behind them. I looked around frantically, testing the door after a moment. It was, of course, locked.

Was I alone? Why would they bring me here again? I thought they were going to kill me.

It was okay. I'd wait for Matthias to return. I could make him bite me, even if it was the last thing I did. Or I could cut myself and jam my bloody fingers in his mouth, forcing him to drink my blood.

The gory image actually helped give me strength.

Then I heard it. A moan. Female.

I warily followed the sound until I reached a room without a door, only an archway. On a large bed was Matthias and a blond woman. She was completely naked and facing me with her eyes closed. He wore pants, but his chest was bare. He kneeled behind her, one hand fanned against her bare stomach to hold her in place, the other squeezing her right breast.

His mouth was on her neck and I could see a trickle of blood slide down to her collarbone. She didn't move, paralyzed by his bite, but the look of ecstasy on her face told me everything I needed to know. She was a very willing victim.

I must have gasped because Matthias pulled away from her, his gaze moving to me and locking there. After a moment, the woman collapsed to the bed, panting.

Matthias grinned at my shock and disgust and wiped his mouth with the back of his hand. "Jillian, what a surprise."

He wasn't surprised. He would have known I was coming. Karen wouldn't dare make a move without his prior knowledge and consent.

He'd wanted me to see this.

"It's unfortunate, though," he said, studying me.

"What is?"

"I decided to feed now, thinking it would diminish your effect on me. But that doesn't seem to be the case. Your blood calls to me." He finally tore his gaze from mine and swatted the blond on her bare ass. "Get out."

She didn't hesitate or argue. She rolled off the bed and, not making any move to cover herself, picked up her clothes off the floor and walked out of the room.

"The door's locked," I said.

"She has a key. She'll let herself out."

"That's convenient."

He smiled. "It is."

What was this? He'd sent his dinner away and now we were alone. I pushed back against the dread that this scenario caused.

He might not know it yet, but he was going to sink his fangs into me in the next ten minutes.

"You look absolutely terrified, Jillian," he said, smoothly getting up from the bed. He walked toward me and I staggered back a step. His smile widened as he moved past me, headed instead for a table holding a bottle of wine as well as grapes, strawberries, and a selection of cheeses. He uncorked the wine and poured two glasses.

"Here." He handed me one glass. I made no immediate move to take it. "It's a very good vintage, I promise."

"I'm not thirsty."

"Are you hungry?"

"No."

"I find that hard to believe. It's been a long time since you were brought here." His eyes narrowed. "Take the wine, Jillian."

The man was intimidating without even raising his voice. His tone held restrained violence and dark strength. He was playing with me again. I didn't like that.

However, if I wasn't even borderline pleasant, he

wouldn't fall for my trap and bite me. I had to be nice. That meant I had to play along. For now.

I took the wine and sipped from it, then ate two strawberries and a piece of cheese. The food slid down to my empty stomach unpleasantly.

"See? That's much better." Matthias took his own glass and held it to his lips, taking a slow sip of the burgundy liquid. "Have some more."

I had another piece of cheese and he watched me carefully—the little mouse caught in his trap.

"You want to ask me questions about what I am, don't you?" he asked. "I can tell you're a curious woman and this is all new to you. Please, ask me anything you wish."

"Are you going to kill me?" It was the first question that came to mind, not surprisingly.

"I haven't decided yet."

"You let Colin die without a second thought." I pulled my hair over my right shoulder and raked my fingers through it nervously. From the pained look on his face, it seemed as if the motion caused a waft of my scent to hit him like a two-by-four.

Good. He could continue to think I was afraid he was going to kill me. Well, I was. Fear was the natural instinct for a situation like this. But it paled in comparison with my end goal.

His grip tightened on his wineglass as he appeared to struggle with keeping his composure. His eyes shifted to black before returning to their spooky light shade.

"Colin was one of my most trusted advisors until I recently learned that he was betraying me. Working behind my back to help overthrow me."

"Then I guess the bastard deserved it."

He studied me. "You feel badly about what happened, don't you?"

"No." I pressed my lips together.

"You do. You're no assassin. So it's true what Noah told me: You don't have any real part in this. You're only a pawn used by those who mean to destroy me."

"I don't know what you want me to say."

"The truth would be nice." He took another sip of his wine and walked toward the far wall on the other side of the bed.

There was no doubt this was a man to fear. His handsome appearance was deceptive. Of course, knowing what he'd done to Declan's mother kept that shiny exterior from affecting me in the slightest. He didn't make any move to put on a shirt to cover his upper body, lean and solid, but less muscular than Declan's. The dhampyr likely outweighed his vampire king father by about fifty pounds.

I didn't want to think about Declan now. All it did was bring a solid lump to my throat that was nearly impossible to swallow past. I had to keep my concentration. If I let it slip, I might lose my nerve completely.

"Tell me exactly what they wanted you to do," Matthias said. "What Monica Gray requested of you."

I licked my dry lips. "How does this work? I answer your questions and you give me a quick, painless death?"

The corners of his mouth twitched. "I'm trying to think where you got such a poor impression of me. Please try to remember that Monica Gray has her own agenda. And she's not above spreading lies in order to meet her goals."

"So you're trying to tell me you're a nice guy and not one to fear. That everything that's been said about you is just to build a nasty reputation?"

"Well, I wouldn't go that far. I'm sure much of what she told you was the truth. I make no claim of being a friend to all humans."

I sipped the wine and tried to look remotely at ease and failing spectacularly, I was sure. "What do you want?"

He slid his hand casually through his dark gold-colored hair. "Many things."

"You know what I am and what I can do. Now what?"

"An excellent question." He downed the rest of his glass of wine and came back over to pour another. He noted my curious stare. "I can drink more than just blood. I can eat, too, if I choose. With effort, many of my kin could fit in very well among the humans. Some already do."

"Then why live underground?"

"Now, now. Let's play fair. You never answered my question. What did they want you to do?"

"Don't you already know that?"

He shook his head. "Noah hasn't related everything to me. He remains resistant to give away all of the secrets of the Nightshade program. He's only shared a glimmer of the truth with me—but it was enough. I assume that even though your involvement with Monica's program was a mistake, they still wished to use you. To push you toward me like a steak offered to a starving lion. But they forget that I'm not exactly starving down here."

So Noah hadn't told him everything. I didn't know exactly what he had told Matthias, though. About the undercover agent? The grand plan? The fusing potion? That Declan was a dhampyr—his son? He hadn't seemed to give a shit when he confirmed to me he was dead. Maybe Matthias didn't care about anything but himself. And Noah had definitely told him the Nightshade in my blood was meant to kill him, but he hadn't believed it. He'd needed to see the proof first.

If he'd known all the answers, it was unlikely he'd be asking me anything right now. I'd already be dead.

It gave me something to work with. A small, very faint, glimmer of hope that I could succeed in my goal right now.

"I didn't want anything to do with this," I said. "Really. This was all a huge mistake."

"Did they think you could enter my domain without my knowledge? Perhaps as a willing human offering? It happens frequently. You think the girl who was in here was kidnapped from her home in the dark of night and forced to let me drink from her?" He shook his head. "She was willing, if that wasn't completely obvious. In fact, she has been known to beg to see me."

I repressed the sour look I wanted to give him, hiding my frown with the wineglass as I took another sip. "Yes, that's exactly what they wanted me to do." I didn't want to hint that there was an undercover agent somewhere down here if he didn't already know about that. I didn't want anyone else to have to die tonight. "But they didn't go into detail about how I was going to do it."

"You spoke to Monica about this."

I nodded.

"She's wanted my head on a platter for a very long time."

"She's not your biggest fan, no."

His lips curved in a sardonic smile. "Tell me, is she still doing her experiments to find a way to produce the perfect hybrid?"

Another subject Noah had neglected to fill the vampire king in on.

My finger tightened on my wineglass. "I don't know what you mean."

"Her Dr. Frankenstein insistence that vampires and humans could produce a being that is the next evolution of mankind. *Dhampyrs*." He cocked his head and his cool smile stretched wider. "You know, Jillian, you must never play poker. You can't bluff very well. You know exactly what I'm talking about. You've probably even seen one of them, haven't you?"

There was no use trying to deny it. Besides, what difference did it make? "I have."

"And what was it like?" he asked, but before I could answer he continued, "A beastly thing not human or vampire? An experiment gone horribly wrong?"

"You must have seen them before. I can't imagine you only bite the naked women who spend time in your bedroom. There has to be some mistakes that happen along the way."

His lips thinned. "They're very rare, but they do happen. And as soon as it's known, the fetus is immediately aborted."

I grimaced with disgust.

"You think that's cruel?" he asked. "What's cruel is letting the dhampyr come to full term. A baby dhampyr already has talons with which they slice their way out of the womb. Even as newborns, they're dangerous to anyone who comes close to them."

"So there's only the one kind of dhampyr?" I asked with mock ignorance.

"Oh, there's also the kind that look like a human but have the strength and agility and healing abilities of a vampire. The kind that can go out into the sun and survive without ingesting human blood."

"You've never seen one of these?"

"Yes, of course. One I remember vividly was a female dhampyr from forty years ago. A child no more than a year old."

She'd be like Declan. My ears perked up. "What happened to her?"

"She was sliced open in a ritual so a former king could

drink what he thought was powerful magical blood to give him true immortality."

I felt physically ill. "This king—he's dead now, I hope?"

"No, but he was imprisoned for his sins."

"Kristoff." I remembered the name from my chat with Dr. Gray. The benevolent king who kept the vampires in check until Matthias came along and ruined everything with his greed and lust for power.

A benevolent king who murdered children so he could drink their blood?

Matthias looked at me sharply. "Monica has many tales to tell, does she?"

"She . . . she said that he was a good king and that you—that you overthrew his reign."

He was silent for a moment before his laughter cut through the room like a knife. "Why am I not surprised? Did that help make you feel that giving your life to take mine was a noble cause? Perhaps so that the good king could be returned to his throne?"

"You have Kristoff hidden away somewhere down here?"

His amused expression disappeared. "He will never be released. Ever."

"If . . . if you feel that strongly, then why wouldn't you just kill him?" I felt his glare at my question like a slap.

"What I do with my prisoners is my business, not yours." He went silent for a moment. "Tell me, Jillian. The man in the car with you. The vampire hunter, Declan Reyes. Were you in love with him?"

My chest ached at the sound of his name and the direct and unexpected question. "I only met him a few days ago."

Matthias came closer and poured me some more wine.

Instead of drinking it this time, I placed the glass down on the table next to the half-empty bottle.

"He's killed many vampires over the years," he said. "He was feared more than any other hunter in recent memory. It helped cull the number of rogues out in the human world."

I swallowed hard. "You call them rogues, too?"

"That's what they are. Those who have pledged allegiance to me are welcome in my kingdom, which offers safety and security and willing blood servants. If they go out into the human world and break these rules, I send servants to bring them back here, where they face punishment. Any others are usually picked off by hunters. However, hunters don't know the difference between those who are truly rogue and those who are not. That's the problem when it comes to indiscriminant hunters like your Declan."

I grimaced. "He wasn't mine."

"He was a beastly-looking man, wasn't he?"

"He wasn't beastly."

He studied me. "You cared for him."

I blinked back the tears that gathered at the edges of my eyes. Then I nodded, soundlessly.

"Such a waste, then, that he's gone." He approached me with effort and reached forward to twist a piece of my hair around his finger. "To earn the affections of a woman like you means he must have been worth something to the world."

Every muscle in my body tensed at having this monster so close to me. I forced myself not to try to escape him.

"Careful," I said. "Get too close and you might want a taste."

In fact, I was counting on it.

"Yes, it's true." His jaw was tight. "Many people have

attempted to take my life. But I'm very, very hard to kill. Perhaps I've begun to feel more powerful than I should. Having you here is a very good reminder of how vulnerable I am."

"So why would you bring me here right now?" I asked. "Was it to kill me?"

"I hadn't yet decided when I asked them to bring you here tonight." He slid his fingers fully into my hair and I watched as the veins framing his eyes and mouth appeared faintly before disappearing.

"And have you decided now?"

"I've decided not to kill you. Not now."

"'Not now,'" I repeated.

A smile played at his lips. "I believe what Noah said— that you're an innocent dragged into Monica's schemes. I can't fault you for that. Not entirely, anyway."

"So what you do want? More answers?"

"No." He shook his head. "I want you to help me."

I cringed as his hand came to rest on my shoulder, just past the edge of my white dress. His skin was dry and cool, like a silk pillow on a hot cheek at night.

"With what?"

"My resistance." His lips parted and I saw the edge of his sharp fangs.

"I don't understand."

"The moment I met you, I wanted to sink my fangs into your flesh and drink you deeper than anyone I've ever known before. The Nightshade is entirely effective as a trap, luring its victim in by seducing their senses. It's nearly impossible for me to resist." His smile widened. "I find that very exciting."

"Then you've got a serious problem."

"Yes. A problem has been presented to me and I like to deal with my problems." His hand slid down my arm.

"I rarely have sex without also feeding. The combination is intoxicating."

A shudder of revulsion went through me. "I don't know much about vampires, but I already know that."

"Gandhi is said to have lain with naked women to test his vow of celibacy. He put the temptation right there in front of him in the form of bare skin and willing bodies. But he never succumbed to his base desires. In his faith, this made him stronger."

I swallowed nervously. "Sorry, I don't quite get the connection."

"If I can control my hunger with you, then I'll have proven to myself that I'm truly meant to be king and those who oppose me are wrong."

I felt panic creep in. When I tried to pull away from him, he took hold of my arm. His strength was enough to keep me in place.

"Look at me, Jillian."

The sharp way he said it should have been a warning. But I did as he asked and looked at him. The moment my eyes locked with his, the panic disappeared. The worry disappeared. The thoughts of Declan vanished.

My mind cleared and a pleasantly warm sense of calm washed over me.

"That's much better," Matthias said. He placed his hand over my chest. "Your heart rate is returning to normal. There's nothing to fear."

"What is this?" My words were slurred as if I'd had a few drinks.

"Vampires of a certain age are able to control the minds of humans to some extent. We can take away your fear when we feed, we can even make it pleasurable for you."

"I couldn't speak when Colin controlled me."

"He was only learning this skill. You may speak with

me, of course. And my grasp on you is not as tight as it could be. No reason for you to lose yourself entirely." His gaze swept over me. "You're feeling better now?"

I exhaled shakily. "Yes."

"Calmer."

I nodded. It was true, after all. I felt as if I didn't have a care in the world. And when Matthias touched me, trailing his fingers lightly over my collarbone, I didn't find it as repulsive as I should have.

"Do you find me attractive?" he asked.

"Yes."

That made him smile before the expression faded. "Your scent is nearly impossible for me to resist. But that's the whole point. I must resist." He raised an eyebrow as his gaze moved to my throat. "And if I fail, then I was meant to fail."

"Bite me," I murmured.

"That's exactly what I'm trying not to do." He took my chin between his fingers and looked deeply into my eyes. "No, Jillian. I'm not going to bite you. I'm going to make love to you. And you're going to enjoy it."

20

THOSE WORDS SHOULD HAVE FILLED ME WITH PANIC, but they didn't. I knew it was because of Matthias's mind control. He was manipulating my emotions—stripping away my common sense.

But he'd said it wasn't a strong hold. I could fight this—I had to fight this.

"You don't want to do this," I said.

"Yes, I do. And if you'd come here without any pretenses and without Nightshade in your veins, I still would have taken you as my lover."

I was unable to look away from his hypnotic gray eyes. "You have a lot of lovers?"

"Many."

"She said your weakness was human women." The mind control was loosening my tongue way too much, as if I'd had the entire bottle of wine instead of just a glass.

He smiled. "I don't limit myself to only women, but it is my preference. Monica certainly knows a lot about me. It's too bad it's not nearly enough to kill me."

I inhaled sharply as his hand slid down my back.

"Take this dress off," he said. "And lay down on my bed."

Instead of revulsion, I felt a sharp twist of lust snake through me, mixed with shame. Unfortunately, it wasn't strong enough to stop me. I was under Matthias's control. It was like I was watching myself from afar and couldn't help but do as he commanded.

If this was only light mind control, I would truly hate to witness the full deal.

I untied the sash at the waist of the white dress. With a shrug of my shoulders, it fell to the floor in a silky pool of fabric. His gaze swept over me, pausing to note the bruises I'd received during my very bumpy few days since becoming a government-funded test subject.

I moved backward as instructed until I felt the bed behind me. I got onto it, laying down on the red silk sheets and bringing my head to rest against a large soft pillow.

"Very good," he purred. "You're beautiful, Jillian."

My friends call me Jill, I thought randomly. But Matthias wasn't a friend. He'd never be a friend. He was monster, a rapist, a murderer who wished for ultimate power over humans. He had me under his control and was able to manipulate my behavior and emotions.

I hated him.

But the thoughts were distant. Muted under a layer of serenity. Not nearly enough to snap me out of this spell he had me under.

He undid his pants and took them off fluidly, effortlessly, and he stood naked in the dim light of the room.

Despite how I knew I should be feeling—fear, revulsion, panic—I couldn't help but feel a dark, unnatural desire for Matthias as he approached the bed.

"That's better," he said. "If anyone should be afraid, it should be me. If I lose control and taste your blood, I could die. Just like that. Four hundred years of life would be over as easily as a candle snuffed at midnight." He crawled onto the bed toward me like a predator, a glimmer of determination in his eyes that fought with the frequent and visible struggle against his hunger.

He could still lose this battle. He could still bite me. This wasn't over yet.

"Yes," he said, running his hands over my bare skin from thighs to hips to stomach. "Beautiful and deadly. And so tempting." He bent his mouth and lightly kissed a bruise on my shoulder. The cool touch of his lips should have disgusted me, but it only made me gasp with pleasure.

The false emotion he'd made me feel was incredibly powerful.

"You're making me do this," I whispered, trying desperately to fight his influence over me—to grasp hold of that piece of me that still had control over my own body. "This is wrong."

"Wrong." He brought his face close to mine, covering my body with his. "There is so much wrong in the world. I don't believe this is one of those things."

I was going to argue with him, but he covered my mouth with his.

"Kiss me," he murmured against my lips when I didn't respond.

"No."

He crushed his mouth to mine again, attempting to coax

a reaction. When he pulled away, his gaze was fully black and the dark blue veins around his eyes and mouth were very prominent. He hissed out a labored breath before the signs of his hunger for my blood disappeared again.

"So tempting," he said. "Every inch of you. It scares me like nothing else I've faced."

"Then stop this." No, that was wrong of me. I should be encouraging this. Pushing him to his breaking point.

"Not yet." He trailed his lips over my throat, his cool tongue traced down the center of my body from throat to navel. He filled his hands with my breasts, squeezing my nipples and making me moan as my body responded against its will. Then his hands moved to my thighs, urging them apart.

Despite my need to get him to bite me no matter what it took, I still wanted to fight against him. But there was no fight left in me at the moment. The control he had over me was too strong.

When I felt his tongue slide against me I think I cried out. Instead of fighting or pushing him away, I reached down to grab hold of his hair as he slowly licked me.

My weakness to fight against my own surge of desire for what he was doing to me disgusted me.

When he kissed his way back up to my mouth, I was panting, scared and aroused and confused to the point of near insanity by what he'd made me feel. He'd succeeded in making me want him, despite what I knew about him and despite what he was.

But when I felt his length press against me, hard and thick, I summoned every last remaining piece of strength inside of me and grabbed on to his shoulders.

"No, Matthias," I managed. "Please don't do this."

"You want me."

"Only because you have the power to make me."

"Your previous lover is dead. There's no reason for you to still feel loyal to him."

The mention of Declan made me squirm in a feeble attempt to get away from Matthias, but the false need I felt for him kept me from moving far.

He groaned as his lips traced against my throat. "You're making me want to bite you as I fuck you. It's nearly worth any price I'd have to pay."

He only needed to push forward and he'd be inside me. My legs were splayed wide apart and he had his hands on the inside of my knees as he rubbed the tip of himself against me.

And at that moment, I wanted him. So badly. I ached for him. But I knew what I felt wasn't real. It couldn't be.

"I never would have agreed to this if you weren't controlling me right now. This is rape. If you do this, you'll be raping me."

"But you're hot and wet for me," he breathed against my ear in a pained tone. This experiment seemed to be more torture than pleasure for him. "You want me inside of you, I know you do."

His grip on me increased, pressing my legs wider apart and he began to enter me. My head fell back against the pillow as my fingernails dug into his shoulders.

But then, without any warning, he suddenly stopped. His expression had grown haunted as if what I'd said had finally registered with him.

"I don't rape women, Jillian," he rasped.

"That—that's not what I've heard."

His eyes narrowed. "Then you heard wrong. I've never taken a woman against her will."

"What do you call this?"

He scowled at me. "You aren't unwilling. The body doesn't lie. *Your* body doesn't lie."

Without another word, he pulled away from me, then got up from the bed and grabbed at his pants, quickly putting them back on.

"My influence just now was only to relax you, to reduce your fear and increase your pleasure. That's all it was." He grabbed my chin again and this time it wasn't nearly as gentle as before. "Look at me."

And I did. The next moment the desire and serenity disappeared and my stress and fear came crashing back at full strength. I grabbed at the bedsheets to cover myself.

He'd stopped. He could have easily finished the job without any more protests from me. Hell, he practically had.

"Who told you I was a rapist?" he asked sharply. "Monica Gray?"

Maybe he'd changed. Maybe he'd been less controlled thirty years ago and had since seen the error in his ways. Now he knew that women would want to have sex with him without being forced.

"No. Declan told me."

"I assume *he* didn't have to take you by force."

I flinched at that, but didn't answer him. It was none of his business what had happened between me and Declan.

"But he told you lies," Matthias said. "And I want to know the source of these rumors."

"It was his mother."

"His mother," he repeated incredulously.

He honestly didn't know anything about this. Noah hadn't told him a thing.

"You raped her twenty-nine years ago. Nearly drained her of blood. She fell into a coma from her injuries, but not until after she told what happened to her."

He stared at me. "That's impossible."

"It's not."

"Yes, it is. It's impossible because I know I never did such a thing." His eyes flashed with anger. "Maybe I did sleep with her. She could have been a blood servant. But something else must have happened to make her create these lies about me."

I was surprised to see such outrage in his expression. "She was pregnant with Declan. She died after he was born."

His gaze snapped to mine. "And it's assumed he was mine? From this alleged rape? Is he a dhampyr?"

I nodded.

Matthias didn't say anything for a very long time. "Get dressed."

He picked the white dress up off the floor and threw it at me. He didn't do me the honor of looking away while I slipped back into it.

I glared at him. Matthias was no gentleman.

"You hate me, don't you?" he said.

"And here I'm trying to hide it so well from you."

"I promise you one thing, Jillian. One day soon you will come to me again." He approached until his face was only a few inches from my own. I held my ground. "And I won't have to use my control in order to make you beg me to fuck you."

I slapped him as hard as I could.

It only made him smile. "I'm not a rapist, whether you choose to believe me or not, but I don't mind a bit of fight in my lovers."

"You're disgusting."

"I'm sure your dhampyr was much better behaved, wasn't he?"

A sob caught in my throat, but I swallowed it down.

"Come with me." He left the bedroom without a glance to make sure I was following and walked to the chamber door. Using a key he pulled from his pocket, he unlocked it and it swung open in front of us.

A man stood there waiting with a dour expression on his face. He recoiled from me with a mix of horror and disgust, his eyes growing black and his upper lip curling back from his fangs.

"So, it's true," he hissed.

"What do you want, Samuel?" Matthias asked sharply. "I have no time for you today."

"*No time*," Samuel repeated with a mocking edge to his words. "I do know how busy you are, Your Majesty. Busy immersed in your hedonistic lifestyle with a new slut—a poisoned one this time. Your selfishness has reached a whole new level today and it hasn't gone unnoticed." He flicked a glance at me. "I know what she is. We all know. And the fact that you allow her to live is unforgiveable."

Matthias glowered at him. "It's none of your concern."

"Not my concern that instead of breaking the neck of a true threat to vampire life at first opportunity, you instead take her to your bed, not only risking your subjects but your own life in the process? On a whim? I heard what you did to Colin."

Matthias didn't flinch at the accusation. "Step out of our way. That's an order."

"It's over," he said, his face tight. "You're not fit to rule us and this situation"—his gaze flicked to me—"is only more proof. We wish to have Kristoff released from his imprisonment and reinstated as king."

Matthias's eyes narrowed. "You wish for the impossible. Turn now and leave, and I'll forget this indiscretion."

"You have to kill her," Samuel urged. "Do that and we might be lenient with you when Kristoff returns."

Karen approached, and Matthias glanced at her. "Take Jillian back to her room. Ensure she is not harmed."

Karen dipped her head. "Yes, Matthias."

"I'll come for you shortly," he said, holding eye contact with me for a moment. "But I must deal with this first."

Karen clamped her hand down on my wrist and pulled me alongside her. I looked over my shoulder to see the heated discussion between Matthias and Samuel continue.

"What was that all about?"

"An uprising amongst the vampires," Karen said. "It's been simmering for some time. Matthias has ignored the threat, thinking nothing would happen. But your presence here has helped bring it to a boil in only a matter of hours."

"Me?"

We got to my room and she opened the door and shoved me inside. I felt tense and on edge and ready to snap. Even worse than that, I still felt Matthias's hands and mouth on me, like he'd branded me with his touch, much like Declan had.

Was it really possible he wasn't as bad as I'd been led to believe? Most of that information had come from Dr. Gray and, granted, she had not proven herself to be all that reliable. But why would Declan's mother make such a claim?

Karen crossed her arms. "Your blood has been shown to kill vampires with only a taste. Matthias insists on keeping you alive and well. That attitude hasn't exactly met with everyone's approval."

"I don't want to hurt anyone," I said.

"Did you fuck him?"

I blinked. "What?"

She gave me a sour look. "Did you have sex with him?

It was obvious to me that that's what he had planned for you."

My stomached churned. "No."

It felt like a lie. Just because he hadn't finished didn't mean it didn't count.

She paced to the bed, glaring at me. "If you think he'll give up the others for you, you'll be disappointed. He has many lovers. I'm surprised his dick even has a chance to dry off."

I felt color come to my cheeks at her blunt statement. "Sounds like somebody's jealous."

"I'm not."

"Don't worry. I'm not interested in having a romantic relationship with a rapist. I do have some standards."

She laughed at that. It sounded like she was mocking me. "You don't really believe Matthias needs to rape anybody, do you?"

"He used his mind control on me."

"Did it work?"

I pressed my lips together and glared at her.

"You are so weak, it stuns me." She shook her head.

"And you are a heinous bitch who needs to get over an unfaithful jerk who obviously doesn't give a shit about you."

"He was faithful to one woman for a short time. Her name was Catherine, a human blood servant he favored. But she ran away from home six months ago. It wounded his precious ego. He's been trying to replace her ever since with a succession of random blonds."

"Sounds romantic. And you're just sorry your particular shade wasn't quite to his liking?"

She studied me for a moment. "You have no idea who I am, do you?"

I shook my head. "Who are you?"

Her eyes narrowed. "That Nightshade in your veins was meant for me."

It took me a moment to process exactly what she meant. When it hit me, I couldn't help but feel a wave of shock. "It *is* you. You're the agent Dr. Gray told me about. But I thought . . . I . . . I'm surprised."

I was right. I'd doubted my first inclination, that she was the agent, but she'd just confirmed it. But—she'd nearly killed Declan the other day with her stiletto heel. Was that something a government agent would do? Kill the same people she was working with to stop the bad guys? However . . . damn, she sure was believable if she'd just been trying to blend in.

She nodded. "I was."

"*Was*? What's that supposed to mean?"

Her expression grew strained. "Dr. Gray believes I still work for her. She's wrong. There's only one person I'm interested in helping."

I felt myself pale. "Yourself."

She smiled thinly. "There's trouble here, apart from anything Dr. Gray envisioned. It's been growing for years and it's reached a peak. The vamps are nearly evenly split. Some are still on Matthias's side, but others want Kristoff back. You heard what Samuel said."

"So have an election."

"It doesn't work that way here. A large percentage of vampires want to kill Matthias so he doesn't stand in the way. Others mean to find where he's locked Kristoff away and make him king again."

"I don't understand why Matthias didn't kill Kristoff in the first place rather than just locking him away somewhere."

"Matthias feels that being locked away, alive and suffering for decades—for eternity—is a much better punishment than simply being executed. It's that simple. And Matthias is that cruel."

I shivered. I supposed that made sense if you were looking at it from the point of view of a sadist. "From what I've heard from everyone but Matthias, Kristoff was a better king."

"Depends on what you're looking for in a king, I suppose. Kristoff was brutal and violent. He wanted to rise up against the humans years ago, but Matthias stopped him before anything major happened."

I was confused. "Why would Dr. Gray make up a story that's the exact opposite of that?"

"I don't know. But she did."

"And the other vamps are okay with Kristoff's plans?"

Her expression had turned amused as she filled me in on vampire politics. "A lot of them would prefer taking action instead of being trapped in Matthias's gilded cage down here—no problems getting blood servants and plenty of other luxuries, but no true freedom is allowed. He sends hunters after the ones that rebel against him. They're either killed aboveground or they're brought down here so Matthias can personally tear out their hearts. A lot don't want to deal with that level of tyranny."

My stomach twisted into knots at the image she presented to me. "So you came down here to settle in, then you were going to get injected with the Nightshade and come back down so you could kill him?"

"That's right."

"Even though it's poison?"

She nodded. "I was willing to give my life to destroy Matthias. Originally, anyway."

"And the two of you were involved."

"Only for a short time. Then he found other uses for me, including being one of the hunters he sent out after rogue vamps."

Well, that would explain the silver stilettos she wore. "And now you don't want to kill him because you fell in love with him?"

Her lips thinned. "Matthias promised to sire me, make me a vampire—eternal life, eternal youth, and endless strength—but it's been a year and I'm still human. My patience has finally worn out. Kristoff would want to build an army of vampires and he wouldn't resist my offer to become one."

I grimaced with disgust. "That's good of you. I'm sure Dr. Gray would be thrilled with your decision."

"You've visited her little lab, have you? Your dead boyfriend's father thinks he runs the show, but it's her baby." Her lips curled. "Interesting choice of words, actually, considering her recent research."

"I saw one of the dhampyrs she has in her lab right now. It was horrible."

"It's a regular baby factory."

My jaw tightened at the thought. "Why would Dr. Gray risk these women's lives?"

Karen looked at me as if I was an idiot. "Because she thinks her research is more important than any one life. Her latest subject gave birth just last night. Dr. Gray contacted me with the news personally—thinks I'm still working for her. That's when she told me about your role in all of this. I never would have guessed your little secret the other day. But then again, I don't have a vampire's sense of smell."

Karen might be a bitch, but she was a fantastic actress. Dr. Gray didn't strike me as either stupid or naïve. "Another monster dhampyr."

"No, not a monster. It's a normal baby girl."

A normal dhampyr child.

"Leave me off the baby shower guest list, please," I said dryly.

"Too bad. I mean, you already know the daddy."

"What?"

I noticed the knife in her hand she'd pulled from the sheath on her belt, the same one she'd pressed against my throat earlier. Ivory hilt, a twin to the one she'd given me to kill Declan that I really wished I still had. It glittered in the near darkness of the room.

"Catherine was the mother."

I inhaled sharply. "Matthias . . . he's the father?"

"You're good at this game. Catherine knew Matthias would make her get an abortion. I alerted Dr. Gray when she ran away and she was picked up."

"You're a pal."

"I do what I can."

"Why are you telling me this?" Why was she telling me *any* of this? I now knew way too much dangerous inside information about her now. And that knife wasn't exactly making me feel as if that was a good thing.

"I guess I just needed a girlfriend to confide in." She smiled. "Feels good to chat."

My eyes flicked to the knife again. "He told you not to hurt me."

"You know, I really would have killed him if I'd been injected with the Nightshade. If I get the chance, I'd be happy to slice this silver blade into his heart to truly show my worth to Kristoff. But first"—she drew closer to me—"let's start with you."

21

I STAGGERED BACK AND SCANNED MY SURROUND-ings for a weapon. The closest I could find was the lamp next to my bed, which I grabbed.

"Matthias should have bitten you," Karen said. "But it seems he was able to resist. Too bad. It only means he'll have to be killed in another way."

She stalked toward me, a trained assassin like Declan. I swung the lamp at her and managed to hit her pretty hard, but she shrugged it off. I swung again and she side-stepped the blow, then swiped the blade, shallowly slicing my arm.

"On second thought, a knife's no good for this," she said, sheathing it again. "If I shed too much of your blood, the vamps will all come running for a taste."

She snatched the lamp out of my hands and threw it to the side. Then she grabbed me, closed her hands around my throat, and started to choke me.

I pounded my fists against her, using every last ounce of my energy to break free. We were about the same height, minus the heels she wore. She responded by pushing me backward until she could slam me into the wall, knocking the wind out of me.

"Just die," she said. "Now you're only wasting my time."

After another moment, my arms fell slackly to my sides as I lost the energy to fight for my life. My vision began to blur and darken.

"Karen." Matthias's calm voice sounded out from behind her. "What are you doing?"

Her eyes widened. "She's going to kill you. It's my duty to protect you."

"Let go of her now."

Defeat flickered over her expression and she released me. I slid to the floor, coughing and gasping for air.

Matthias didn't look at me. His attention was all on Karen.

"You would kill her to protect me?" he asked.

"Of course."

"I finished with Samuel. He won't be causing any more problems."

Her expression tightened. "You killed him."

"Like I said, he won't be causing any more problems."

"He shouldn't have said those things to you," she said. "It was disrespectful."

"Rebellion. Uprising. Releasing Kristoff from where I placed him twenty-nine years ago. Those things?"

"That . . . that's right."

"You said Catherine was pregnant when she left." Still, his voice was so calm, it was eerie. At her look of shock, "You know my hearing is good enough to listen through doors. It's unfortunate my sense of smell was not keen enough to detect a change in Catherine's body chemistry when she was still here. That would have changed many things. She must not have been very far along at all when she left me."

Karen let out a shaky breath. "I should have told you, but she made me promise I wouldn't."

"But you told Monica Gray. You work for Monica Gray. I also heard that. You were supposed to carry the Nightshade in your blood, not Jillian." He held up his hand when she tried to say something. "It was only a complete and utter fluke that the formula ended up with her."

"I had second thoughts. I came to respect you too much to follow through."

"You asked to be in my bed, to be my willing blood servant. And you were upset when you were not to my liking. Did that make you feel like a failure, Karen? Did your jealousy when I discarded you for Catherine lead you to conspire against me with the likes of Colin, Samuel, and the others, or was it simply because I refused to sire you and gift you with eternal life?"

"Matthias . . ."

"Just answer me. Would you have let them kill me? Or would you have killed me yourself? You can't lie. I won't let you."

His gaze was focused on hers and I assumed he was using some of his control over her to make her tell the truth. However, if he'd been listening in, he already would have heard it.

"Yes," she said. "I would have killed you, you selfish fucking bastard."

She reached for the dagger on her belt, but her hand didn't even get a chance to touch it before Matthias reached out, took her face gently between his hands, and then, with a sharp twist, snapped her neck.

She fell to the ground in a heap.

Matthias's spooky gray eyes flicked to me. "I don't like traitors."

My heart pounded as I looked between him and the dead woman.

"I just saved your life," he said. "Please don't forget that."

I nodded my acknowledgement of this. My throat felt crushed and my vision was still unclear. The fear I'd felt when Karen was trying to kill me didn't seem to be in any hurry to go away.

"She said that the baby had been born, didn't she?" he asked.

I tried to swallow. It hurt. "She did."

I couldn't read anything in his expression to tell me what he thought of the news that he was a father.

"A girl," he said.

I just nodded.

He held his hand out. "You need to come with me right now."

I looked at him warily. "Where are we going?"

"There's someone I need you to see."

The last time someone said that to me, they'd locked me in a room with a hungry vampire. But this time it was the vampire telling me to come with him. A vampire I was extremely conflicted about. One I knew was a murderer. One that had psychically seduced me into having sex with him—well, *almost*. One I'd pledged to kill even if it was my last living act.

He'd just saved my life.

That made things even more confusing than they already were.

I held out my hand and he helped me to my feet. He pushed at my hair to look at my throat where Karen had choked me nearly to death, and his gaze flicked to mine.

"You can stand being this close to me now with no problem?" I asked.

"It's a big problem for me, actually." He raised an eyebrow. "But I'm able to put on a good front, don't you think?"

"Very believable."

"However, my abilities to withstand the Nightshade won't impress anyone. Seems my popularity level here has taken more of a beating than even I thought it had. I may need to find another home while I figure out my next move. Now, come with me."

He didn't pull me along, instead letting me walk on my own. Which meant I either had the choice to stay where I was and babysit Karen's dead body or follow Matthias.

I followed Matthias.

The hallways definitely gave the underground lair the feel of a subterranean hotel. They were just as lavishly decorated as the rooms and painted in deep burgundy—a color that reminded me of my tainted blood—with gold trim. It was truly a palace. We entered a cavernous room with a massive chandelier hanging from the thirty-foot ceiling. Several support beams looked like thick Grecian columns. There was a wall of large bookcases in here as well.

"Lots of time for reading?" I asked absently as we passed it.

He nodded. "I collect books on magic."

"Magic?"

"Houdini was a good friend of mine for many years, and he helped spark my interest in the world of magic." A smile played at his lips. "I offered to make him into a vampire, but he refused. He thought he could achieve immortality by other means. As far as I know, he may very well have succeeded."

"He died."

"That's what everyone believes. However, he was the best escape artist the world has ever known, so I'm still not entirely convinced he's gone forever."

"Where are we going, Matthias?"

"To get someone to help us."

"Help us with what?"

"I need to go aboveground." His jaw was tight.

The awareness of what he meant sunk in. "The baby. You're going to go get her, aren't you?"

"I am."

"Why? Catherine ran away from you. That's got to tell you something, doesn't it?"

"Despite what Catherine wanted, I won't turn my back on my daughter now that I know she exists."

"Dr. Gray will take care of her."

His eyes flashed with anger. "You have no idea who Monica Gray is. She's devoted her life to making people believe I'm a monster. But *she's* the monster in this scenario, whether or not she even realizes it. I told you about Kristoff and the child dhampyr, didn't I?"

I'd been trying very desperately to forget about that. "You did."

"Kristoff was part of a secret society of vampires called the Amarantos, whose members believed that a female dhampyr baby's blood would give them true immortality. As it is, a vampire has the potential for a very long life without succumbing to any human ailment, but they're still vulnerable. Kristoff believed in the immortality ritual and he worked very hard to create such a child with many women—willing or unwilling. When he finally succeeded, he killed his daughter and drank her blood and he forced one other vampire to do the same."

His voice was tight as he said this. There was deep anguish in his eyes at reliving this horrible memory.

"The other vampire was you, wasn't it?" My voice shook.

"He had me held in place as he force-fed me the blood." He looked away from me and didn't elaborate further.

I shuddered. "So is it true? Are you completely immortal?"

"I don't know for sure. All I know is it was a waste of a small life. I'd known he was evil before that, but I'd never actually seen the evidence for myself. His followers believed everything he said. They've lain in wait all these years for the chance to find him and make him their leader again. They think I'm a hedonist who cares nothing about my people, but they're wrong. I must feed on sexual energy as much as I do blood—without it I grow weak. Kristoff is the same."

I was confused. "Do all vampires feed on sex?"

"No. Not the younger ones. But such needs increase over time and affect those like my brother and I."

"Wait a minute, Kristoff's your *brother*?" I said, stunned.

"Yes."

"And you locked him away somewhere so he couldn't hurt anyone."

"I couldn't kill him, despite what he'd done. But he had to be dealt with." He nodded soundlessly, his face extremely tight and pale. "Female dhampyrs are the ones sought after for the immortality ritual by the Amarantos Society. The males are thought to be useless. All I know right now is that my daughter is in great danger and I have to protect her."

It was at that moment that all my doubts about Matthias vanished. The fear remained as sharp as ever, but my prior opinion of him—based on a certainty that he was a remorseless rapist and abuser of women—was gone.

He hadn't raped Declan's mother. Declan had been lied to over the years. He'd been told stories to build his hatred for a man he'd never met, helping to create an unstoppable weapon to use against the vampire he held responsible for ultimately killing his mother.

"Will you help me?" Matthias asked.

"Yes." It was a very simple word to describe how strongly I felt about this. Did Dr. Gray know how dangerous it was to have a baby dhampyr in her possession—especially a girl? If anyone found out, they would try to take her. Kill her. Drink her blood in the belief it would make them indestructible.

She was the exact opposite of me.

My blood meant a vampire's instant death. The baby's blood meant eternal life.

We passed several people along the way, but Matthias looked neither to our left nor right. We didn't travel through the area unnoticed. Whomever we passed gave us their full attention. I noted wariness in their expressions, some fear, and a great deal of anger to see dangerous, unwelcome me freely walking alongside their current king.

When we left the large room with the columns and bookcases, we headed down a staircase to a lower level, and down a hall. When we turned a corner, two men blocked our path.

"Matthias," one said. I was dismayed to see it was Davis. He held a knife in his hand. "I'm afraid I can't let you pass."

"This is her?" the other man asked. His breathing was labored and his eyes had already turned black to show he was a vampire. "The carrier of the Nightshade?"

"It is," Matthias confirmed.

"Why the hell haven't you killed her yet?" Davis asked. "If you did that, you might be able to get out of this alive. Even still, if you tell us where Kristoff is locked away, I might not have to kill you."

"You'll never find my brother," Matthias said simply.

"You're wrong. And when we do, he'll give the blood servants immortality and we'll help him rise to the surface and take what we want from the humans. Kristoff's time has come."

"Get out of our way."

"No."

"Look at me," he said to Davis.

"So you can use your mind tricks on me and force me to do your bidding? I don't think so. Not anymore."

Matthias glanced at the vampire who was eyeing me like I was an ice-cream cone he was dying to lick.

"I tasted her," Matthias said. "I couldn't resist. The fang marks on her throat show that I've marked her. It did nothing. It was all a trick to make us fear our enemies aboveground."

"You lie," the vampire said.

"No, I don't. Her blood is as delicious as it smells. Do you think even I could resist?"

"Wait, no . . . ," Davis began. "It wasn't Matthias who—"

But before he could get the rest of the sentence out, the vampire had me in his grip—his control was nowhere close to Matthias's. He pushed my head to the side and eagerly sank his fangs into my neck.

There was no mind control this time to make it pleasant, and the pain was sharp and immediate. Tears welled in my eyes, but I couldn't fight him since I was immediately paralyzed by his bite.

"Yesss," he hissed against my throat. "So good . . ."

My gaze was fixed on Matthias as Davis lunged at him with the knife. Despite Davis being a good hunter and fighter, he was no match for the vampire king, who easily snatched the knife away from him. His hand was a blur as he slashed Davis's throat. Davis brought his hands up to stop the gush of blood, his eyes wide with surprise at his own inescapable death.

The vampire released his hold on me, my dark red blood drizzling down his chin and dripping to the floor.

When I was able to move again, I clamped my hand to the side of my injured throat.

The vampire's gaze moved to Matthias.

"You were right," Matthias said, wiping the blade off on his black pants. "I was lying. Hope you enjoyed the taste of death."

It didn't take long for the flames to consume the vampire's body. His screams stopped a moment before he burst into fiery ash.

I glared at Matthias. He looked surprisingly amused given what had just happened.

"What's so damn funny?" I snapped. "You made him bite me."

"You'll heal. He won't."

"Still not finding the humor."

"When there's nothing to laugh at, that's when you should laugh the hardest."

He was a regular vampire Confucius. "You're fucking insane, do you know that?"

"Come. We're almost there."

"Why the hell don't you have bodyguards?"

"Those were my bodyguards."

Without another word, he turned and began swiftly

moving down the hallway, then down a flight of stairs into another more dimly lit corridor.

A man stood at a doorway with his arms crossed. There was no one else in the area.

"I need to see him," Matthias said.

"I've been instructed to no longer acknowledge you as my king." He uncrossed his arms and clenched his fists at his sides. "I'm sorry, but I can't follow your orders."

"Then I'm sorry, too," Matthias said before he plunged the silver dagger into his chest. The man's eyes widened before they filled with flames and he exploded into ash.

Guess he'd been a vampire. It was surprisingly hard to tell from a distance. When I recovered from the shock of another vampire death, I grabbed Matthias's arm.

"Who's in that room?" I demanded.

"This is where we bring prisoners."

"Karen told me how you kill rogue vampires. Was she lying about that?"

Matthias's intense gaze was on me. "Would you like me to tell you she was?"

"I just want the truth."

He looked at the door. "I'm the king, so their betrayal is betrayal against me. So, yes, I carry out the execution myself, as Karen said."

My stomach turned. "You rip their hearts out with your bare hands?"

"Sometimes."

I shuddered. "That's barbaric."

"I can do many things with my hands that aren't quite as barbaric," he said, his lips curving at the sides. "As you now know."

I crossed my arms protectively in front of me. "I want to forget about that."

"All I want is for you to acknowledge that the desire you felt for me wasn't entirely forced upon you. Will you do that?"

There was no time for this. Why would he even bring it up now?

"Just say it, Jillian. You desired me then. Just as you desire me now. Admit it."

He wasn't going to do anything else until he got an answer out of me.

I bit my bottom lip. "It's not true."

"As I told you before, never play poker. It's too easy to see when you're bluffing."

He took the chain of keys off the ground, which was the only thing remaining from the guard other than a small scattering of ash, and used it to open up the door.

I gasped.

Inside the room, with his hands chained up above his head, was Declan.

—— 22

DECLAN BLINKED AGAINST THE BRIGHT LIGHT FLOOD-
ing into the dark room. Then his good eye began to grow
wider at the sight of me.

"Jill . . . my God, it's you."

I was so stunned that for a moment I couldn't think or
act. But then I quickly entered the room until I stood in
front of him. His face was bloody, but there were no cuts
as far as I could see. Whatever may have been there had
already healed and scarred. He wasn't wearing a shirt and
there was also blood on his chest, evidence of healed damage there as well.

However, he was *alive*.

"Declan." I reached up and touched his face very gently
with a trembling hand. Relief that he was still alive flooded
over me. Then I shot an angry look over my shoulder at
Matthias. "What the hell have you done to him?"

"Normal procedure for an enemy. He was detained for questioning. Although, I'm told he refused to talk."

"You told me he was dead."

"Karen told you that."

"You confirmed it."

His expression didn't change. "I needed your full attention, Jillian. Knowing your lover was still alive would have been more distracting for you than thinking he was dead."

"Release him."

"Not yet."

I looked at Declan again. They'd chained him up like an animal. And all this time I thought he'd been killed in the car accident and I'd been trying desperately to come to terms with that.

"He suffered for nearly twelve hours calling for you, but you never came to him." Karen must have been laughing at me, knowing the truth the whole time.

I didn't think of myself as a vengeful person, but I was glad the bitch was gone.

"They told me you were dead as well," Declan said and pain slid through his gaze. "The accident. I woke up here and you were gone. They said you went through the windshield and you died instantly."

"They're liars."

"I know that now."

I finished inspecting him for injuries and was relieved when I found nothing that looked major. I took a moment to gently touch his face. More confirmation he was alive and right in front of me. His eye patch had shifted since he'd been chained up so I put it back in place.

"Thank you," Declan said, then looked past me to glare fiercely at Matthias. "Who the fuck are you?"

"I'm surprised you don't already know the answer to that." Matthias entered the room to come and stand in front of Declan next to me. He studied the dhampyr's scarred face. "I am Matthias."

Declan's chains rattled as he strained against them, fury radiating through his expression. "I'm going to kill you!"

Matthias rubbed his hand over his mouth, pondering the dhampyr in front of him. "Let me guess why. Because I raped your mother?"

"You disgusting bloodsucking bastard, I'll tear your throat out."

"No, you won't. You're chained and at my mercy right now."

"It's okay," I said, my hand on Declan's chest as if shielding him from the vampire king.

Declan looked at me with confusion. "What the fuck is going on, Jill? What has he forced you to do?"

"Interesting question," Matthias said. "But there's no time for games. You need to listen to me, dhampyr, and listen well."

"Jill," Declan rasped. "You need to get out of here. Go now."

"Not yet." I glanced nervously at the open door, expecting a dozen angry vampires to arrive at any moment. "Matthias, please hurry up."

Matthias moved me out of the way and grabbed Declan's face, forcing him to look the vampire king in the eye. "What you were told about me is a lie. I didn't rape your mother. You are not my son. I may be many things, but I am not a rapist."

"You're lying." Declan tried to wrench his head away, but Matthias held him firm.

"I'm not lying. Your mother must have been taken by Monica Gray so a child dhampyr could be harvested to aid her research program."

"Dr. Gray didn't raise me."

"But she gave you to someone who could, didn't she? Someone close to her whom she trusted to keep a secret? And she's continued to experiment in vampire/human hybrids at the cost of several human lives since then."

"Women who've come to her for help."

"And she helped them by allowing them to come to term only so the dhampyr could claw its way out of its mother's fragile body. Monica would have clearly seen that it was a monster dhampyr by a simple ultrasound. She could have ended these pregnancies while there was still time to save the mother's life, but she didn't."

Declan's face remained stony. "It doesn't change who you are."

"I'm not your father."

"I know what I was told."

"You were told a lie in an attempt to make you hate me. Monica Gray has conspired to destroy me for nearly thirty years. The development of Nightshade is only her latest attempt."

"She wants to destroy all vampires, not just you."

"So she might have you believe." Matthias paced the small dark room. "But I'm not entirely convinced that's true."

"She's a good woman," Declan insisted.

"Not sure about that." I let the doubt I'd been feeling up till now show. "She's the one who gave me the fusing potion rather than the blood cleanser, remember? She didn't care if I lived or died. You knew that, too, or you never would have tried to take me out of there."

Doubt crossed Declan's expression at this reminder.

"You're the only dhampyr of your age I'm aware of," Matthias continued. "But there's another one who's just been born. A girl. My . . . *daughter.*" He hesitated after using that word. "Monica also has her. A female dhampyr child's blood is thought by some very powerful and greedy vampires to imbue true immortality. If my daughter's existence is discovered, she'll be taken and sacrificed so these vampires can drink her blood."

Declan shook his head. "You're wrong."

"I'm not wrong."

Declan's brow was deeply furrowed. What Matthias was saying was getting through to him. Maybe not entirely, but some of it was filtering in. His eye flicked to me, his expression now filled with doubt.

"I believe him," I said. "I didn't at first, but it makes sense. I feel like it's the truth and now we have to do something about it."

His gaze flashed at me and there was pain there. "He had me chained and tortured for more than a day, while letting me believe you were dead."

"You're my enemy," Matthias explained. "An enemy is rarely greeted in my kingdom with open arms. You've killed many of my people, led only by your prejudice against vampires, which has been instilled in you since birth. Your name is well known. However, I had no idea you were a dhampyr." He shook his head. "Your scars . . ."

"What about them?" Declan growled.

"If I didn't heal as I do, I would look very similar to you from all I've been through."

"Lucky for you, you don't heal like me. Wouldn't want to jeopardize that kingly face of yours." Declan glowered at him. "I don't know what I believe."

"It doesn't matter if you believe everything I've told you. The only thing that matters is my daughter. I need to get to her and her mother as soon as I can. Before it's too late."

"Carson wouldn't be a part of something like this," Declan reasoned.

"Maybe he doesn't know," I said, although I didn't entirely believe that statement.

Matthias reached up to Declan's shackles and unlocked them, using one of the keys he'd taken from the dead vampire guard. Declan's arms fell down to his sides and he slumped against me. His body felt knotted with tension and barely restrained violence.

"Are you going to be okay?" I asked, stroking his face again.

He looked at me fiercely. "They told me you were dead. I believed them."

"I know. But I'm not."

"Your blood—"

"Still deadly to vampires," Matthias said. "Everyone here insisted I kill her, but I didn't. Consider that another mark of good faith between us, since it seems to have triggered a very inconvenient rebellion against me."

"Can you walk?" I asked.

Declan nodded. "Yes."

"So you see, Jillian?" Matthias said. "I help you rescue your dhampyr, and you help me rescue mine. A fair trade?"

He sounded so calm, but I could tell he wasn't. A responsibility he'd never thought he'd have, coupled with being ousted as king by the subjects he'd ruled for three decades—well, that had to be wearing heavily on him.

That he'd tried to make me admit that I wanted him just before revealing that Declan was still alive hadn't gone unnoticed by me. It amused him to play with my emotions.

Matthias wasn't a nice guy who'd just helped me rescue Declan out of the goodness of his heart. It was at his command that Declan was chained and tortured in the first place. He was an opportunist and a manipulator. Even still, I didn't doubt his sincerity at wanting to rescue his daughter before something truly horrible happened to her.

Once Declan grew steadier on his feet after being chained up for so long, he approached Matthias and grabbed the front of his shirt, bringing their faces close together.

"If I learn you've lied to me about any of this, I will personally rip off your head with my bare hands."

"Fair enough," Matthias replied calmly.

Declan let him go, then turned and searched my expression, carefully touching my neck, which showed the signs of two vampire bites as well as Karen's attempt to strangle me. It still surprised me that someone who looked as dangerous as Declan could be so gentle.

"Did he hurt you?"

"No," I replied, my throat tight. "He actually saved my life."

"And you believe what he's said."

I nodded. "I do."

"We have to leave immediately, before we're discovered," Matthias said, an unpleasant edge to his voice. "Some of my people will need time to sort out their issues before I can return. There are places I can go aboveground where they won't find me."

"Because if they find you—" Declan began.

"They'll kill me. Or, at least, they'll try to."

"You don't seem too concerned."

"I prefer to think about one problem at a time. And the

problem at hand is getting to my daughter." His smile faded and a shadow of desperation slid behind his gaze. "Will you help me?"

Declan considered the vampire who stood before him. Comparing the two men, it looked as if the more muscular Declan would have no problem in a fight to the death with Matthias. However, I wouldn't want to put money on it. Matthias was lethal and ancient, and I'd seen him kill without any remorse. Both were very different, but very dangerous men.

"I need answers, too," Declan said. "So, yes, I'll help you."

"Then come with me." Matthias turned and left the room, walking briskly down the hallway. "It's nearly three in the morning. There isn't a great deal of time before dawn. This must be finished by then."

I remembered what Declan told me about vampires and sunlight. The myth was that sunlight would kill a vampire, but in reality, the sunlight caused them to go blind. There was no sunlight underground. It would have made this real estate very desirable. Other than that, from what I'd seen of Matthias's kingdom, he'd spent a lot of money on making it extremely livable.

We reached a large silver door with a keypad next to it. Matthias punched in a series of numbers and the doors opened.

"This elevator will take us to the surface," he said. "All other exits will be guarded right now to prevent me from leaving. I'm a very firm believer in having alternate escape routes for just such an occasion."

Declan was silent, warily watching the man he had believed all his life to be his father. I had no idea what he was thinking right now. But then his gaze turned to me and his expression relaxed a little.

My eyes stung with tears. "I'm so glad you're not dead."

His grip on me tightened. "The feeling's mutual."

"How adorable," Matthias said dryly, watching us as he leaned against the back of the elevator as it began to rise. "You know, the three of us could have a great deal of fun together if this all works out."

I glared at him, but stayed silent.

The way Matthias looked at me was unnerving. Like he knew what I was thinking. Like he assumed I wouldn't be able to put the moments we'd spent together out of my mind. He was convinced I wanted him. But he'd *made* me feel that way. It hadn't been real.

I was the first to look away.

"I don't understand how you can be near her," Declan said, choosing to ignore the generous offer of a threesome. "Doesn't Jill's blood affect you?"

"Yes, of course. But I already knew about her before she arrived. I was ready to withstand her many . . . charms."

Declan frowned. "How did you know?"

"Noah," I said, the taste of his name like bile on my tongue. "He's been Matthias's informant all this time. He's the one who gave word that we left Silver Ridge the other night."

Declan's eye widened and fury flashed across his expression. "That's impossible."

"Don't blame Noah," Matthias said. "I had him captured shortly after he began working for Carson Reyes and let him know in no uncertain terms that I would expect answers from him about the research they did there. I never trusted him entirely—which is why I felt the need to test the formula before I believed the claims about it. However, Noah was very helpful when it came to information about Jillian since she arrived in your little town earlier this week. He disagreed with much of what the research program stands for."

Declan looked stunned. "I can't believe this."

"And Karen, the blood servant who hurt you at the gas station the other day," I said. "She's the one who was the original Nightshade agent. But she switched sides. She tried to kill me."

Declan's eye narrowed. "Where is she now?"

"Dead," I said. "Matthias . . . he saved me from her."

Declan took a moment to let this sink in. "You'd save a woman who could mean your ultimate destruction?"

Matthias smiled. "I guess I'm simply drawn to black-haired human beauties who've gotten themselves in way over their heads. It's my weakness."

The elevator jerked to a halt as we reached our destination. The doors opened into what looked like a cave. The temperature was hot, much hotter than underground, which was well air-conditioned. Karen hadn't called it a gilded cage without reason. It might not have been fresh air down there, but it was the next best thing.

Without waiting for us, Matthias began walking out of the cave and into the desert. The night sky overhead was a canvas of black velvet studded with stars and a crescent moon.

A couple hundred yards away, there were two cars hidden by beige tarps. Matthias pulled the protective layer off one of them to reveal an SUV.

"Do you know how to jump-start a car?" he asked. "Didn't have much of a chance to grab the keys before leaving."

"I'll handle it." Declan set to work.

I felt Matthias's gaze heavily on me again and it made me uncomfortable. He wasn't close. He was currently twelve feet away from my scent, but it felt as if he was standing only inches from me.

The car roared to life a few moments later, thanks to Declan fiddling with some wires under the dashboard. He was a pro at grand-theft auto.

Matthias approached and opened the passenger-side door. "After you, Jillian."

As I was about to get in, his hand curled around my waist and he pulled me against him so he could whisper in my ear.

"Just remember my promise," he said. "This changes nothing."

I pushed away from him and got into the car. He closed the door behind me.

His promise. I wanted to pretend I didn't know what he was talking about, but I did. It was the only promise he'd made to me since we'd met.

"One day soon you will come to me again and I won't have to use my control in order to make you beg me to fuck you."

The memory was now a distraction I didn't want or need.

My priorities had shifted. Before I was all about myself—finding a solution to the poison in my veins. As far as I knew, it still could kill me. I hadn't been stricken by any debilitating pain since nearly dying from the fusing potion. My blood had changed. I didn't know if there was anything I could do about this or if it was too late for me and this was how I'd be until the day I died.

For all I knew, that day was today. I felt like I'd been on the verge of death since leaving the office on Tuesday— my temp job answering phones seemed like it belonged to someone else's life now—and my fateful meeting with both Carl Anderson, the parachemist, and Declan Reyes, the dhampyr assassin. It was the moment my life changed forever, and I'd been worried about my own life, my future, ever since then.

But now I was worried about someone I'd never even known about before today. A baby who'd allegedly just been born, whose chance at life was truly in jeopardy.

As Declan drove through the desert, finally bringing the car onto a paved road headed toward Silver Ridge, I knew then that despite who her father was and what might stand in our way in order to get to her, I'd be willing to give my life in order to save that baby's.

It was kind of funny, actually. I'd never really been the maternal type.

23

THERE WAS SOMEONE WAITING FOR US WHEN WE arrived at Carson's house. Noah stood in the shadows, wringing his hands nervously as he watched our approach.

"I messaged him that we were on our way," Matthias explained. "He can help us."

Declan increased his pace so he easily arrived first. He grabbed Noah and pushed him up against the wall.

"You've been working with Matthias all this time?" he growled. "And you said nothing to me?"

"Dec . . . I can explain—" Noah began.

"He's our enemy."

"We don't have time for this," I said tightly.

"And what did Matthias promise you to gain your loyalty for selling us out?" Declan asked, not loosening his grip on his former friend. "Did he promise to sire you? Make you into a vampire so you can live forever?" Declan shook him. "He did, didn't he? Haven't you learned anything since coming here?"

"Hey, take it easy. You're going to hurt him." I grabbed his arm until he looked at me and his tense expression relaxed a fraction.

His jaw clenched. "Noah's involvement in this could have gotten both of us killed."

"I know. I'm not trying to justify what he did, but it's in the past now."

Declan glanced at Noah again before finally releasing his grip. "We'll talk about this later."

Noah shot me a worried look. He was looking in the wrong direction if he wanted total forgiveness and a warm hug.

"Noah," I said, "You didn't tell Matthias everything, did you? He didn't know Declan's a dhampyr or he was allegedly his son."

Noah shook his head. "Matthias wanted to know what Dr. Gray was up to. That's all. I didn't elaborate much beyond the Nightshade formula and what was up with you."

I looked at him dryly. "Yeah, thanks for that."

"There was a great deal more you knew that would have helped me immensely, Noah," Matthias said. "We'll have to discuss your shortcomings later."

His tone was even, but his message came through loud and clear for Noah, who flinched. He now had a vampire angry at him for not saying enough and a dhampyr furious at him for saying anything at all.

"Yeah . . . uh . . . later." Noah cleared his throat. "Speaking of Nightshade . . . you're feeling better, Jill? Last time I saw you, you were at death's door."

I grimaced at the memory. "Nobody answered when I rang the bell. Still breathing. For now."

"I've been reading through a ton of files since you left," Noah said. "Hacked into all the top-secret archives. I know even more things I'm not supposed to know."

"Do you know where my daughter is being kept?" Matthias asked tightly.

Noah nodded with a sharp jab of his head. "Dr. Gray set up a nursery downstairs."

"And Catherine? Her mother?"

Noah's lips thinned and he shook his head once. "I'm sorry, she died just after the baby was born."

A shadow of grief flitted over Matthias's face. "She never should have run from me."

A shiver went down my arms. "I'm so sorry." I looked at Noah. "But the baby's okay?"

"She is. Currently sleeping like a . . . well, a *baby*. On the other hand, there's another dhampyr baby downstairs that took a couple fingers off one of the guards earlier today. He's lucky that's all that happened," Noah made a face. "Once a newborn gets a taste of human blood—hell, even a good sniff—it's usually an automatic death sentence."

"Sounds adorable," I said with a shudder.

Noah's eyes flicked to Matthias. "But yours . . . well, she's not like that of course. No sharp teeth. Just gums. And diapers. And, uh—"

"Let's go." Declan keyed in a series of numbers into the side lock. For half a second, I expected an alarm to go off, but there was only silence. I followed him through the door and down the hall inside.

"Dec," Noah said under his breath. "There's something you need to know. Something I found out by reading through more of the files."

"What?" he snapped, glaring at him.

"It's about your mother."

Declan stopped walking. "What about her?"

Noah looked as if he'd aged from mid-twenties to mid-forties since the last time I'd seen him. Whatever he'd been reading had worn heavily on him—not to mention the revelation of his being Matthias's part-time informant.

"I found files that looked like they'd been duplicated and adjusted. The first set was what I'd already seen. Your father, uh, *you know who*," he nodded at Matthias, "and what he allegedly did to your mother before she was found and hospitalized for the remainder of her pregnancy."

"Matthias isn't Declan's father," I said.

"You're right. He isn't. That was added later. A woman named Chloe was listed as the mother."

"It's a lie. I don't remember any Chloe from that long ago." Matthias's gaze flicked to me. "Just because I've had many lovers, doesn't mean I forget them."

God, how many women—and men—had been in his bed during his lifetime? Thousands? Tens of thousands? More?

"You don't remember Chloe because she didn't exist. She was only a cover for the real mother's name." Noah swallowed. *"Monica."*

It took me a moment to make the connection. But when I did, I literally gasped out loud. "You're not saying that Dr. Gray—"

"—is Declan's real mother," Noah finished for me. "Yeah. It's in the files, and it's one I'm sure she probably thinks was destroyed."

Declan stood in silence for a long moment, next to the house he'd lived in for the past six years. "She can't be my mother. She's alive."

"Not all dhampyr births end in death for the mother. That's only a definite outcome in the monster births."

Noah grimaced. "There were pictures with the files of the corpses after the dhamps escaped their mothers' bodies. Nothing I want to see again outside of old sci-fi movies starring Sigourney Weaver."

"But Catherine died." Matthias said the name of the mother of his child tightly.

Noah cleared his throat nervously. "I . . . don't think she died from childbirth."

Matthias's lips thinned. "Monica has much to answer for."

Catherine had been killed after giving birth? What was Dr. Gray doing here? Her focus had been on helping others through her research. Did that now include murder?

I grabbed hold of Declan's hand and looked up at him. "It doesn't matter who your mother is."

"It *does* matter," he said softly. "If Monica Gray is my real mother, why would they have to make up lies that have haunted me my entire life? Why would they have told me my mother died giving birth to me and that her condition was caused by a violent rape? Dr. Gray's been around since I was a child, and she's barely looked at me except to pass some unsatisfied judgment. But she's my mother? Carson never said a word to me about this."

"Maybe he didn't know the truth." What kind of a man would let his "adopted" son believe such horrible things all his life?

This hadn't been an easy couple of days for Declan and he didn't even have the serum to help dampen his emotions against all of this. My heart ached for him, but I didn't know what I could do to help him through this.

After another moment, Declan shook his head as if to clear it.

"We need to keep moving," he said. Then he continued walking through the large house until we got to the staircase, and went single file down it. The lights were off downstairs.

"The baby was this way," Noah whispered. "I'm not a big fan of the thought of kidnapping, but in this case, I think it's definitely justified. I just read all about some vampire society Dr. Gray's involved with. The baby's not safe here."

"I knew it," Matthias bit out, fury entering his previously controlled expression. "The reasoning behind her dhampyr research program. She's trying to supply the Amarantos Society with blood for their immortality rituals. And now she has my daughter."

I looked at Declan, who appeared confused by all this. Then his expression hardened.

"There's no question that we need to save this child," he said.

I nodded and my heart swelled for him. He was willing to put his own prejudices aside to do the right thing tonight. Helping Matthias went against everything he'd ever been led to believe. If he was still on the serum, he'd never be able to see that this was the right thing to do.

But if it was true and Dr. Gray was helping the Amarantos Society, why would she create Nightshade—something that would kill the very same vampires?

We turned down the long hallway I remembered from the other day. The one leading to the observation room where I'd been placed in with the vampire for an experiment to see if my blood was as lethal as they thought it was. There were several other rooms along the hall. I stopped at a door when I felt as if someone was staring at me. A small window showed large black eyes set into the pale white face of a dhampyr, who stood closely up against the door watching us pass.

"Is that the baby you were talking about?" I asked, a shiver coursing down my spine at the dead look in its eyes. "The one who bit the fingers off the guard?"

Noah looked at the holding cell. "Yeah. Cute, right?"

"Not even slightly."

"She's keeping my daughter in this section with that *thing* close by?" Matthias sounded disgusted. He glared at me. "Why are you smiling?"

My cheeks were shaky with the apprehension I felt, but I was definitely smiling at him. "You'll make an interesting daddy. Overprotective, probably."

His harsh expression softened. "My daughter will never want for anything."

"Just hold off on the pony for a while, okay? She'll get spoiled."

"Here it is," Noah said when we reached a door thirty feet down the long hallway. Then he froze in his tracks. "Shit. Somebody's coming."

A breath caught in my chest.

A guard turned the corner up ahead, moving toward us, although he seemed completely at ease at the sight of Declan and Noah. He had a foam cup of coffee in one hand.

"Don't tell anyone I left my post for a minute," he said. "Had to get some caffeine. It's been a hell of a night."

"You're telling me," Noah said nervously.

"Are you guarding the new dhampyr baby?" Declan asked.

"Both of 'em. However, one gets a bottle when it cries. The other gets a tranq dart." He laughed.

Declan punched him in the face and the coffee went flying. The guard shook his head, then began reaching for his gun, but Declan grabbed the front of his shirt and slammed his head against the concrete wall. The guard dropped to the ground, unconscious.

He glanced at me. "Never liked the guy. Total slacker."

"Can you open this door?" Matthias asked, stepping over the guard.

"Yeah." Noah had to step over the body in order to punch in a bunch of numbers. Matthias grabbed hold of the handle and opened the door, crossing the small room in an instant to get to the crib against the wall in the otherwise undecorated room. My heart pounded wildly, but I followed him inside.

Matthias pulled out a teddy bear—the entire contents of the crib.

"Where's the baby?" I asked, my stomach sinking.

He looked at me with knowledge filling his gaze. "This was a trap."

I shook my head. "It can't be."

"They knew we were coming."

I looked over at Noah, who stood at the doorway.

He looked stricken. "I didn't say anything. I swear. She was in here earlier. I don't know where they would have taken her." He turned to look at something down the hall and he raised his hands up to his sides. "No . . . please wait. I have to—"

I heard a gunshot and Noah staggered backward. He turned to look at Matthias and me with wide eyes. There was now a red patch on his white T-shirt. He fell to his knees and then dropped fully to the ground, gasping for breath.

"Noah!" I yelled, panic ripping through me. "Declan!"

But Declan didn't move from where he stood in the hallway to get out of the line of fire, and his gaze was fixed on someone approaching. He held his hands clenched at his sides, a look of fury on his face.

"What the fuck is going on here?" he demanded.

"Declan—" Carson came into view of the doorway. "Just remain calm."

"Why would you shoot Noah? He's unarmed."

"He's a traitor working for vampires, stealing our information so he can give it to them. This is how we deal with traitors."

I ran toward the entrance of the room. Matthias put his hand on my shoulder to prevent me from entering the hallway completely.

I looked at him. "Do something."

He shook his head. "First I need to know where my daughter is."

Carson's gaze flicked to me and widened with surprise. "You're still alive. The fusing potion worked."

"You told me it was a blood cleanser," I said, a ghost of the anger I'd felt after that little incident still haunting me.

His expression looked strained. "It had to be done. You were unwilling to help. Sometimes hard decisions must be made to serve the greater good."

"'The greater good'?" Declan repeated. "Is that what this is?"

"Of course." Carson's words were earnest and edged in pain. "Everything I've done has been to help protect humans from the threat of vampires. You know that."

"I thought I did."

"Don't doubt me now, son."

"*Son*," Declan said bitterly, pacing a few steps down the hallway and then back again. I moved closer so I could see. "Is that what I am to you?"

"Yes, of course you are."

"Is it true? Is Dr. Gray is my real mother?"

Carson looked surprised, then cast a stern look down at the injured and pale Noah. He struggled to breathe as he pressed his hand against his gunshot wound to try and stop the flow of blood. I desperately wanted to go to him, to help him, but Matthias's grip on my shoulder held me in place.

"No matter who you are or where you came from, you're my son and an integral part of this mission. Don't allow yourself to be swayed by the opinions of others."

Declan raised his hand and pointed at Matthias. "He's not my real father. That was a lie you've told me my entire life so I'd hate him and follow your orders to kill other vampires without question."

Carson's jaw tightened. "You're not taking your serum anymore, are you?"

"Is it that easy to tell?"

"Yes. Your mind is unclear, therefore your choices are becoming erratic, including bringing that *vampire*"—the word was spat out as if it was a curse—"into my laboratory. The new serum I've been developing for you is finally ready. While untested, I truly believe it'll prevent any slip-ups like this in the future. How long has it been since your last dosage?"

Declan's eye flicked to me before returning to his adoptive father. "I'm not taking the serum any more. Or the new one, either."

"Declan, you're not thinking straight. You must take it or you will begin to act more like one of the other dhampyrs. Your hungers will rule you."

"It's been almost three days and I feel fine without it."

"No, you don't. You're struggling with this." Carson shook his head. "I know it's difficult for you to accept, but the serum is vital for your survival and your ability to not unleash the violence inside of you on innocents."

I glared at him. "Just leave him alone for once in his life, will you?"

Carson's eyes narrowed. "This has nothing to do with you."

My disdain for the man who'd oppressed the real Declan all these years sped right past the fear I felt at being caught trying to save Matthias's daughter. "You brainwashed him all these years to take that serum, so you could make him into your puppet. Well it's over. He's going to make his own decisions from now on."

"That's not possible, I'm afraid. My number one priority is protecting human life. And that includes making sure Declan is not a threat."

"You never even gave him a chance."

"Another successful dhampyr from years ago was the most dangerous creature around. He killed many innocents and had to be put down like a rabid dog. If he'd been put on the serum, either of his own free will or forcefully, it would have saved many people's lives. Trust me, Jillian. I know what's best for Declan. I've *always* known what's best for Declan."

"You suck at being a father."

"Thank you for your opinion," he replied tightly, then nodded at a guard entering the far end of the hallway.

Declan turned and stormed at the guard, getting twenty feet before I heard a grunt, and then Declan stopped moving. He pulled a small dart out of his shoulder and threw it to the side. Then he slammed his fist into the guard's face, sending the guard down hard.

Declan glanced over his shoulder. "What the fuck did he just shoot me with?"

"It's a tranquilizer," Carson said, walking down the hall toward him. "It will help to allow me to do what I must."

Declan collapsed to his knees in front of the dhampyr's holding cell two doors down from where I stood, then braced his hands against the floor, his breathing labored. "Don't do this, Carson."

I tried to run toward him, but Matthias held me back.

"He has a gun," he reminded me.

"I have to help him."

"You can't stop this."

"No, but—but *you* can. We can get your daughter later. Why aren't you doing anything to help?"

His expression was stony. "I can't."

"You can't? You mean you don't want to." I tried to push away from him, but he held tight to my wrist. I almost broke my arm trying to get away from him to go to Declan's side. But all I could do is watch.

Carson nodded at someone else who'd appeared in the hall behind Declan. The man in a white lab coat approached with a syringe filled with a light green liquid.

"No!" I yelled.

"Do it," Carson snapped.

The man in the lab coat reminiscent of Anderson's injected Declan in the side of his neck.

24

CARSON CROUCHED DOWN IN FRONT OF DECLAN. "Thanks to this new scrum, you'll feel control again. Permanently. No more three hour doses for you to deal with— this one shot is all that's needed." He nodded as if he was reassuring himself of what he'd just done. "You'll thank me when you start to feel better. More like yourself again."

"Go to hell," Declan growled, but then his rapid breathing began to slow. He looked down the hall toward me, and I watched as his strained, furious gaze began to flatten out. The next moment, the tranquilizer took over completely, and he crumpled to the floor unconscious.

Whatever fury Declan just lost, I gained. I was livid— so angry that Carson would do this that I was literally shaking. No free will. Just a perfect soldier ready to carry out any order his father figure gave him. Now and in the future.

"You son of a bitch," I snapped. "How could you do this to him?"

"I value Declan too much to lose him." Carson looked over toward me. "He's dangerous without the serum whether he wants to admit it or not. But it's okay now."

"It's not okay. This is as fucking far from okay as I can deal with."

"It's done?" another voice asked. It was Dr. Gray. I felt Matthias tense up next to me. I was furious with him—why hadn't he helped? He was a fucking vampire king with mental control abilities and he hadn't even moved an inch.

"I'm going to kill her," Matthias growled under his breath.

Finally, some kind of tangible reaction. I was beginning to think he had slipped into a coma.

But then he let out a shallow gasp when she came into view holding in her arms a baby wrapped in a thin pink blanket. A hulking, armed guard was at her side.

Matthias's daughter was being cradled by his enemy.

"Yes, it's done," Carson replied. I assumed she was asking about Declan's new permanent serum. I cast a worried look at his unconscious form. I wanted to go to him, but I stayed right where I was.

Carson's gaze flicked to the holding cell for the monster dhampyr down the hall since it sounded as if the creature had thrown itself at the door. He swore under his breath. "We've disturbed it."

"Deal with it," Dr. Gray instructed curtly. "Now. There's no more time to waste."

"Deal with it," Carson repeated. "Now?"

"Yes, now. Kill it. Put it out of its misery. We'll try again another time. I can handle this." She entered the room, passing Matthias and myself in the doorway and sidestepping Noah's body to enter. She hadn't even looked at where Declan lay at Carson's feet. I cast a last look at him before I turned my attention to Dr. Gray. I looked up at Matthias's tense face as he glared at the woman who'd stolen his child, now standing within an arm's reach of him.

"Isn't she beautiful?" Dr. Gray asked, gazing down at the bundle in her arms before gently laying the baby down in the crib.

"What have you done, Monica?" Matthias's jaw was tight.

"Long time since I last saw you face-to-face. You've been keeping a very low profile, haven't you?" Her gaze flicked to me. "Doesn't Jillian have any effect on you at all?"

"Look at me, Monica."

Her lips curved. "And let you attempt to influence me? I don't think so. I would never in a million years look a vampire like you directly in the eyes."

Fear flooded me at the sight of the woman I'd genuinely liked until she'd tricked me into taking the fusing potion. Until I'd found out her ulterior motives for everything she'd done. Until I'd found out she was Declan's real mother and had hidden that fact from her son, instead allowing him to be used as a weapon to kill vampires.

I hated her.

She was seemingly without a worry about the danger of being so close to Matthias, whose hands were fisted at his sides, lips curled back to expose his sharp fangs.

I waited for him to reach out and snap her neck as he'd done with Karen. But he didn't. He didn't move. What was he waiting for?

Maybe he knew that she wasn't as helpless as she looked. Sure, he could kill her, but there were guards. Security systems. I didn't know what other safety precautions they took here, but I imagined it was enough to keep a small community of researchers safe from a clan of vampires only a few miles away.

But I didn't know for sure. And not knowing what was going to happen next was torture.

Carson didn't enter the room. He was following Dr. Gray's orders to kill the monster dhampyr. The silence outside was deafening.

I couldn't see Declan in the hallway from here. But I could see Noah. And blood. Lots of blood.

I had no idea what to do, what to say to make this better.

It was too late for better. All I could hope for now was that it wouldn't get any worse.

Dr. Gray eyed me. "My goodness. The Nightshade has certainly settled in, hasn't it? The poison is so fixed in your body that it literally changed the pigment of your hair and eyes. Fascinating."

"You owe me a new wardrobe. I think I'm a winter now."

She smiled. "It suits you. The blond made you look much too inconsequential and harmless. Then again, that was a nice camouflage."

I clenched my hands at my sides. "The fusing potion you gave me nearly killed me."

"It had to be done."

That sure as hell wasn't much of an apology.

"It didn't even do what you wanted it to," I said. "Matthias didn't bite me."

"Go to her," Dr. Gray said to the vampire king, choosing now to ignore me. "I know you want to gaze at the face of your daughter, even if it's just for a little while."

He didn't budge. "What did you do to Catherine?"

"She was very angry with me near the end when she

knew I'd be taking the baby. It's sad, really. When I had her brought here originally, she was ready to help. She was convinced you were a beast who needed to be destroyed. A lover's spat, I assume?"

"She caught me with someone else in my bed. She didn't like it. But my hungers must be satisfied on a regular basis or there would have been a heavier price to pay than dealing with a jealous woman." He sounded certain, but his tone did hold regret.

"Mmm. In any case, she wasn't executed if that's what you think. She was shot by a guard when she tried to escape with the baby. It couldn't be helped."

"You heartless bitch."

"I didn't pull the trigger, Matthias."

"You may as well have."

"You want to tear out my throat, don't you?" she asked. "Try it. Both you and your daughter will be dead before a drop of my blood hits the floor. And you know it, don't you?"

An empty threat? Or a promise?

I didn't know. But Matthias didn't budge. He knew her—from a long time ago. He knew what she was capable of. If she'd left a vampire king known to tear the hearts of traitors from their chests with so few options at the moment, it didn't put my mind at ease that we were all going to get out of here alive.

My gaze moved to Noah again to see that his eyes were now glassy and his inhales were short, jagged breaths. He'd lost a lot of blood, so much of it pooled next to him that I felt a fresh panic surge through me.

"Noah needs medical assistance," I said, my voice strained. "Please."

Dr. Gray shook her head. "He chose his fate by helping Matthias. There is no other end for him than this. Let him suffer." She looked at the guard stationed outside the door who'd glanced in at us. "That's an order."

He didn't budge, his expression revealed nothing but obedience.

Would Declan still be willing to help us when he woke up? Or had the serum changed him back to someone only able to follow orders and be obedient, too? What was taking Carson so long? Why did the dhampyr have to be taken care of right now?

Dr. Gray gazed in the direction of the crib. "She's a miracle, really. You should be very proud of yourself, Matthias."

"You need to release my daughter into my care and let me leave here in peace," he said. "There doesn't have to be any further bloodshed tonight. And believe me, there will be if you don't stop this right now."

"How do you feel, Jillian?" Dr. Gray asked me, switching her attention again so she could ignore the vampire king. "Now that the Nightshade has worked its way completely into your system?"

"I feel pissed off," I snapped. "To put it extremely fucking mildly."

"Physically, though," she said. "Are you running a fever? Has there been any more nausea? Joint aches? Pain of any other kind?"

"No."

"There may be in the future. The fuser may not last forever, and when your blood cells begin to separate from the formula, this may cause . . . severe complications."

A chill went down my spine. "Like what?"

"It's very likely you'll die from it. Despite how you may feel right now, you're not out of the woods yet. Nightshade is untested except on you. The effects on a human body are still unknown. I assume it's only a matter of time before it begins to break down. For something so powerful to kill a vampire, I can only imagine what it will do to a human if given enough time."

My heart raced. "You're trying to scare me."

"Is it working?"

"Yes. But since I know you're a fucking liar, I'm having a really hard time believing anything that comes out of your mouth."

She gave me a patient smile—seemingly totally at ease with this situation; a dying man outside the doorway, a motionless vampire king who looked like he wanted to decapitate her where she stood, and a poisoned human woman who hated every single moment of this standoff. "I'm not lying about this. I can help you, though, by giving you regular doses of the fuser and monitoring your vitals."

"In return for what?"

"You will work for me as an assassin—a vampire hunter who doesn't need to know how to use any weapon other than her own body. They'll be drawn to you like bees to pollen." She glanced at my injured throat. "Just because Matthias can resist you doesn't mean others can."

"This was going to be Karen's job?" Matthias asked.

"That's right."

"Karen's dead."

Dr. Gray didn't look surprised by this. "Karen was strong of body, but weak of mind. Her end was not unexpected."

"You're kind of a heartless bitch, aren't you?" I said.

She smiled. "Women who have power are often thought of as bitches by those who don't understand."

"You've done all this to kill vampires?" Matthias asked.

"Of course."

"If that's the case, then what about the Amarantos Society?" he asked. "You're one of their human members, aren't you?"

She looked at him sharply. "Who told you that?"

It was beginning to make some small amount of sense to me. Matthias might be concerned for his daughter's life, but he wasn't afraid to take deadly force when necessary. Even when it wasn't necessary. He wanted answers—important answers that went higher than just personal gain or loss. Answers Dr. Gray couldn't give him if he killed her.

"Humans are allowed entry, but only those associated with high-level members. You've been attempting to create a female dhampyr for years in order to supply them for their immortality rituals, haven't you? And they've been very patient with you."

"It's important to have powerful friends. And when one does make friends, one will do anything to help them. Like your brother."

"What about him?" he growled.

"You stole his throne."

"He was a monster who had to be controlled." Matthias drew in a breath. "Wait a minute. It's him, isn't it? Kristoff is your connection to the Amarantos Society."

She gave him a wistful smile. "He'll be restored to his rightful place now that you're gone."

I watched her carefully, her body language, the joy and determination that lit up her face when she spoke about Kristoff. I stifled a gasp as I made the connections, like puzzle pieces in my mind.

"Kristoff—" I said. "He's—he's Declan's real father, isn't he?"

Her eyes narrowed on me. There was only a short pause before she answered. "Yes, he is."

"Did he rape you?" Part of me was willing to be sympathetic to someone who'd gone through abuse. There could be reasons why she had turned into a power-hungry bitch. But my sympathy didn't last long.

She let out a short bark of laughter. "Of course not. He was my lover. I gave him my blood and he offered to give me everything else in return, including immortality. That is, until Matthias trapped him away somewhere— somewhere I couldn't find him. Kristoff deserves to be king again. And he *will* be king again. I'll see to it personally."

Matthias stared at her blankly for a few long moments before he began to laugh. "Oh, Monica, you're absolutely precious. And what do you think will happen when and if Kristoff is released and restored to his full strength after thirty years of imprisonment? That he'll take you as his lover again? I hate to break it to you, but you have the body and face of a sixty-year-old woman. Not to his tastes, I'm afraid. At thirty, you were already too old for him. Even if he gave you immortality, you would remain frozen as this haggard witch for all eternity."

Anger shadowed Dr. Gray's face and she clenched her hands at her sides. "He'll reward me for my devotion to him. Especially when I offer up your daughter to help him regain his strength."

It was all she'd needed to say to snap Matthias's thin veneer of control. He'd held himself back until now, but she'd finally crossed the line.

Matthias flew at her, grabbing her tightly and slamming her against the wall. "I'll kill you first."

The guard stormed in and used a taser to get Matthias to release his grip. He staggered backward and fell to the ground, twitching from the electricity that coursed through his body. Dr. Gray brushed herself off and composed herself again.

I couldn't believe it had been that easy to stop him. What was going on here?

Dr. Gray glanced at me and smiled at my confusion. "This is the floor where all of our dhampyrs are kept. All of our vampire prisoners are brought here as well. Every wall is infused with silver. It works best on vampires—weakens them. Perhaps Matthias didn't want you to know that he's no stronger than a human male here. He's currently powerless."

Silver walls. I looked around at the shiny surfaces that I'd barely noticed since entering here. It was the reason he hadn't done anything. Because he *couldn't* do anything that wouldn't get him and his daughter killed.

Matthias and I exchanged a glance before he looked away. "Enough of this, Monica."

"Yes, I agree," she said. "Enough. I was ready to give you a pleasant enough death. Look at Jillian. She's lovely, isn't she? Not who I'd originally planned to use against you, but she would have served her purpose well enough. It doesn't take a great deal of talent or strength to be a meal for a vampire when one has a lovely body and face. But you refused this gift."

Matthias shakily pushed himself to his feet. "Death is not a gift."

Dr. Gray crossed her arms. "I'm glad you didn't taste her. I'm glad you're still alive."

Matthias cocked his head to the side, now bemused, despite the silver that currently helped to imprison him. "Trying to mend ways between us? It's a little late for that, I'm afraid."

"You produced a perfect dhampyr female. That means you have something special inside of you." She approached him and drew a finger down his chest, not stopping at the waistband of his pants as she cupped him. "I can use you in further reproductive testing. I'd say, a year at the most and I'll have all the answers I need. Then I'll lock you away like you've done to Kristoff and let you wither and fade with no blood or sex to fuel you. Thirty years of solitude in a locked silver box should be enough to drive you completely insane, wouldn't you say?"

What was taking Declan so long to wake up? Where the hell was Carson? Why wouldn't he be here right now, side by side with his vampire-researching gal pal, Dr. Gray? What would they both say if they heard Dr. Gray's plans? Everything she'd done up till now, everything she'd done for the last thirty years, had been in an effort to kill Matthias and have Kristoff put back in place on his throne.

Her devotion to the ex–vampire king was seriously insane.

"I hold your daughter's life in my hands and you know it." She walked a slow circle around Matthias. "You're powerless now and getting a taste of how Kristoff would have felt as you passed judgment on him. Your own brother. Perhaps you should have killed him when you had the chance."

Matthias's jaw tensed. "I tried. He wouldn't die."

"The Amarantos ritual," she murmured. "Are you saying it worked?"

"All I know is when I sank a silver dagger into his heart, it did nothing but slow him down."

I inhaled sharply. The immortality ritual. Kristoff drank the blood. But Matthias drank it, too. What did that mean? Was he immortal? Both of them?

"This is very good to know. I know he'll regain his strength quickly when he's released." She exhaled and it sounded like a sigh of relief. Had she thought it was a possibility that Kristoff was completely gone? That she'd been holding on to a pipe dream all these years? "Now, you'll have to come with my guard and we'll fit you with a nice set of silver handcuffs. You understand we must take precautions with you. You'll make an excellent stud. I think I can create many dhampyr sacrifices, thanks to you."

"I'm no one's slave. I'm a king."

"Not anymore."

He was silent for a moment, his expression stony. "Will you let me say good-bye to Jillian before you take me away?"

She cocked her head. "How romantic. If I didn't need her for other reasons, I might have made her the first incubator for your future spawn."

Matthias turned to me and closed the distance between us in two steps, his gaze intense and without even a glimmer of humor.

I wanted to pound my fists into his chest and wake him from whatever stupor he'd fallen into. The silver walls shouldn't mean anything. He was a vampire. Dr. Gray was only a human. Why wasn't he fighting this? He was just going to accept this—why? Because he feared he wouldn't be able to protect his daughter?

I shook my head, my chest tight as my loose hold on hope began to slip away completely. "It can't end like this."

Fight this, I thought, flicking a look at the large guard with the taser. *Do something. Don't give up.*

"You need to promise me to look after my daughter," he said quietly, glancing toward the crib. "Don't let any harm come to her."

I didn't know how I could promise that, but I knew I had to. "Yes, of course. I promise. But, Matthias, you need to—"

He took my hands in his. "I didn't want it to end this way tonight if I had a choice, but I always make sure to have a Plan B. And it will serve me well. Better even than I thought it would." He glanced at the crib and at the baby whose face he hadn't yet seen up close. "She's beautiful, isn't she?"

"She is."

"You're beautiful, too, Jillian." His mouth curled a little at the side. Then he leaned closer and whispered something in my ear.

I frowned. "What are you—"

But before I could say anything else, I felt his mouth against my throat and the sharp sting as his fangs sank into my flesh.

25

"NO! MATTHIAS, DON'T!"

I tried to stop him, tried to push him away, but it was too late. His bite had temporarily paralyzed me. My blood spilled into his mouth and he drank quickly and eagerly before he was yanked away from me by the guard. I felt the blood oozing down the side of my neck. He'd drank so greedily that the dark blood ran over his bottom lip and onto his chin.

He touched his chin and then looked at the blood on his fingertips.

"Just as I knew it would be," he said, meeting my gaze. "Delicious."

Before I could say anything, shout anything, scream anything, he convulsed in pain. The fire erupted, quickly consuming him, and he vanished in a cloud of ash.

My chest constricted. "Matthias!"

But it was too late. He was gone. But—no. He—he took

part in his brother's ritual. The immortality ritual. Yet, my blood still worked. He was gone.

The silver—had it been enough to counteract the ritual? His immortality?

Dr. Gray swore and glared at me. "You killed him."

I was in shock. I couldn't believe what had just happened and so quickly. He knew what could happen if he drank from me and he did it anyway. Why? So Dr. Gray wouldn't have power over him? He didn't want her to use him for her dhampyr experiments. I couldn't say I blamed him, but why did he have to die? There had to be another answer. He could have stopped her. He could have killed her. I knew he could have.

But he didn't.

He said he'd lived for four hundred years, but now he was gone. And it was because of my blood.

"I only did what you wanted me to," I choked out. "Matthias is dead because of your precious fucking Nightshade."

She smacked me hard across the left side of my face, making my ears ring and pain burst through my face, but then she slowly appeared to regain control over herself.

"Matthias was meant to die," she said, then nodded toward Noah. "Much like that one is. I knew it, but I tried to fight it after everything was already in place. And it all turned out the way it was supposed to. Do you see that it's all fate?"

My eyes burned with tears. "All I see is a woman who's made some really bad choices in her life."

Her gaze flicked back to me. "No. I'm a warrior in this fight. And so are you."

"A warrior."

"Yes. Like Amazons." She slid her fingers over my bleeding throat while I stood there frozen, still in shock.

She smiled as she painted her nose and forehead with my unnaturally dark blood like a tribal chief. "It's interesting how humans can't smell what vampires can in your blood. It's got to do with special preternatural pheromones."

Seeing this woman speaking so calmly, yet painting herself with my blood like an Amazon warrior, sickened me.

"What do you think I should name the baby?" she asked, looking over the edge of the crib.

Matthias's daughter's eyes opened up. They were gray, a couple shades darker than her father's. Then her face screwed up and she began to cry.

There was a horrible sound then, a heavy metallic ripping noise, followed by a scream—a man's scream.

It was a split second before the alarm began to sound.

"Carson!" Dr. Gray exclaimed and worry crossed her gaze. "What the hell is he doing out there?"

She grabbed hold of the sleeve of my dress and directed me to the door past Noah's still body. I noticed the first guard whom Declan had knocked unconscious was nowhere to be seen—he'd likely come to and run away. I didn't really blame him. As soon as I stepped fully outside the room, I saw the problem and my breath caught in my chest.

Carson lay in the hallway thirty feet away, his throat slashed. He held his hands around it as blood gushed out. The guard who'd injected Declan with the new permanent serum lay nearby in a pool of blood. Declan was now awake and standing over his father with a knife in his hand.

At the sight before me, I stopped breathing. My chest tightened.

For a moment I thought he'd done it, that he'd knifed his father and the guard, but there was no blood on the blade. There was a long cut on Declan's forearm, which dripped blood to the ground. He looked over at me and our eyes met.

"Stay where you are," he said loudly so he could be heard over the alarm. "Don't come any closer."

The door to the other dhampyr's room had been torn from its hinges and the dhampyr slowly emerged from the holding cell.

"Damn it. I told him to kill it. It's been done dozens of times before," Dr. Gray whispered. "Carson prefers to euthanize the dhampyrs. Prefers to end their lives humanely. But this—" she swore under her breath. "That stupid, stupid man."

Her orders to kill the dhampyr had led to this. Carson had tried to humanely end its life, but that only gave it a chance to attack. To slash and gore. To kill.

Declan lunged at it, but the dhampyr effortlessly knocked him out of the way. Declan hit the wall hard and slid to the ground. He didn't move for a moment, a tear now on his shirt showing an alarming welling of blood that made me shriek and clamp my hand over my mouth. The dhampyr approached him, dripping blood from its talons. Declan's blood. Carson's blood.

It was going to kill him.

"Declan! No!" I yelled.

The dhampyr's head whipped toward me and it sniffed at the air. It smelled me. That was enough to draw its attention and it approached slowly down the length of the hallway. My first impulse was to run, but Dr. Gray dug her fingernails into my arm.

"Don't move," she instructed. "Stay very, very still."

Dr. Gray's personal guard ran at the dhampyr, still gripping the taser that had worked to stop Matthias from killing Dr. Gray, but the dhampyr easily slashed his throat with its talons. The guard fell. The silver walls down here seemed to be no defense against it. I hated to think about how strong it would be outside of here.

My gaze shot to Noah, now laying between us and the monster. His blood pooled on the smooth tiled floor. He was still alive, though. His chest moved, and he made a weak attempt to scramble back from the dhampyr as it approached. Its black eyes moved from me as Noah's movement caught its attention.

"Blllooooddd," it rasped.

"Noah," I whispered. "No."

I couldn't let the dhampyr tear him apart. He was so helpless just lying there. He couldn't defend himself.

"No!" I yelled louder. "Over here, you freak! Look at me! My blood's way better!"

"What the hell are you doing?" Dr. Gray snarled.

Good question. In order to save Declan and Noah, both bleeding and vulnerable, I'd forced the dhampyr to change its course and come directly for me.

I guess I'd chosen to die after all. Funny, it was what I'd been trying desperately to avoid since all this began.

Funnier still that it felt like exactly the right decision.

The dhampyr would bite me, drink my blood, kill me—and I'd kill it.

So be it.

Matthias's baby would live, Declan would live, and, well, I hoped like hell that Noah would also live despite the bullet in his chest.

This was fate. All of it. Everything that had happened had led me here.

I had been asked to kill the vampire king. I'd done it, although not in the way I'd ever intended.

And now I was going to kill a dhampyr who wanted to kill the people I'd grown to care about.

I didn't need a weapon. I *was* a weapon. Whether I liked it or not.

Still, as the monster drew closer, I couldn't help but feel the resolve begin to leave me like water draining out of a leaky boat.

Dr. Gray clutched my arm. "Stupid," she hissed. "You're ruining everything, do you know that?"

Yeah. I kind of figured that. But screwing up her plans to use me as her own personal assassin really wasn't that much of a victory for me at the moment.

The dhampyr was close now, studying me carefully. Its tongue slid out of its mouth and it licked its white lips. It reached out a clawed hand toward me. I braced myself. Declan shakily began to rise to his feet again. He stood at the far end of the long hallway as he spotted the dhampyr in front of me. I couldn't read his expression but he held the knife tightly.

Please stay back, I begged silently. *I don't want you to die, too.*

Then a horrible thought occurred to me. What if the dhampyr killed me, but my blood didn't kill it? The Nightshade killed vampires, but a dhampyr was only half-vampire. Then it would continue on, unstoppable, and hurt everyone else.

No, this had to work. It had to. My sacrifice couldn't be in vain. *Please.*

"Stop," Dr. Gray said firmly to the curious dhampyr when it had drawn close enough that I could feel its hot breath on my skin. "Bad boy. You will go back where you belong now and behave yourself."

Was she cocky enough to think she could reason with this thing? She was crazier than I thought she was.

"Bloooddd," the dhampyr said in a broken, screechy voice.

"Yes," Dr. Gray said. "Blood. Jillian's blood smells good to you, doesn't it? But you can't have any."

The dhampyr's gaze now moved to Dr. Gray as if mesmerized by the sound of her voice. "Monnniccaaa."

Her eyes widened a fraction. "Yes. You know my name. How . . . wonderful."

It reached its pale, thin, taloned hand up to touch her face.

She looked triumphant for a moment before fear flickered in her eyes.

"Monnniccaaa," the dhampyr said drawing even closer so its tongue could flick out to slip over her cheek. "Blloooddd."

I suddenly realized what was happening. My blood—it was on her face. She'd painted it there herself to look like a warrior. There was more of my blood on her skin than there was on mine.

"Jillian," she said sharply. "Get its attention away from me. Do it now."

No, actually, I didn't think I would. I backed away from her, as slowly and quietly as I could, moving toward Noah.

"Jillian," she snapped. "What are you doing?"

"I'm leaving you to your research. After all, it's more important than the life of any one woman, isn't it?"

"Wait," Dr Gray said to the dhampyr now lapping at the blood on her face like a gruesome puppy. "No! Get away from me now or I'll—"

It was the last thing she said. The dhampyr closed its mouth filled with razor-sharp teeth over her throat and I heard a horrible crunching and tearing sound. I staggered farther backward, horrified, finally dropping to the floor and shielding Noah's prone form from the carnage.

The dhampyr was so busy feeding on Dr. Gray that it didn't notice Declan's stealthy approach. He was able to slice his knife into its back, deep enough to pierce its heart. It screamed before it collapsed heavily on top of Dr. Gray's body.

I ran into the crib room to check on Matthias's daughter, but she was fine. Still crying, her little gray eyes welled with tears. I carefully picked her up and cradled her against my chest before emerging back into the hallway.

Declan walked over to Carson's body, looking silently down at his adoptive father's glazed-over eyes. I went to his side.

"Declan . . ." I could barely breathe. "I'm so sorry."

He turned to look at me with a flat, emotionless expression. "Thank you."

"Are you feeling—"

"I'm feeling fine," he said.

I wanted to touch him, comfort him, but he moved out of arm's reach.

"I need to deal with this," he said, flicking a glance at what was left of Dr. Gray. "I didn't get a chance to ask her why she never told me the truth. That she was my mother and that she lied about my father."

It was on the tip of my tongue to tell him—tell him his real father was Kristoff. But I bit the words back. This wasn't the time for a revelation like that. Too much had happened. I didn't want to cause him any more pain.

"I'm sorry," was all I said instead.

His flat gaze moved to Noah. "He needs help."

"Declan—" I moved the baby in my arms so I could reach for him again, but didn't manage to make contact.

"I'm glad you weren't killed," he said. Then he was gone, walking briskly and methodically down the hall. My heart broke into a thousand pieces to see that he was just as emotionless as the first moment we'd met.

I hugged the baby against me until she stopped crying

and then I stayed with Noah until someone arrived a few minutes later with a stretcher for him and several body bags for Dr. Gray, Carson, and the guards.

It was my blood on her face that had made Dr. Gray so appetizing to the dhampyr that had torn out her throat. She'd smeared the target on herself.

She'd wanted me to be death personified. She just didn't know I'd be *her* death.

Seemed fitting, actually.

"I FEEL LIKE SHIT." NOAH GROANED, PROPPED UP IN A hospital bed in a neighboring building eight hours later as I walked in his room.

"You look like shit," I confirmed.

"Thanks so much."

I smiled for the first time in recent memory. "I don't think Carson wanted to kill you. If he had, he would have aimed for your head."

"You have a questionable bedside manner, you know that? I don't suggest a career in nursing."

"You're going to be okay."

"From your lips to God's ears."

"Are you religious?"

"No. I just like the saying." He swallowed, his face pale. He fiddled nervously with his IV as the doctor left the room after checking Noah's bandages. "Jill, listen to me . . ."

"What?"

He grabbed my hand tightly in his. "It's not safe here. Not for you."

My heart began to pound harder. "What do you mean? Dr. Gray's dead and so is Carson."

"It doesn't matter. You need to get out of here. Take my

car. The keys are under the front seat. Just go and don't look back."

"Why?" He was scaring me. I thought I'd already met my daily quota of fear, but I guess I was wrong.

"Where's the baby?" he asked.

"In the nursery. A new one that's been set up downstairs—monster free this time."

He nodded. "Carson tried to keep your involvement really quiet, so not everybody knows who you are. Most of the guards are under the impression you were Dr. Gray's new research assistant for the dhamp babies. They're under that impression because that's what I told them."

"So what's the problem?"

"A couple people do know who you are and what you have in your veins. And a lot of them, like the two men who were observing the other day from the government, subscribe to the same crazy magazine that Dr. Gray did. They'll want to use you as a weapon to kill certain vamps whether you like it or not. Like I said, I read the files. As soon as I'm able, I'm taking off, too, and I'm not coming back. I know way too fucking much about this place."

It was true. My situation hadn't changed at all. I still had Nightshade-infused blood. Some people might find that a reason to keep me around against my will. "What about Declan?"

Noah shook his head. "He's on the new serum Carson had made for him. No more shots required. He was raised here, this is his life. He'll keep taking orders like the well-trained dhampyr he is."

"But . . . he's different now. He has to be." I heard the strain of desperation in my voice.

"I'm not so sure about that."

Declan hadn't said two words to me after he'd left the

bloodbath downstairs. I'd tried to find him, but he obviously didn't want to be found. Not by me, anyway.

I thought it all through. "I have to take the baby with me. I gave Matthias my promise she'd be safe."

Noah nodded. "Do it. Just go. You're only wasting time now."

I gave him a shaky grin. "You're all bossy with a bullet in your chest."

"Bullet's out." He grimaced in pain. "But the painful memory remains."

"But . . . but wait. Dr. Gray told me I needed to get regular treatments with the fusing potion or I'd die."

"I'll look into it. Try not to worry about that yet. Here's my email address." He pressed a small scrap of paper into my palm. "Get in touch when you can and don't go back to San Diego where you might be recognized. Now get the hell out of here before it's too late."

"Yes, sir." I leaned forward and kissed his cheek. Then I went to get the baby from a pair of guards who believed the lie that I was Dr. Gray's research assistant. I told them I wanted to take the baby outside for some fresh air. They let me.

Swallowing back any second thoughts or doubts, I left.

DR. GRAY SAID I'D LIKELY DIE WITH THE NIGHTSHADE inside of me. She said I'd need her help and regular doses of the fuser in order to stay alive. She'd said it to get me to behave and go along with her plan to turn me into a reluctant vampire slayer.

Honestly, though? I didn't think she'd been lying.

But she was dead now and I couldn't say I was sorry about that. She'd justified everything she'd done, every choice she'd made in the past thirty years, due to her allegiance to Kristoff. How many women had died in childbirth, terrified until their last breath by what was clawing its way out of them? And Dr. Gray had stood by and let it all happen.

I cradled Matthias's daughter in my arms, desperately wishing I had a baby carrier to safely put her in, as I quickly made my way to Noah's Mustang. It was nearly noon, exactly four days after I'd first been injected with the Nightshade.

Four days of fighting for my life. And it didn't look like it was over yet.

I had to get out of there. I didn't know where I was going to go, all by myself with a baby. I had no supplies for her, I was a terrible babysitter, and had zero maternal instinct, but I knew I had to do this. I'd protect her, no matter what.

I ignored the urge to go back inside and hope for the best.

Noah was right. If there was anyone in there who sided with Dr. Gray, then I wasn't safe here. And this child wasn't, either.

"Where are you going?" A deep voice stopped me in my tracks.

It was Declan. He was following me.

Strong resolve filled me as I turned to face him. "I'm leaving."

"Are you?"

"Yes."

"You're going back to San Diego?"

"No, I—I'm not sure where I'm going." I swallowed hard.

He glanced back at the house. "They want you here.

There are more tests that can be done with your blood. You're a part of this research program now whether you like it or not."

I shook my head. "I can't stay."

His gaze dropped to my arms. "Do they know you're trying to take the baby?"

"Just let me go, Declan. Please. It's dangerous here. The baby's in danger. I promised Matthias I'd take care of her. Don't try to stop me."

He studied me for a long moment with that familiar blank expression I'd grown to hate. "I'm not trying to stop you."

"You're not?"

"No."

"Then what are you doing out here?"

"Isn't it obvious?" he asked. "I'm coming with you."

My eyes widened with surprise. "What are you talking about?"

He glanced around again and I noticed this time it was with wariness. "Get in the car before someone sees us."

I didn't argue. I got in, holding the baby on my lap since there was nowhere else to put her. Declan got in the driver's side and grabbed the keys from under the seat. It was as if he knew they'd be there.

"Noah—" I began.

"He told me."

"But he said you were—but . . . but the serum . . ." Confusion made my thoughts cloudy. "I don't understand."

"Do you honestly think the serum changes anything?" he asked stiffly, pulling the door closed behind him and sliding the key into the ignition. "It works to dampen my emotions—*a lot*—but I still know the difference between right and wrong. And it doesn't make me forget what I've experienced. They can't make me do anything I don't agree with. And whether I'm on this new serum or not, I know what I want." He snorted humorlessly. "Although, it might take me a long time to get it."

"What do you want?" I asked.

"You," he said simply. "And I want you to be safe. It's my fault you're a part of this. The least I can do is make sure you're okay."

I was stunned. "Declan—"

"I understand if you want to get rid of me as soon as possible."

"Of course I don't want to get rid of you." Tears welled in my eyes as I allowed relief and happiness to flow through me—relief that he was here, with me, happiness because I never would have believed this could happen. "I thought you were gone, that this new serum had taken you away forever."

"I never went anywhere. But this serum, it's still a problem. I want to be with you, but it's not an option for me right now. I don't know when it will be again."

The memory of being with him the other night came back crystal clear into my mind. While he was on the serum, that wouldn't happen again. Carson had said the new serum was permanent, but I refused to believe that was true.

"Trust me. I can be very patient." I leaned toward him and kissed him, but he didn't kiss me back. It reminded me of being with Matthias. I'd refused to kiss him as well, although it hadn't been because my emotions were repressed.

Declan pulled the car onto the road and headed out of town. The baby felt warm in my arms, so small but so full of life.

"For a dhampyr, she doesn't seem to be all that drawn to my scent," I said.

"That makes one of us." Declan glanced at me again.

"We'll have to stop and pick up some supplies. Formula, diapers."

I made a face. "Me, changing diapers. Not exactly something I'd planned on. Then again, I hadn't planned on any of this, had I?"

"I think you'll do just fine. And we'll keep an eye on things from afar and check in with Noah in a couple of days. I made him promise to look after Molly."

That he'd make sure his cat was okay made me smile. "See? You're still a softie."

He raised an eyebrow. "Being responsible for those I've chosen to take care of doesn't make me a softie."

"If you say so."

"Also, we'll keep tabs on the vampires and when they manage to find and release Kristoff. Now that Matthias is gone, it's only a matter of time."

A fresh surge of dread moved through me. "You really think so?"

"I do. And we'll also keep an eye on you. If the Night-shade bothers you again—"

"Then what will we do?"

"We'll deal."

I allowed myself to grin at that. "You're pretty optimistic for an emotionless dhampyr assassin with a baby on board."

He raised an eyebrow, but kept his attention on the road. "Trying to be."

This wasn't over, I knew that much. The image of Matthias with my blood on his lips a moment before he burst into ash haunted me.

But something else haunted me as well, in an entirely different way. It was what he said before sinking his fangs into me. I cringed as I touched the raw marks on my throat.

"I'll find you."

That was what he'd whispered to me. He'd made me promise to look after his daughter and then he'd said, "I'll find you."

Not exactly the typical last words of a man about to die.

I couldn't help but remember his books on magic and his friendship with Houdini, who'd been a master of escape and illusion.

I remembered him speaking with disgust about being forced by his brother to drink the blood of another female dhampyr child in an Amarantos ritual.

Immortality, I thought as Declan began to drive us east toward the sunrise. *True* immortality.

It just might be something worth dying for.

Turn the page for a special preview of

Bloodlust

by Michelle Rowen
Coming soon from Berkley Sensation!

RAVENOUS WAS THE PERFECT NAME FOR A PLACE LIKE this.

I'd arrived at the seedy North Hollywood bar a half hour ago. A friend had sent me an email earlier today asking mc to meet him here tonight at ten o'clock because he "had to talk to me about something very important." So here I was—ready, willing, and able to talk.

But by ten thirty he still hadn't shown. And I was getting worried.

Maybe he's dead, a little voice in my head whispered.

My chest tightened at the thought. No, he was too smart. Too wily. Too young and cocky. I refused to allow myself to believe he'd let himself get killed. Tonight he could possibly have the information that would help get my back life to normal.

Where are you, Noah?

My attention shifted to a blond guy in a leather duster

approaching the far left of the small dance floor. A heavy metal tune had begun to blare through the speakers, making it difficult to concentrate. Even in the dim light of the club, his skin was so pale it seemed to faintly glow, easily making him stand out from the rest of the crowd. He scanned the few dancers, coming to rest on a petite redhead wearing a micro-short leather skirt.

When he smiled I saw the subtle glint of fangs beneath his upper lip.

She noticed him looking and smiled back at him, thrusting her ample chest forward—the universal easy-girl's signal for "come and get me, bad boy."

The girl had no idea this bad boy was a vampire.

"For fuck's sake," I said under my breath. "Don't be so stupid."

Two weeks ago I thought vampires didn't exist. But they do. There were those who preferred to keep their distance from humans, but others like this one, well . . . they were just really hungry.

The redhead was going to die.

I wasn't psychic. I had no special supernatural powers, no superstrength, no otherworldly abilities—but I knew her fate. I saw it in the vampire's pale gaze as he flicked a smug look at his friend also standing at the edge of the dance floor.

A large part of me didn't want to get involved. I had my own vast and varied problems to deal with. Plus, not to judge a book by its cover, but girls like this one, seemingly alone and vulnerable at this kind of dive, would likely find trouble sooner or later. If she couldn't protect herself, if she had no one around to keep an eye on her, then I didn't think her future was a bright one.

But it didn't mean I was just going to let this monster make her his nightcap.

After another quick scan for the missing-in-action Noah, I slid off the tall stool and began weaving my way through the rough-looking crowd toward the exit. The vampire and the girl were now dancing together, if you could call it that. His hand closed on her ass under her short skirt, pulling them groin to groin as he pressed his lips to her throat. It looked sexy—kind of romantic, even—but I knew it wasn't. Or it wouldn't be for long.

I froze in place as a horrible thought occurred to me. He was going to bite her right in front of everyone.

I wanted to walk away, pretend I hadn't seen the vampire, leave this club, and contact Noah another night, but I couldn't do that. I'd never be accused of being a sweet and softhearted woman who wanted to help the helpless, but if there was a problem that was standing right in front of me and I might, possibly, be able to do something about it, then I had to. My conscience wouldn't allow otherwise.

"I really don't want to do this," I whispered to myself.

But I did it anyway.

I forced myself to walk close enough to brush against the vampire. He immediately caught my scent and released the girl.

I kept walking. I didn't have to look over my shoulder to know he was now following me. He was the mouse and I was the cheese. It didn't really matter what I looked like, how I filled out the thin white tank top I wore, or how long my legs were under my skirt. I was irresistible.

Believe me, I wasn't saying it to be vain. I wished like hell I didn't have this particular effect on the bloodsuckers.

I exited the club. Even though it was hot air that brushed against my bare arms and legs, I still shivered. I picked up my pace, ignored my racing heart, and walked toward the parking lot out back of the bar.

"Hey beautiful," the vampire said from close behind me. "What's your name?"

I forced myself to look coyly over my shoulder. "Sorry, I don't talk to strangers."

"Oh, c'mon, don't be like that." He was right next to me now and he stroked a long strand of black hair off my forehead, pausing to roll it between his fingertips. He held it up so he could inhale its scent, and his eyes darkened with lust and hunger. "Damn, you smell good. Where are you going, honey?"

I shuddered. "Back to my motel room."

"We can keep you company." He glanced at his friend—dark hair, sallow skin, and a slow smile stretching his gaunt cheeks. He bared his sharp fangs as if he didn't care who saw that beneath his human facade he was a monster.

I'd just wanted to lure the vampire away from the girl. I didn't want this, but it did come with the territory. I tried my best to stay calm. "I don't want company. Really, just leave me alone."

"And what if we don't want to leave you alone?"

"Then you're in serious trouble."

He grinned at that, then inhaled deeply, and thin, dark veins branched along his jawline and down his neck. Each vampire showed their hunger slightly differently—it was like their fingerprint, and along with their fangs it revealed them to be much different from human. The black of his pupils spread out to cover the pale gray of his irises.

His hand shot out and he grabbed me by my throat. I clawed at his arm as he dragged me around the corner into an alleyway, and then he threw me roughly at his friend.

"Hold the bitch still," he snapped.

I tried to struggle against him. I'd hoped very hard it wouldn't come to this, but I'd overestimated how much control a hungry vampire had. Fear laced through me as the blond's lips peeled back from his fangs.

"No, wait—my blood—" But I wasn't able to finish my sentence. He wrenched my head to the side so violently he easily could have snapped my neck. I gasped in pain as his fangs sliced into the soft flesh of my throat.

The vampire's friend had grabbed my left breast and was squeezing it so hard that tears sprung to my eyes.

"She tastes incredible," the blond growled as he slurped at my blood.

A moment later, he gasped and pulled back from me, his black eyes registering surprise now that he realized that my incredible blood came with a bit of an aftertaste.

"What's wrong?" his friend asked.

"I don't know." The vampire's mouth gaped open and he touched his lips, looking down at the unnaturally dark crimson color of my blood on his fingertips. His brows drew together in confusion before he staggered back a few steps from me.

When he screamed, fire poured out of his mouth. In mere seconds, the only thing that remained of Thirsty Vampire One was a fall of fiery ash, turning the hot July night into a Christmas card from hell.

The paralyzing effect disappeared and I clamped my hand to my neck to stop the flow of blood. I felt weak and my legs threatened to crumple beneath me. I had to struggle to remain standing. The vampire's friend moved his shocked gaze to look at me. His hunger showed along his hollow cheekbones, the sallow skin etched with a spiderweb of dark blue veins, his eyes soulless and black as pitch.

"You're the one I've heard about, aren't you? Your blood is poison to us." His voice was a whisper, but his hands were clenched, his jaw tight. Anger and grief flashed through his eyes as he came at me, not waiting for my answer.

He wasn't going to bite me. He was just going to kill me as I'd killed his friend.

Before his hand did more than brush against my throat, someone grabbed him, spun him around, and a scarred fist slammed into his jaw, knocking him backward.

"Don't fucking touch her," the man attached to the fist growled. His gaze flicked to me, resting on my injured throat for a split second, before returning to the vampire.

I pressed back against the cold wall as the vampire recovered quickly and launched himself at his attacker. Silver flashed, too fast to fully register. The blade sank into the vampire's chest right up to the hilt. He attempted to pull it out, but didn't have enough time. His hands burst into fire along with the rest of his body and he exploded outward into another ashy cloud.

The knife clanged to the pavement and the man crouched to snatch it up and slide it into the sheath he wore at his hip. Then he glared at me through his right eye. The left was covered by a black patch. He'd lost the eye a long time ago in another fight with a vampire in which he hadn't fared quite as well as this.

I hadn't realized I'd been holding my breath. I finally released it and inhaled shakily.

He was well over six feet tall, heavily muscled, and covered in ragged scars, including those on his face, branching out from where his eye patch sat, down his cheek and jaw and along the left side of his neck. His dark hair was cut very short, almost shaved. He wasn't the type of man you wanted to meet in a dark alley like this. Not if you valued your life. Declan Reyes was scary as hell.

My hero.

I finally allowed myself to relax just a little bit and I wiped my tears away.

He came toward me and roughly brushed the hair back off my neck. "Let me see."

I reluctantly pulled my hand away from the bite wound.

"Damn it, Jill." His lips thinned. "What the hell did you think you were doing just now? Trying to get yourself killed?"

"They were going to kill a girl in there. Right in front of everyone."

"So you offered yourself up as a willing sacrifice instead?"

"I thought I could distract them without getting bit. I guess I was fooling myself."

"Where's Noah?" He pulled a clean rag from his pocket and held it against my throat.

"He hasn't shown yet."

"Then you shouldn't have stuck around." He glanced over his shoulder in the direction of the bar. "You need to stop trying to protect others all the time. You have to focus on protecting yourself."

Declan had a tendency to see me as way more altruistic than I actually was. "So I should have just stood by and watched them tear her throat out?"

"Next time come find me first before you decide to play the pied piper to vampires." He touched my face gently. "Are you okay?"

"I'll be fine." I searched for some emotion on his battle-scarred face—anger, fear, maybe even annoyance—but came up empty.

"We need to go."

"But Noah—"

"Isn't here. Something must have gone wrong. We'll wait for him to contact us again."

"Don't you think we should wait just a little while longer?"

"No. Best to cut our losses and try again later."

I felt the thud of disappointment push away the small amount of hope I'd allowed myself to feel earlier. Declan had chosen to remain outside when we'd arrived just before ten o'clock. While it wasn't the classiest bar in Los Angeles, the way he looked—like death incarnate, which as a vampire hunter he came by honestly—might have gained us a bit too much attention.

Declan was a dhampyr—human mother, vampire father. While this gave him a great deal of extra strength, it wasn't nearly the same as being fully vampire. He healed much faster than a human, but every single time he received a flesh wound it left a scar behind as a reminder of the horror he'd been through.

It was Declan who'd kidnapped me, kicking and screaming, from my normal life two weeks ago. It may as well have been two years by how different I felt and looked. It was the Nightshade formula I'd been injected with that had changed my hair and eyes to black. It was the Nightshade that meant any vampire who drank my blood would die a horrible, fiery death.

Declan stopped a dozen feet away and glanced over his shoulder at me. "Are you coming?"

When I moved closer to him he turned his face away so the scarred side would stay in shadows, away from the light shining down on us from the streetlamp. The undamaged side of his face showed the man he could have been in a different life—a handsome, if a bit rough around the edges twenty-eight-year-old. Same age as me. Very different lives.

I wanted to touch him, but I restrained myself. "Don't hide from me."

"I'm not hiding."

"You asked me how I was feeling, so now I'll do the same. How are you feeling right now?"

His jaw tensed. "I'm fine."

"The new serum is—"

"Holding strong. Much better than before."

Better. It wasn't exactly the word I'd use to describe the experimental drug he'd been pumped full of more than a week ago.

His now-deceased adoptive father, Carson Reyes, had been very concerned about Declan's dhampyr nature. So much so that he'd developed a special serum that had to be injected every three hours since Declan was a child. This serum was meant to curb any vampiric tendencies he might have—violence, bloodlust, erratic behavior of any kind. The serum also restrained his emotions so much that he appeared to have none. This made him the perfect weapon who could follow orders to the letter and not give his father or anyone else any problems. He'd been an effective killing machine who felt nothing apart from getting the job done.

Shortly after he'd met me he'd been forced to stop taking his serum regularly when it was stolen. I'd been worried that the violence and need for blood might overwhelm him, but it hadn't. Instead I'd met a different Declan, one who felt emotions strongly and wanted more from life than merely being a blunt instrument sent out to kill monsters.

Carson was still convinced he was right, that dhampyrs like Declan were dangerous and unpredictable. He'd been developing another serum—one that was meant to be permanent. He'd forcibly injected Declan with it hoping it would save his son from giving in to any bloodlust.

Ever. But that also meant that his emotions—including love, compassion, and sexual desire—would be permanently dampened.

I needed answers. "I'm going to check the bar one last time."

Declan shook his head. "Not a good idea."

I felt the resolve flow through me. It helped me to ignore the stinging pain from the vampire's bite. "Five minutes, I swear. Wait for me here."

"Jill, no—"

Before he could stop me, I turned and quickly re-entered the dark and musty interior of Ravenous. Keeping a close eye on my surroundings, wary of anyone who looked suspicious—and admittedly, a lot of people did—I made a beeline to the bar where I'd been sitting earlier. The newspaper I'd been flipping through still lay closed on the scarred wooden bar top. On the top of page twenty-two I'd seen a small black-and-white picture of me and a heartfelt plea from Cathy, my older sister, asking anyone who knew my whereabouts to please contact the police immediately.

I forced myself to look away from the newspaper and toward the bartender.

"Have you seen a guy in here tonight?" My words came out in a rush. "Early twenties, about five-ten, sort of thin. Light brown hair. Looks a bit like a frat boy?"

He eyed me as he ran a wet rag along the countertop. "Not a lot of frat boys come in here."

"No shit." I hissed out a sigh of frustration.

"But, yeah, I think I've seen the guy you're looking for."

My breath caught in my chest. "Really? Where?"

His gaze moved over my shoulder. "Right behind you."

I spun around to see Noah standing ten feet away after coming out of the restroom on the right side of the club.

A wide smile spread across his boyish features, and he

closed the distance between us in a few steps. "Jill, I wasn't sure if you were here or not."

I hadn't realized until this very moment how incredibly worried I'd been that he was hurt . . . or worse. The last time I'd seen him he'd been recovering from a bullet wound.

"Where the hell were you? You said you'd be here over a half hour ago."

His smile widened. "Good to see you, too."

I hugged him tightly. "I thought you were dead."

"I'm not. But, ouch. Be careful. I'm still recuperating."

"Sorry." I released him and he placed a hand over his chest wound hidden under his dark blue shirt.

"Don't worry about it. But if this was a normal world I'd likely still be in a hospital bed slurping up Jell-O cubes." His amiable expression faded and he touched my face. "Christ, you look like hell."

I'd have taken it as an insult if he didn't look so concerned. "I feel better than I look, believe it or not."

"You're paler than last time I saw you. Maybe it's just the new hair color. I mean, don't get me wrong. You're still hot. You're a hot chick who looks like she hasn't slept in about a decade."

"I'll go heavier on the under-eye concealer the next time I enter polite society."

"Are you in any pain?"

Having poison in my veins came with a whole set of issues, a couple of which were excruciating pain and nausea. I'd been given another drug, a fusing potion, meant to bind the Nightshade with my blood on a cellular level. Since then, things had been better.

"Other than feeling headachy and weary, kind of like a constant low-level hangover, I haven't experienced any severe pain since taking the fuser."

"Not yet, you mean."

I cringed. "Thanks for the reminder."

"I got more fuser for you so you can take it regularly. I know it doesn't exactly go down easily, does it?"

"It sure doesn't."

The fuser ramped up the pain I felt about a hundred-fold before it started to work. As the saying went, it was always darkest just before the dawn.

"A spoonful of sugar helps the medicine go down," he said.

"Thank you, Mary Poppins. If I didn't have to inject it, I'd be happy to swallow a bucket of sugar with it." I reached for his sleeve to draw him closer when some other rough-looking bar patrons moved past us. "Is that what you wanted to see me about tonight? The fusing potion? I thought you might have some other answers."

His expression tensed. "Not yet, I'm afraid."

I felt a stab of disappointment at his answer. "Oh."

"Where's Declan?"

"Waiting vigilantly outside. Armed to the teeth."

"That's surprisingly reassuring to know." He glanced at my neck as I twisted a lock of hair around my finger. "Making new friends?"

I touched the fresh fang marks. Luckily for a newly designated pin cushion like myself, a vampire's bite healed in a matter of a few days leaving no scars behind. It was small comfort since they stung like a bitch. "You kept me waiting too long. I met a couple guys who liked the way I smelled."

He grimaced. "Sorry. I take it they're gone now?"

"Permanently." I glanced around. "Now that you're here, I do want to talk to you about Declan's new serum."

Noah looked nervously over his shoulder. "Yeah, sure. But . . . listen, Jill, there actually *is* another reason why I needed to see you tonight. And it's not because I enjoy the dulcet tones of Black Sabbath and the smell of sweaty leather."

"What is it?"

Noah shot another look over his shoulder. "Jesus, Jill, when he contacted me yesterday it scared the shit out of me. It was the last damn thing I expected. He wants to see you, but he didn't want me to mention that until you got here."

My heart sped up. "Who?"

Noah met my gaze and held it. "Matthias."

There was a long moment of stunned silence before I gathered my thoughts together enough to answer him. "He—he's alive?"

Noah nodded.

Fresh panic raced through me. "And he's here? Right now?"

"In the flesh."

I had the sudden urge to turn and run, to escape this bar as fast as my feet could carry me. But my legs felt like lead.

Matthias was alive. It couldn't be possible. It *shouldn't* be possible.

I turned as if in slow motion to see the vampire king in question step out of the shadows to my left, his pale gray gaze trained on me. My mouth fell open in shock. I couldn't help but be stunned to see him again—alive and well and standing right in front of me.

After all, I'd been the one who'd killed him.

YASMINE GALENORN

Harvest Hunting

The D'Artigo sisters are sexy supernatural operatives for the Otherworld Intelligence Agency. It's Samhain, and the Autumn Lord calls Delilah to begin her training with the Death Maidens. . . . And she finds that she likes it. But the sisters have problems: Werewolves are going missing and a new magical drug, Wolf Briar, is being used as a weapon. But most dangerous of all: Stacia Bonecrusher has put a bounty on their heads. Now it's a race to take out the demon general before she realizes the sixth spirit seal is within her reach. . . .

**Explore the outer reaches
of imagination—don't miss these authors
of dark fantasy and urban noir who take you
to the edge and beyond . . .**

Patricia Briggs	**Anne Bishop**
Simon R. Green	**Marjorie M. Liu**
Jim Butcher	**Jeanne C. Stein**
Kat Richardson	**Christopher Golden**
Karen Chance	**Ilona Andrews**
Rachel Caine	**Anton Strout**

penguin.com/scififantasy